ROWE IS A PARANORMAL STAR!" ~J.R. WARD

D0841754

"[a] thrilling entry into romantic suspense... Rowe comes through with crackling tension as the killer closes in." ~ *Publisher's Weekly*

PRAISE FOR CHILL

"*Chill* is a riveting story of danger, betrayal, intrigue and the healing powers of love... *Chill* has everything a reader needs – death, threats, thefts, attraction and hot, sweet romance." ~ Jeanne Stone Hunter, *My Book Addiction Reviews*

"Once again Rowe has delivered a story with adrenalin-inducing action, suspense and a dark edged hero that will melt your heart and send a chill down your spine." ~ Sharon Stogner, *Love Romance Passion*

"*Chill* packs page turning suspense with tremendous emotional impact. Buy a box of Kleenex before you read *Chill*, because you will definitely need it! ...*Chill* had a wonderfully complicated plot, full of twist and turns. " ~ Tamara Hoffa, *Sizzling Hot Book Reviews*

PRAISE FOR NO KNIGHT NEEDED

"*No Knight Needed* is m-a-g-i-c-a-l! Hands down, it is one of the best romances I have read. I can't wait till it comes out and I can tell the world about it." ~*Sharon Stogner, Love Romance Passion*

"*No Knight Needed* is contemporary romance at its best....There was not a moment that I wasn't completely engrossed in the novel, the story, the characters. I very audibly cheered for them and did not shed just one tear, nope, rather bucket fulls. My heart at times broke for them. The narrative and dialogue surrounding these 'tender' moments in particular were so beautifully crafted, poetic even; it was this that had me blubbering. And of course on the flip side of the heart-wrenching events, was the amazing, witty humour....If it's not obvious by now, then just to be clear, I love this book! I would most definitely and happily reread, which is an absolute first for me in this genre." ~*Becky Johnson, Bex 'N' Books*

"*No Knight Needed* is an amazing story of love and life...I literally laughed out loud, cried and cheered.... *No Knight Needed* is a must read and must re-read." ~*Jeanne Stone-Hunter, My Book Addiction Reviews*

Ghost
ISBN 10: 1940968062
ISBN 13: 978-1-940968-06-3
Copyright © 2014 by Stephanie Rowe.

Cover design ©2014 by Peter Davis. Cover design, book layout, and epub creation by Peter Davis. Cover photos courtesy of iStockphoto.com.

Please be a leading force in respecting the right of authors and artists to protect their work. This is a work of fiction. All the names, characters, organizations, places and events portrayed in this novel or on the cover are either products of the author's or artist's imagination or are used fictitiously. Any similarity to real persons, living or dead, is purely coincidental and not intended by the author or the artist. For further information, please contact Stephanie@ stephanierowe.com

Acknowledgements

Special thanks to my beta readers, who always work incredibly hard under tight deadlines to get my books read. I appreciate so much your willingness to tell me when something doesn't work! I treasure your help, and I couldn't do this without you. Hugs to you all!

There are so many to thank by name, more than I could count, but here are those who I want to called out specially for all they did to help me with this book: Leslie Barnes, Alencia Bates, Kayla Bartley, Jean Bowden, Shell Bryce, Kelley Currey, Holly Collins, Ashley Cuesta, Kelley Curry, Denise Fluhr, Sandi Foss, Valerie Glass, Christina Hernandez, Heidi Hoffman, Jeanne Hunter, Rebecca Johnson, Dottie Jones, Janet Juengling-Snell, Deb Julienne, Bridget Koan, Felicia Low, Phyllis Marshall, D. Alexx Miller, Jodi Moore, Evelyn Newman, Judi Pflughoeft, Carol Pretorius, Emily Recchia, Kasey Richardson, Karen Roma, Tracy Sasso, Caryn Santee, Julie Simpson, Summer Steelman, Regina Thomas, Linda Watson, and Denise Whelan.

And lastly, thank you to Pete Davis at Los Zombios for another fantastic cover, and for all his hard work on the technical side to make this book come to life, and for the most amazing website. Mom, you're the best. It means so much that you believe in me. I love you. Special thanks also to my amazing, beautiful, special daughter, who I love more than words could ever express. You are my world, sweet girl, in all ways. And of course, to my awesome dog, who endured such hardship sleeping next to me in his big armchair while I worked, just so that I would have company. What a dog!

DEDICATION

This book is dedicated to all those who have faced tragedy and yet found the strength within themselves to keep going. My heart and admiration goes out to you on every level.

GHOST

Alaska Heat

STEPHANIE ROWE

CHAPTER 1

"What are you running from?"

Ben Forsett froze at the unexpected question, his hand clenching around the amber beer bottle. For a long second, he didn't move. Instead, his gaze shot stealthily to the three exits he'd already located before he'd even walked into this local pub known as O'Dell's in Where-the-Hell-Are-We, Alaska. He rapidly calculated which exit had the clearest path. A couple of bush pilots were by the kitchen door. They were large, rough men who would shove themselves directly into the path of someone they thought should be stopped. His access to the front door was obstructed by two jean-clad young women walking into the foyer, shaking snowflakes out of their perfectly coiffed hair. The emergency exit was alarmed, but no one was in front of it. That was his best choice—

"Chill, kid," the man continued. "I'm not hunting you. I've been where you are. So have most of the men in this place."

Slowly, Ben pulled his gaze off his escape route and looked at the grizzled Alaskan old-timer sitting next to him. Lines of outdoor hardship creased his face, and wisps of straggly white hair hung below his faded, black baseball hat. His skin hung loose, too tired to hold on anymore, but in the old man's pale blue eyes burned a sharp, gritty intelligence born of a tough life. His shoulders were encased in a heavy, dark green jacket that was so bulky it almost hid the hunch to his back and the thinness of his shoulders.

The man nodded once. "Name's Haas. Haas Carter." He

extended a gnarled hand toward Ben.

Ben didn't respond, but Haas didn't retract his hand.

For a long moment, neither man moved, then, finally, Ben peeled his fingers off his beer and shook Haas's hand. "John Sullivan," he said, the fake name sliding off his tongue far more easily than it had three months ago, the first time he'd used it.

"John Sullivan?" Haas laughed softly. "You picked the most common name you could think of, eh? Lots of John Sullivans in just about every town you've been to, I should imagine. It'd be hard for people to keep track of one more."

Ben stiffened. "My father was John Sullivan, Sr.," he lied. "I honor the name."

Haas's bushy gray brows went up. "Do you now?"

The truth was, Ben's father was a lying bastard who had left when he was two years old. Or he'd been shot. Or he'd been put in prison. No one knew what had happened to him, and no one really cared, including Ben. "I'm not here to make friends," Ben said quietly.

"No, I can see that." Haas regarded him for a moment, his silver-blue eyes surveying Ben's heavy whiskers and the shaggy hair that had once been perfectly groomed. Ben shook his head so his hair hung down over his forehead, shielding his eyes as he watched the older man, waiting for a sign that this situation was going south.

He would be pissed if Haas turned on him. He needed to be here. He was so sure this was finally the break he'd been waiting for. He let his gaze slither off Haas to the back wall of the bar where an enormous stuffed moose head was displayed. Its rack had to be at least six feet wide, its glazed dead eyes a bitter reminder of what happened to life when you stopped paying attention for a split second.

Beside the moose rack was the battered wooden clock he'd been watching all evening. Adrenaline raced through Ben as he watched the minute hand clunk to the twelve. *It was seven o'clock.*

"What happens at seven?"

Ben jerked his gaze back to Haas, startled to realize the older man had been watching him closely enough to notice his focus on the clock. "I turn into a fairy princess."

Haas guffawed and slammed his hand down on Ben's shoulder. "You're all right, John Sullivan. Mind if I call you Sully? Most Sullivans go by Sully. It'll make it seem more like it's your real name."

Ben's fingers tightened around the frosty bottle at Haas's persistence. "It is my real name."

Haas dropped the smile and leaned forward, lowering his voice as his gaze locked onto Ben's. "I'll tell you this, young man, I've seen a lot of shit in my life. I've seen men who look like princes, but turn out to be scum you wouldn't even want to waste a bullet on. I've seen pieces of shit who would actually give their life for you. You look like shit, but whatever the hell you're running from, you got my vote. Don't let the bastards catch you until you can serve it up right in their damn faces. Got it?"

Ben stared at Haas, too stunned by the words to respond. No one believed in him, no one except for the man who had helped him escape. He'd known Mack Connor since he was a kid, and Mack understood what loyalty meant. But even Mack knew damn well who Ben really was and what he was truly capable of. Mack's allegiance was unwavering, but he did it with his eyes open and ready to react if Ben went over the line.

He had a sudden urge to tell Haas exactly what shit was going down for him, and see if the old man still wanted to stand by him.

But he wasn't that stupid. He couldn't afford for anyone to know why he was here. "I don't know what you're talking about," he finally said.

Haas raised his beer in a toast. "Yeah, me neither, Sully. Me neither." As Haas took a drink, another weather-beaten Alaskan sat down on Haas's other side. This guy's face was so creased it looked like his razor would get lost if he tried to shave, and the size of his beard said the guy hadn't been willing to take the risk. Haas nodded at him. "Donnie, this here boy is Sully. New in town. Needs a job. His wife left him six months ago, and the poor bastard lost everything. He's been wandering aimless for too damn long."

Ben almost choked on his beer at Haas's story, but Donnie just nodded. "Women can sure break a man." He leveled his dark brown gaze at Ben. "She ain't worth it, young man.

There are lots of doe around for a guy to pick up with."

Ben managed a nod. "Yeah, well, I'm not ready yet."

"We gotta get him back on the horse," Haas said. "Got any ideas?" With a wink at Ben, he and Donnie launched into a discussion about the assorted available women in town and which ones might be worthy of Ben.

As the two old-timers talked, Ben felt some of the tension ease from his shoulders. In this small town in the middle of Alaska, he had an ally, at least until Haas found out the truth. Shit, it felt good to have someone at his back. It had been too damn long—

The door to the kitchen swung open, and a cheerful female voice echoed through the swinging door. Her voice was like a soft caress of something...damn. He realized he didn't even know what to compare it to. His mind was too tired to conjure up words that would do justice to the sudden heat sliding over his skin. But a seductive, tempting warmth washed over him, through him, like someone had just slipped hot whisky into his veins, burning and cleansing as it went.

Ben went rigid, adrenaline flooding his body. It was seven o'clock. Based on what he'd pieced together about her schedule and her life, she would be coming on duty now, walking out of the kitchen *now*. Was it her? *Was it her?* Her hand was on the kitchen door, holding it open as she finished her muffled conversation. She was wearing a black leather cord with a silver disk around her wrist. On her index finger was a silver ring with a rough-cut turquoise stone and a wide band with carvings on it. Her fingernails were bare and natural, a woman who didn't bother with enamel and lacquer to go to work. Her arm was exposed, the smooth expanse of flesh sliding up to a capped black sleeve that just covered the curve of her shoulder. She wasn't tall, maybe a little over five feet.

Son of a bitch. It might actually be her. *Come into the bar,* he urged silently. *Let me see your face.* He'd never heard her talk before. He'd never seen her in person. All he had was that one newspaper picture of her, and the headshot he'd snagged from her family's store website before it had been taken down. But her trail had led to O'Dell's, and he was hoping he was right. He *had* to be right.

The door opened wider, and Ben ducked his head, letting his hair shield his eyes again, but he didn't take his gaze off her, watching intently as the woman moved into the restaurant. Her back was toward him as she continued her conversation, and he could see her hair. Thick, luscious waves of dark brown.

Brown. *Brown.* The woman he'd been searching for was *blond.*

The disappointment and frustration that knifed through his gut was like the sharp stab of death itself. He bowed his head, resting his forehead in his palms as the image flooded his mind again, the same memory that had haunted him for so long. His sister, her clothes stained with that vibrant red of fresh blood, sprawled across her living room, her hand stretching toward Ben in the final entreaty of death. *Son of a bitch.* He couldn't let Holly down. He couldn't let her down *again.*

"Are you okay?"

He went still at the question, at the sound of the woman's voice so close. She still had the same effect on him, a flood of heat that seemed to touch every part of his body. He schooled his features into the same uninviting expression he'd perfected, and he looked up to find himself staring into the face he'd been hunting for the last three months.

He'd never mistake those eyes. The dark rich brown framed by eyelashes so thick he'd thought they had to be fake, until now. Until he could see her for real. Until he could feel the weight of her sorrow so thickly that it seemed to wrap around him and steal the oxygen from his lungs. Until he looked into that face, that face that had once been so innocent, and now carried burdens too heavy for her small frame.

Until he'd found her.

Because he had.

It was her. Yeah, maybe she'd ditched the blond and let herself go back to her natural color, which looked good as hell on her, but there was no doubt in his mind.

He'd found her.

Son of a bitch.

He'd found her.

Mari Walsh froze under the intense stare of the man at her counter. His gaze was so penetrating, so relentless, and so unforgiving that she could almost feel his hands on her, gripping her shoulders, trapping her. His dark hair was ragged and messy, swept down into his eyes as if he'd just walked out of the storm that had ripped apart her house yesterday. His face was angular and rough, framed by dark whiskers so thick they seemed to obscure any sense of humanity about him. But it was his eyes that she couldn't tear her gaze away from.

They were a vibrant green, so electric they looked as if they were lit from within. She'd never seen eyes that color. In fact, she'd never even seen that color at all, in any form. It was simply magical. His stare was unflinching, probing her without apology, without finesse, and without grace. Just with pure, unforgiving focus.

"Yeah," he said quietly. "I'm okay." His voice was rough and deep, cultured with tones too rich for a native Alaskan...but at the same time, there was a roughness beneath. An edge, as if he'd once spoken differently, and had spent years trying to erase who he had once been.

"You are?" She then recalled that she'd asked him if he was okay. "Well, then, that's good. I just thought...you looked..." Her words faded at the darkening expression on his face, one that clearly warned her not to remark upon the fact that one minute ago, he'd been hunched over, every line of his body shouting exhaustion, weariness, and a hopelessness so deep that it seemed no person could withstand it. She cleared her throat. "Can I get you something? I'm on duty now. I'm taking over for Jessica."

"Yeah." His gaze was still unwavering on her face. "Can I order food at the bar?"

"Of course." Her hands suddenly felt clammy, and she wiped her palms on the white apron that reminded her too much of a life she couldn't bear to recall. Unexpectedly, tears burned in her eyes, and she had to look away at the ugly old moose head on the wall. Everyone called him Big Buck, which was just silly since the poor thing was dead. She'd been told that he'd been killed trying to run down a truck that had come too close to his herd, so she always felt sort of comforted by his presence, like he would jam his antlers into anyone who messed with his place.

Of course, she knew that moose didn't live in groups so the story couldn't be true, but that almost made her like him more. It was as if Big Buck was telling her that even if she was alone, there was still a big, badass moose ready to run down anyone who messed with her.

"Steak and fries. Medium," her customer said, drawing her gaze back to him. "And another round for Haas and Donnie."

She glanced at the two old men sitting beside him, and she felt some of her tension ease. "You know them?"

"Damn right he does," Haas announced, slamming his hand down on the man's shoulder as if he'd been listening to the conversation the whole time, planning the right moment to interfere. Which, she mused, he probably had. "He's been in town even less time than you have, but he's a good 'un. Mari, this here is John Sullivan, but he goes by Sully. Sully, meet Mari Walsh."

John Sullivan? The name was far too innocuous for a man of such intensity. His name should be Damien or something like that, a half-devil, half-man hybrid that no one dared approach.

John nodded at her. "Nice to meet you, Mari."

She swallowed. "Yes, you too." A customer at the end of the bar gestured to her, and she started to turn away, but one final question burned in her. "Are you...are you in town for long?" She didn't know why she asked. The man exuded roughness and danger, which she didn't want in her life. But at the same time, he was inexplicably compelling, and a part of her wanted to just plunk down and stare at him, losing herself in his tormented strength.

Again, those green eyes seemed to see right through her, past all her secrets, as if he understood exactly why she'd asked. Did he? "I'll be here a while," he said.

She couldn't suppress the relief that rushed through her at his answer. *A while.* That meant he wouldn't leave the moment she turned away. She didn't know anything about him, but she knew she wasn't ready to have him vanish.

"Sully needs a job," Haas said. "Got one for him?"

Mari laughed softly. Gone were the days where she was in a position to offer anyone a job. "No, sorry, I'm fresh out of those at the moment, unless you can rebuild my house that got damaged in the storm—"

"I can do that." John's reply was so quick that it startled her. "I used to work construction."

"You?" She looked quickly at Haas, tension leaping through her. Did she really want this intense stranger inside her house? "I don't know—"

"You worked construction?" Haas was looking at John with interest. "Well, now, it's damn good to be skilled with your hands out in these parts. The storm that blew through here yesterday did a lot of damage. It'll take months to get everything put back together." He looked over at Mari. "And you're probably damn low on the list, aren't you?"

Mari's cheeks flushed, well aware that as an outsider, her needs had barely warranted notice when she'd started calling around for someone to fix her house and get the tree out of her living room. Gone were the days when people looked out for her. Yes, it had been her choice to come here and start a new life, but it wasn't as if she'd had a lot of other options. She'd been so desperate that Alaska had felt like her only option.

And yesterday, when she'd sat in bed all night, listening to the sounds of the outdoors that were separated from her only by the blanket she'd tacked up over the hole in the side of her house, her decision to move here hadn't felt so right. "Well, yes, I have had trouble getting someone to fix it, but—"

"What's the damage?" John said.

"The tree came through my roof and destroyed the southeast wall—"

"I'll come by tomorrow. Eight o'clock too early?"

She hesitated. Did she really want John showing up at her place with all his brooding torment and raw masculinity? She didn't even know him, and the way he looked at her was unnerving. But yet, there was something more to him. Something intriguing. Something that called to her. Maybe it was the vulnerability and grief she saw in the lines of his face. Maybe it was the utter desolation that had consumed him when she'd first seen him hunched over with his head in his hands. She knew what that felt like. She'd battled it every day for the last year. Somehow, someway, she had a connection to him…which was unsettling.

She didn't want to be connected to another man, especially not one who exuded so much strength, suffering, and allure. She swallowed, unsure what to do. But did she really have a choice? She couldn't live without a roof and a wall for another month, not in Alaska, not with winter bearing down on them, and not with her own nightmares chasing her so relentlessly. She swallowed, then made her decision. "Well, no, eight isn't too early, if you're sure?"

"It's not too early, and yeah, I'm sure." A brief grin flashed across John's face at her acquiescence, a smile so fleeting it was gone almost instantly, yet that brief glimpse had been so laden with relief that she half expected him to collapse right on the bar, as if he'd suddenly released a thousand years of burden.

"She's at the end of Miller Road," Haas said. "The old Hogstead place. Just follow Wilson Lane from the end of the town, and turn right after about fifteen miles."

John nodded. "I'll be there."

Mari glared at Haas. "You're giving my address to a stranger?"

"Sure am. You can thank me by bringing me another beer."

One of her customers waved at her again, and the bartender gave her a nudge. "Get on it, Mari," he said.

"Yeah, okay." She looked again at Haas and John. "We'll talk about this later."

Haas grinned, but John simply nodded with the calm confidence of a man who already knew he was going to get his way. Frustrated, but at the same time, energized by an unfamiliar awareness she hadn't felt in too long, she turned away.

Her face feeling hot, she hurried toward the end of the bar, away from the dangerously oppressive air that seemed to be swirling around John. She quickly refilled two drinks, and she was just setting them down when a hand grabbed her arm. "Mari!"

She jumped, stumbling back so quickly she crashed into the edge of the bar.

Charlotte Murphy, the hostess, gave her a surprised look and held up her hands in a gesture of surrender. "Whoa, girl. I'm not going to attack you."

Embarrassment flooded Mari's cheeks as she rubbed her hip where she'd crashed into the sharp corner of the bar. Charlotte was about her age, and she'd always been warm and outgoing, the kind of person she could become friends with, if she wasn't so messed up. Maybe someday, if Charlotte didn't give up on her by then. "I know. Sorry. Just a little jumpy."

Charlotte gave her a knowing look. "I'm sure. I'd be jumpy too after getting all worked up over him."

"Him?" she echoed blankly. What him?

"Of course *him*. He's dreamy, you know." Charlotte rested her elbows on the bar, watching John. "Who in heaven's name is that steaming hunk of sexuality making eyes at you? We don't get new guys in here much. He really adds to the scenery, don't you think?"

Mari didn't turn around to look at John, her heart pounding at the idea of him making eyes at her. Was Charlotte right? Had John been watching her? The thought made her shiver…both in anticipation and in fear. Damn. He was too intense, as was her reaction to him. She didn't want him in her house. "Listen, Charlotte, during the storm last night, a huge tree fell on the back of my house. It took out the roof and the back wall. Do you know anyone who could fix it?"

Charlotte stood back up, sighing dramatically as she tore her gaze away from John. "Oh, you'll have to get in line, Mari. There was a ton of damage from the storm. My brother's company is already backed up for a couple months repairing damaged structures. Maybe three."

"Two or three months?" Mari stared at her, unable to keep the dismay out of her voice. "Really? Is there anyone else?" Of course, she'd called more than ten places earlier, but Charlotte was local, so maybe she would know someone.

Charlotte shook her head. "I doubt it, but I'll ask around. Hey, can you take a couple of the tables? We're a little busier than usual tonight, and it would help if you came off the bar a bit."

"Yes, sure." Relief rushed through Mari. She wouldn't be stuck in John's shadow all night. But even as she ducked out from behind the bar, she couldn't help but steal another glance back at him. He was talking to Haas, but watching her.

Chills ran down her spine, and she turned away, but she could feel his gaze on her the entire time. It was dangerous and a little threatening, but at the same time, a relief. John Sullivan gave off the distinct aura of being a man who could handle himself and anything that came his way. With his attention on her, she felt as if she had a safety net. If something happened, John would know instantly, and he was the kind of man who could stop it. Who *would* stop it.

The front door opened and a heavily-jacketed man walked in, but for the first time since she'd started working there, she didn't jump, and her heart didn't stutter in fear. She just looked over at John and saw him check out the latest customer. He was watching, too. He would know before anything happened.

John Sullivan might be too intense, a complete stranger, and uncomfortably compelling, but he made the bar feel safe tonight. For that, she just might let him work on her house.

Then she thought of how his eyes had seemed to reach into her soul, right past all her barriers. She shivered at the sudden ache of longing that seemed to pulse low in her belly, the tingle of being a woman that she'd shut down for so long.

Or maybe, sleeping with only a thin sheet tacked up over the hole in her wall was less dangerous and less scary than allowing John Sullivan into her house.

CHAPTER 2

Midnight scared her now.

Mari paused on the steps of the bar, peering out into the dark parking lot. She'd been unable to find a nearby spot when she'd arrived at seven, and now her vehicle seemed too far away. The walk across the asphalt felt long and exposed.

John had left an hour earlier, when they'd closed down for the night, as had Haas and Donnie. The only cars left were hers, Charlotte's, and a couple that belonged to the kitchen staff.

"Good night for tips?" The door behind her opened, and Charlotte stepped out, still zipping her parka up.

"Pretty good." Mari hesitated. "Where'd you park?"

"Last row. You?"

"Me, too." Mari hurried down the stairs to stay beside Charlotte as they headed toward their cars. Not that the brunette would be much help if someone leapt out from behind the building with a gun, but it was better than walking alone. "So, did you come up with anyone who could fix my house?"

Charlotte raised her eyebrows at her. "No, but I heard Haas saying that new guy could do it."

Heat fused Mari's cheeks at the thought of John showing up at her house in eight hours. "Yeah, I know. I was just hoping, well—"

Charlotte rolled her eyes as she tugged a black hat over her hair. "He's handsome. What's there to wonder about? Let him fix your house and then invite him in for a hot chocolate… or a foot massage or something even more interesting." She gave

Mari a wink that left no doubt what she meant by interesting.

Mari zipped her coat up higher and buried her chin in the fabric, trying to shield herself from the bitter cold. She couldn't deny there was some sort of raw masculinity to John that was appealing, in that bad-news kind of way, but it wasn't enough to tempt her. "Well, I just…I'm not ready to date."

Charlotte sighed, a knowing look in her eyes. "You've been here three months, sweetie. Whatever bastard you left behind, it's been long enough."

Mari hugged her purse tighter under her arm, ducking her head against the biting wind. "It's not like that. It's different."

"It's always different," Charlotte said softly, "but in many ways, it's always the same. No matter how bad it was, you have to find a way to keep living. You really do." She tucked her arm through Mari's as they neared the old Cherokee Mari had bought shortly after she arrived. It had four-wheel drive and worked, but she still wished she'd found a car that wasn't black.

Black was just so devoid of hope.

"Tell you what," Charlotte said, squeezing her arm. "My younger sister is getting married next weekend, and pretty much the whole community is invited. You should come. Get to know people. Start to make some friends."

Mari's chest started to hurt at the idea of being in a crowd. "Thanks, but—"

"No buts. I'll give you the details on Monday." She winked. "I have the weekend off. I met a guy a few weeks ago, and we're going to Seattle for a mini-vacation."

Guilt tore through Mari at her inability to accept Charlotte's overture. She was so tired of being afraid. Suddenly, she just wanted to get out of there and get home. She had to regroup. She had to find a way out of the black hole that was trying so hard to consume her. "Well," she managed, "have a good time." She fumbled for her keys, managing a wave as Charlotte hopped into her pickup truck.

Before getting into the car, Mari checked the back seat and luggage area. No one was hiding back there, of course. But still, she quickly locked the doors as she got in, starting the engine and pulling out of her space quickly, not lingering. She didn't relax until she made it onto the main road, by herself again.

But as she watched the taillights of Charlotte's truck head in the opposite direction, an almost overwhelming sense of longing welled up inside her. She was envious that Charlotte was brave enough to date. She wanted to accept Charlotte's invitation. She wanted to walk into the party and meet people, get to know the people who lived in her town, start to build her new life.

As badly as she wanted it, however, the thought of being in that crowd, trapped, unable to escape, was simply too overwhelming.

She couldn't do it.

After three months of healing in Alaska, she wasn't any better than she'd been the day it had all happened.

⚅⚅⚅⚅

Ben draped his forearms over his steering wheel, his engine idling almost silently as he watched Mari pull onto the main road after leaving work. He'd been waiting for her to leave for an hour, and he'd been starting to get concerned until she'd finally walked out with the hostess.

Mari had driven off alone, and he liked that she'd been smart enough to check the backseat of her car. Did she know the same thing he knew? Was she watching as carefully as he was?

He waited, his headlights off, carefully scanning the area for any sign of movement.

A car's engine turned over, and his adrenaline surged. He slouched lower in the seat, watching as a black pickup truck pulled out of the parking lot across the street from O'Dell's. It turned onto the road behind Mari's car.

Son of a bitch. Tension hammered at him, and he eased his truck onto the asphalt, keeping far back from the other two vehicles. The black truck stayed behind Mari, trailing from a distance, but not turning off onto any side road.

Mari got out of town and picked up speed, and so did the black truck.

Ben eased his foot onto the gas, keeping to an unobtrusive distance, but staying close enough to get involved if he needed to. Instinctively, he reached below his bench seat and felt the cool hardness of the rifle he'd stashed under there. Still there. Still ready.

For twenty-one minutes, the three trucks drove in silence. There was no sound except the humming of his tires on the asphalt and the whine of his engine.

Then Mari's brake lights went on. She slowed, and then turned off the main road. As she reached the woods, he saw her slow down, as if she was watching the car behind her to see what it did.

So was he.

For a split second, it seemed to slow down, and then it sped up, cruising past her road. Ben considered turning down after Mari, and then decided to follow the truck a little further. He sped past Mari's road as her taillights disappeared into the woods. The moment he passed her road, fear began to hammer at him.

Whoever was in that truck couldn't hurt her, because he was driving away from her house. But if someone was waiting for her at the house, she would be in immediate danger, while Ben was hauling ass *away* from her.

He'd made the wrong choice with Holly. Not again.

With a muttered curse, he hit the brakes and pulled a U-turn across the highway, gunning it to make it back to Mari's road. The moment he reached it, he careened across the oncoming lane and bounced onto her street. He turned his headlights off immediately, slowing the truck down to a crawl as he entered the woods.

Within a couple minutes, he saw the faint glow of lights ahead. He quickly pulled the truck off the road, driving deep enough into the woods to hide it. Then he swung down from the driver's seat, grabbed his rifle, and broke into a steady, stealthy run toward her house.

※※※

One of the spotlights was out.

Mari sat in her truck, staring apprehensively at the ominous, dark woods to the right of her house. The day after she'd arrived, she'd bought six huge spotlights and outdoor extension cords. By nightfall, her house had been surrounded by a ring of light that dove deep into the dark woods in all directions.

But one of the lights wasn't working anymore, the one on the side of the house where the tree had broken through her wall. On that side of her home was an eerie combination of shadows leaching into the impenetrable blackness of the forest. What if someone had broken the light to give them a veil of darkness so they could sneak up to her house? What if—

"No. Stop it!" she said aloud, her voice stark in the silence of night. "You're turning into a crazy woman. There's no one hiding in your woods." Slightly aggravated with her overreaction and still fuming at her inability to muster the courage to accept Charlotte's invitation, she shoved open her car door and stepped outside. Her feet crunched on the ice balls still left from the storm, and she hurried up the steps to her house, quickly unlocking the door and sliding inside.

The interior lights were blazing, and she sighed with relief as she locked the door behind her. But as she did, a slight rustling noise caught her attention. It was coming from the living room.

For a moment, she froze, terror hammering at her, her heart exploding into overdrive. Not moving, not taking a step, she leaned forward ever so slightly to peer around the corner. One of the blankets she'd nailed across the opening had come loose, and it was flapping. Dried leaves and snow littered the floor in front of the opening, drifting across the room as if a wind had blown them around...or someone had tracked them in.

Argh! Again with the drama! "There's no one here," she announced aloud. "This is Alaska, for heaven's sake, not some urban crime area." Then again, it wasn't as if Maple Street on the southern coast of Oregon had been a heavy crime area either. "Stop it!" she ordered herself, forcing her mind away from the past. Dammit. She couldn't keep doing this. She couldn't live like this anymore!

Frustrated, she stormed through the house, making herself look in every closet, in every cabinet, and under every piece of furniture, until even she had to admit that there was nothing dangerous lurking in her house. She was safe. *She was safe.*

After tacking up the blanket with more nails, she walked into her bedroom and yanked down the shades. Tonight she was going to sleep. No more staying awake listening to every sound, being afraid of the nightmares sleep would bring. Nightmares couldn't hurt her. Only guns and bullets, and there were none of those in her house or the surrounding woods right now.

But when she climbed into bed ten minutes later, she could already feel herself tensing in anticipation of the flashbacks that would come when she slowed down enough that her mind was free to wander.

She thought of how safe she'd felt in the bar when John Sullivan had been there with his watchful eyes and brooding looks. That's what she needed: John camped out at the foot of her bed, being her eyes so she didn't have to be so vigilant.

At the memory of John's intense green eyes, she shivered, pulling the blankets closer around her. There was something about him that was so dangerous, so hunted, so...dark. She knew she should be afraid of him, but she couldn't stop thinking about the way Haas had put his hand on John's shoulder.

Haas trusted him. Haas, who knew almost every secret in the entire region, according to Charlotte and everyone else who knew and admired him. Haas, who had disappeared for fifteen years in the eighties and nineties, and then reappeared fifty pounds lighter, packed with muscle, and sporting a haunted clarity in his eyes that no one had ever been able to explain. Haas was too wise to misjudge someone, and he clearly thought John was one of the good guys.

Haas was the first person she'd met when she'd arrived, and he'd gotten her the job at O'Dell's. She trusted Haas, and Haas trusted John.

Was it enough for her to invite him into her room to sit at the foot of her bed to keep her safe? No. She would never be ready for such intimacy with another man.

But at the same time, she thought with a small smile as she rolled onto her side, Haas's faith in John did mean that she had decided to allow him to work on her house. In less than eight hours, John Sullivan would be at her door, and she would be able to relax—

A loud crack sounded outside, and Mari bolted upright,

her heart hammering at the sound. Had that been a gun?

She waited, frozen, barely able to breathe through the terror as images cascaded through her mind, terrible memories. She didn't move, waiting, counting the seconds.

Ten.

Twenty.

Thirty.

There were no more cracks. Just the one. Had it merely been a sound in nature? She let out a shaky breath and leaned back on her pillows, but she knew that the chance had been lost. Sleep was not going to come, not tonight.

So, she closed her eyes and concentrated on the one thing that had brought her peace since her world had exploded a year ago: the pair of brilliant, unblinking, jade-green eyes that she'd seen for the first time tonight.

⋈⋈⋈⋈

Ben gripped the rifle loosely as he watched Mari's bedroom light turn off. The shades were drawn, but he'd caught a glimpse through the windows before she'd pulled them down. He knew that was her bedroom, and that she'd made it in there alive.

For a moment, he didn't move from his hidden position, surveying the woods one more time for the source of the loud crack that he'd heard, but there were no more sounds, other than natural whispers of the woods at night.

Slowly, he eased himself out of the tree he'd perched in and walked carefully across the yard, stepping over the broken branches and debris from the storm. He reached her bedroom and crouched under the window, listening intently.

There were no noises from inside. No reassuring domestic sounds that told him she was alive and safe. Swearing, he eased himself to his feet and angled himself so he could see inside through the crack by the shade. The faint light from the moon slid through the cracks at the edge of the blinds and illuminated the. He could see the outline of her face as she lay in bed, her eyes open as she stared at the ceiling. There was no one with her. Just her, alone, in a bed that looked too big for her. She was on the near side, and the rest of the bed was empty, yawning in desolate abandon as it stretched across the room.

Her face looked so young in the dim light, streaked with silver from the moon. She was wearing a long sleeved sweatshirt with the hood over her head. Her arms were folded across her chest as if she was trying to ward off the world instead of relaxing into sleep.

Protectiveness surged over him, and suddenly, it wasn't about Holly any more, about trying to fix the past, about all the other shit he was carrying. Just like that, it suddenly became about the woman lying in her bed five feet from him. A woman who was still alive, just like his sister had been fourteen months ago. A woman who, if he was correct, had no idea of what was coming for her.

No one did.

Only he knew.

Only he stood in the way of a repeat of what had happened to his sister.

Mari bolted upright suddenly, staring right at the shade where he was. Swearing under his breath, he jerked back, pressing against the house. He heard the shade fly up, and the window opened.

Shit. She must have sensed him. All she had to do was stick her head out, and she'd see him hovering by her window like a stalker. He held his breath, not daring to make a sound. He could hear her breathing, and suspected that she had her face up against the screen, staring out into the night. He glanced back across the clearing, lit by her floodlights, and he saw the faint indents of his footsteps across the debris-laden snow. Shit. Would she see them?

For a long moment, there was no movement, and then he heard her sigh, a delicate, feminine sigh of weariness. "There's no one out there, Mari," she told herself, her voice so soft and gentle that Ben had to close his eyes to keep from leaping out from his hiding place and begging her to repeat it, just so he could hear her voice again.

He had no idea why her voice affected him so deeply, but it did. There was a vulnerability to it that he hadn't heard in so long. A yearning. A realness.

Then he heard the window close, cutting him off from

her...except it wasn't closed all the way. He could still hear her, the soft padding of her bare feet across the floor. The creak of her bed as she climbed in it. Another sigh as she slipped under the covers.

He leaned his head back against the wall, relief pouring through him. Now that he could hear her, he didn't have to see her to know what was going on in her room. His legs suddenly exhausted from so many months of pushing so hard, he slid down the side of her house and sat down on the ground, his rifle resting across his bent knees.

He leaned his head back against the wall, surveying the landscape, as he kept his hearing attuned intently to Mari's bedroom, listening for every sound, his body tensed in readiness to leap up if he heard the sound of an intruder.

He didn't like the floodlights she'd installed. They made the dark woods too impenetrable, and he was too obvious sitting there. Someone could be yards away, watching him, and he would have no idea.

Tonight would not be about catching the bastard.

Tonight was about keeping Mari alive.

Tomorrow he was going to have to convince a woman on the edge to trust him, a man who could do nothing but lie to her.

CHAPTER 3

At ten minutes before eight, a large black pickup truck drove up to her house.

Mari couldn't suppress the leap of anticipation as she peered out the kitchen window. John was driving an oversized Ford that looked like it had several hundred thousand miles and a few decades on it. It was splattered with mud that had been kicked up from the huge tires, and it was the same haunting black that hers was. His truck was old and battered, the kind of vehicle that had survived dozens of battles and had decided not to give up yet.

Then the driver's door swung open, and he stepped out.

In the dim light of morning, John loomed even larger than he had last night in the bar. He wore a heavy black parka down to his hips, and his insulated boots came up nearly to his knees, almost obscuring the faded jeans. His dark hair was even longer than she remembered, still tossed carelessly about. He slammed the door shut and turned toward her, his attention going instantly to her kitchen window and meeting her gaze as he strode toward her front door.

Even from this distance, she could feel the intensity of his green stare, and she shivered, unable to stop from reacting to him as his boots crunched across her yard. He was so rugged and male, a tightly coiled sphere of strength. What was she doing letting him into her house? He was a stranger and—

He knocked on the door, a single heavy rap that made her jump back.

For a split second, she considered not answering it, and then had to laugh at herself. He'd looked right at her, and he knew she was there. Seriously? She was going to hide and pretend she wasn't there? Was she really that wimpy? No, no, no. She definitely wasn't. But that didn't stop her hand from shaking as she turned the deadbolt and pulled the door open.

John was leaning against the railing on her porch, his hands on either side of his hips, as if he were bracing himself. His whiskers were even thicker this morning, but his eyes, God, his eyes were absolutely riveting. "Good morning," he said pleasantly, a greeting far too innocuous for the intensity of her reaction to him.

He'd spoken only two words. That was it. Nothing more. And yet they seemed to leap through her like some sort of electric shock, ricocheting through her almost violently. She swallowed. "Hi."

He averted his gaze, looking out across her property. "You've got a gem here."

Mari followed his gaze, studying the mountain range in the distance. It was barely visible in the darkness of the morning, but there was just enough glow from the sun to showcase the mountain peaks. She smiled, unable to resist the awe in his voice. "That's why I chose it," she admitted. "I loved that the house is perched above the valley with the view of the mountains. It makes me feel free. Like nature has opened its doors to me and invited me in..." Her voice trailed off as John looked sharply at her. Her cheeks flamed at how much she'd rambled on about the house. "Yeah, you probably didn't want that much information—"

"No. It just reminded me of the first time I saw mountains. I felt the same way." He looked past her again, and this time, there was a softness to the lines around his eyes, as if he was seeing things in his mind that weren't in front of him. "Freedom," he said softly. "It's a concept beyond comprehension. You don't grasp it as a kid, and then it's too damn late by the time you figure it out."

She frowned at the undercurrent to his voice, a rich, haunting melody of suffering. His pain was evident. He was clearly tormented by whatever he was thinking about, and suddenly her own loss seemed to spill through her in response.

She recalled the vast sense of loneliness that plagued her, and how it had eased up when she'd first walked onto this land. She'd felt hope the first time she'd seen that vista, a desperate faith that somewhere in this rugged land she would find the peace and security that had been ripped from her. But three months later, the pain had not abated. She was still staggering through her days, fighting for the willpower to survive one more day, to take one more step.

Suddenly, tears brimmed in her eyes, and she had to turn away. "So," she said, clearing her throat and injecting some level of forced cheerfulness into her voice. "Do you want to take a look at the damage?"

"I'm not that profound," he said.

She looked sharply at him in confusion as she started down the steps. "What?"

"I said, I'm not that profound." He levered himself off the railing and vaulted down the three steps to land on the ground beside her. Right beside her. So close she could almost feel the heat from his body. Why was she so aware of him? Loneliness, again? Because that was just not a good enough reason to notice how broad a man's shoulders were. She'd made that mistake before, and she wasn't going to repeat it. Seriously. Especially when he was babbling about things she didn't even understand. "What are you talking about? I didn't say you were profound."

"This is true." He was looking past her, surveying the woods. His face was no longer in relaxed awe. Now, it was intent and focused, as if he were searching the woods for some specific purpose. "However, when I made the comment about freedom, which was fairly insightful, I must admit, you started to cry." He looked back at her, one eyebrow cocked in question. "As I said, I'm not that profound. I can't imagine any circumstances in which I would come forth with an observation so rampant with meaning that it could spur a spontaneous tear from a listener."

She stared at him, even though a part of her wanted to laugh at the boldness of his statement. "You're sort of rude, aren't you?"

A sardonic grin curved his mouth unapologetically. "It's among my many flaws. What clued you in?"

She couldn't stop staring at him, at his vibrant green eyes and unabashed face. He really didn't care? "Most people would just respect my privacy and pretend they didn't notice the tears."

His face darkened. "My sister cried. I pretended not to notice. And now she's dead. So, yeah, I don't really care if I'm rude. You cried. I want to know why. Life is too short to be polite."

His words hung in the crisp air like a thousand daggers burdened with grief. Embarrassment flooded her cheeks at her callousness in the face of his tragedy. Her throat tightened with his pain, and with hers. "I'm sorry," she whispered, the words sticking in her throat. "I'm so sorry."

For a second, she thought he was going to respond with another flippant comment, but then some of the tension seemed to soften in his face. "Thank you."

She nodded. "I cried," she whispered, scraping out the words she had never been able to say to anyone she'd met in Alaska, the words that were too painful to speak, the words that she didn't want to see reflected in anyone's eyes when they looked at her, because it would hurt too much to see them, "because I lost my parents and sister almost a year ago, in a tragic—"

She was going to say accident, but she couldn't belittle the truth when it had been a killing so intentional she still didn't understand it. But at the same time, she couldn't burden some stranger with what had really happened. So, instead she simply shrugged, kicking aside tree branches from the storm. "They were in the wrong place at the wrong time," she said. "Sometimes the pain comes back when I'm not ready for it." As the truth tumbled out, she felt a strange sense of relief, mingled with fear. Relief that the secret she'd bottled up for so long was finally out, and fear that he would respond in some way that would make it worse, that would make the pain insurmountable.

He regarded her silently for a long moment, and she could do nothing but stand there, riveted to her spot, waiting.

Finally, he said, simply, "There are no words."

It was perfect. It was everything, without saying anything, because he understood what it was like to lose someone he loved. "There are no words," she agreed, and just like that, all her fear of him seemed to dissolve. He was a stranger from a rough place, or a rough time, but there was a depth to his soul. She'd felt it, their connection, their shared, unspoken bond based on the kind of scars that would never go away.

He nodded, and then a slow smile curved his mouth. A real smile this time, not a sardonic grin. "I'm guessing your mom would want you to have a back wall on your house?"

She blinked, then a smile seemed to take root somewhere inside her. Somehow, it was the perfect thing to say. "I think she definitely would. She was never a fan of me camping out in the backyard in a trash bag, you know?"

He grinned. "Smart mom." He gestured toward the back of the house with a low bow that had just enough flourish to make her giggle. "After you, m'lady."

She laughed, her heart lightening for the first time in months. "You are way too grungy to be pretending to be a fairytale knight."

He flashed her a smile of perfect white teeth. "Back in the middle ages, I'm guessing all those knights were rank, underfed, and generally unpalatable, so I think I actually have some more backsliding to do before I could adequately pull one off."

"More backsliding?" She raised her brows at his word choice. "So, there was a time when you were all spiffed up? Short hair? Ironed slacks? Polished shoes?"

His smile flickered, so quickly she almost didn't see it happen, then the witty grin was back in place. "Ah, I'm so sorry to disappoint, but the last time I had ironed pants was at my grandpa's funeral when I was four. My mom lost the battle from then onwards." He turned away then, focusing on the tree that was lodged in her house, hiding his face and ending the discussion, but she wasn't blind.

She knew something had just happened. Had he just lied to her about something as simple as whether he'd ever worn dress slacks? That made no sense. She must have imagined it—

But even as she had the thought, she saw him carefully scan her woods yet again, his focus a little too intense and a little too careful. Chills crept down her arms, and she followed his glance. "What are you looking for?"

He glanced at her. "Deer."

She turned to face him. "No, you're not." She set her hands on her hips. "What's going on, John? I want to know."

⚜⚜⚜

Ben's first thought was that Mari was extremely pretty when she was mad.

His second thought was that she was also too damned perceptive.

It was too soon for the rest of the truth. Much too soon. He couldn't risk it. So, instead of deflecting her query with another lie or deception, he asked the question that had been haunting him for so long. "Do you live here alone?"

Her eyes narrowed. "I have a six-foot-six lumberjack husband with a shotgun collection that takes up our whole living room. He'll be home any minute. Why?"

He didn't believe she had a husband. Not for a minute. Not based on what he knew about her. "Because," he replied, easily sliding into the story he'd thought of during his vigil beneath her window, "Haas said that there have been a few break-ins around here, mostly targeted to houses in isolated situations. He asked me to check and make sure your place looked secure." He intentionally let his gaze go to the blanket flapping in the wind over her back wall. "It doesn't." He met her gaze. "Haas said he thought you lived alone, but he wasn't sure. If you really have a huge husband, then you're all set. If not..." he shrugged. "I can check your woods for footprints to see if anyone's been casing it."

When her face went sheet white, he instantly regretted his words. But at the same time, he steeled himself. If Holly had known to be wary, maybe she would still be alive today. Mari needed to know...at least as much as he could tell her. "I'll check around, okay?" he offered. "And I'll get the exterior secured as soon as possible."

"Today?" she asked, her voice high-pitched. "Can you get it sealed off today?" Her panic made it clear that there was no husband coming home to keep her safe tonight...and he was too damned pleased by that little piece of info.

Shit. He wanted Mari to be unattached, didn't he? He

grimaced, but he couldn't shake that feeling of satisfaction that she was solo. Hell. He was a complete ass, and stupid, too. He was in no position to be thinking about the marital status of the woman he had to keep alive.

Dragging his gaze off her, Ben turned his full attention to her house before he answered her. He'd need a chainsaw to hack up the tree, and rebuilding the wall would take time. It wasn't something he could even begin to accomplish in one day, which was good, because it gave him an excuse to shadow her. He started to shake his head, and then saw the flicker of real fear in her eyes, and he swore under his breath, unable to make himself add to her stress. Turning away, he walked around the tree, rapidly assessing. "I can get some plywood sheets and nail them onto the existing house, using the tree trunk as the frame. It means the tree will still be in your living room, but it would at least be secure. I can rebuild during the day, and secure it back at night."

She nodded quickly, and Ben suddenly recalled how he'd heard her unlock the deadbolt when she'd answered the door upon his arrival. The woman had a blanket for a back wall, and she was still locking the front door? He studied her with renewed interest, wondering if maybe, she actually did know exactly how much danger she was in.

He made the decision then.

He'd use today to build trust, and then tonight, he would tell her the truth...or as much of it as he could without risking them all. He managed a grin that was lighter than he felt. "You ready to do some shopping?"

She stared at him blankly. "Shopping?"

"Yeah. I need to get some wood and supplies, and we need to stop at Haas's place. He said I could borrow his tools. I don't have any with me." He raised his brows. "Haas bragged that he makes the best chili in the state. I think he wants to show it off for us. You okay with that?" A couple hours with Haas spouting on about how great John Sullivan was would go a long way for laying the foundation of the story he was going to tell her tonight. "Giving the old man a little company is a fair trade for borrowing his tools."

She stared at him, and then nodded slowly. "Old school

values," she said.

"Something like that."

Mari took a deep breath, and she pulled back her shoulders, fusing strength into her body. It was startling to see her recover, to realize how deep her fear was, and how much control she exercised over it. Admiration coursed through him, and he couldn't halt the surge of interest. She was an intriguing combination of vulnerability that made him want to sit under her bedroom window all night to protect her, and of immense inner strength that made him want to get down on one knee and salute her. Put all her attributes together and...damn. He wanted her, didn't he? He was here on a very specific mission that held both of their lives and his sister's spirit in the balance, and he was actually attracted to her? The first time he'd felt any kind of interest for a woman in too damn long, and it was *now*?And it was *her*? Yeah, getting involved with her sounded like a brilliant idea, because getting personal with the woman whose life he was trying to save wouldn't screw things up beyond all recognition, right? Yeah, *right*.

"Do you really need me to go shopping with you?" she asked. "It's my day off—"

He was tempted to free her, he really was. He had a bad feeling that spending the day with this woman would lead him further into temptation than he could afford to go, but Holly had been killed at two o'clock in the afternoon. Daytime was not a defense. There was no chance in hell he was going to leave Mari alone until this situation was resolved. He needed to keep her safe until it was over. So, instead of cutting her loose and giving them both some breathing space, he pulled her even closer, with words that gave her no choice but to align herself with him. "You really want to stay here alone?"

She glanced at the woods, then sighed. "Am I too wimpy?"

He grinned, laughing softly at her aggravation. "Sometimes, wimpy is sexy as hell—" Oh, shit. Had he really just said that?

Mari's eyes widened in shock, and the air between them suddenly crackled with electricity. The tension grew thick, and he became too damned aware of her pulse hammering in her throat. "You're trouble," she said softly.

His grin widened. "Yes, I am." He couldn't lie to her about that. He was far too attracted to her, and he knew that if he spent as much time with her as he was planning to, things were going to get heated, and she had to know what he was really like. He was trouble. He'd been accused of having no morals many times. And he had never been the kind of guy who deserved a woman like her.

She let out her breath. "I don't need trouble in my life right now."

He studied the tense set to her mouth, and the wariness in her eyes, and shook his head. "I think that maybe you do."

CHAPTER 4

John might be dangerously sexy, carry a boatload of trouble, and exude an undercurrent of violence, but he was also hilarious, charming, and witty, much to her dismay. The man was disarming her defenses, and that was just not a good thing.

Despite her best intentions, Mari couldn't help but laugh as John and Haas held up a massive piece of plywood between them, both men sporting comically serious expressions on their faces. "You're sure this is the decor you like?" John asked. "Because we could always go with the slightly more woody brown instead."

She grinned. "It's exactly the shade I've been dreaming of since I was a little girl, and imagining the plywood remodel I would get to do on my dream house. Let's buy a lot of them. If we have extra, maybe you could build me a new bed out of it, too—" She cut herself off a second too late when John's eyebrows shot up. Bed? She had to make a bed joke? He would think she had her mind...well...exactly where it had been all day since she'd seen him effortlessly lifting Haas's heavy machinery into the back of his truck. The man was sheer strength, the epitome of the Alaska guy stereotype.

John grinned, a smirk of self-satisfaction that no doubt suggested he was being a typical guy and loving the bed talk. "I think you're making a great choice," he said, as he and Haas loaded the piece onto one of the industrial-sized carts at the home supply store. "And yeah, sure, I'd be happy to work on your bed for you."

Heat flared in her cheeks. "Um, yeah, okay—"

He winked at her and turned back to Haas, as the two men started negotiating prices with the sales guy. The closeness between John and Haas was evident. From what she'd gathered, John hadn't been in town long, but the two men had evidently found some sort of common ground. Haas had absolutely insisted on joining them on their shopping trip, and his good humor had eased some of her tension about being alone with a man who was so... intense? Unsettling? Sexy as hell?

Something hard slammed into her hip, and she jumped with a yelp. "What—" She cut herself off when she saw that she'd just been rammed by a rather slouchy and unusually large older woman trying to wheel a cart full of carpet samples.

"I'm so sorry, my dear," the woman said, trying unsuccessfully to redirect the cart away from Mari. She was wearing an ankle length housedress, and her snow boots were sticking out from the hem of the skirt, making Mari smile. Her hair was a fiery red that definitely wasn't natural, and her chin and jaw sank into several layers of skin on her neck. Her head was ducked slightly as she fought with the cart, a battle she was clearly losing.

"Oh, it's okay. I'm fine." Mari quickly grabbed the front of the cart and pushed it back toward the middle of the aisle, her hip still throbbing from the impact.

"Mari! Is there an outdoor socket by the back of the house?" John called over to her. He was holding a massive extension cord that looked big enough to power a lighthouse on the northern coast.

"Yes, there's a number of them," she replied, knowing exactly where they were after having set up all her spotlights.

"Ohh..." The cart-assaulting-lady peered past Mari at John. "Isn't he handsome? Is that your young man?"

Mari glanced over at John again, and a sudden longing washed over her. It wasn't that he was handsome, because he was actually a little rough looking. It wasn't the way his deep voice seemed to call to her, though she had to admit there was a certain decadence about it. It was more the simple feeling of shopping with him, of knowing that she had someone to bounce ideas off of and discuss solutions with.

It was a basic thing, really, to have a partner in one of the mundane tasks of life. She'd forgotten how nice it was to do something so basic with someone else. It made her miss her family, and the life she used to have. Being with John and Haas reminded her of what she didn't have anymore. Not that there was any sense in dwelling over it. Life was what it was, and she had to find a way to move forward. That was why she was in Alaska. She had to find her footing again, and that meant not relying on anyone else to make her happy. With a deep breath, she mustered a cheerful smile. "No, unfortunately, he's simply my contractor."

The woman snorted. "Sweet honey, that man is not your contractor. He's got sex written all over his face when he looks at you." The woman arched one painted-on auburn eyebrow. "And you look at him the same way. If you two aren't a couple, my name's not Sally Sands."

Heat flushed through Mari. Was she really that transparent with how John affected her? It wasn't like she was actually considering doing anything about it. She wasn't in a place to date anyone. For heaven's sake, she still couldn't sleep at night! "I don't know what you're talking about—"

"Mari!" Charlotte hurried up, grinning cheerfully. "What are you doing here?"

Mari was relieved at the interruption, still disconcerted by Sally's assertions about her and John. "I'm here with John and Haas, buying supplies to fix my house. John's going to do it."

"John?" Charlotte echoed, looking past Mari. Then her eyes widened. "Oh…*that's* John?" She looked back at Mari. "*He's* working on your house? You really hired him?"

Mari cleared her throat, shifting restlessly at the gleam in Charlotte's eyes. Was she going to start in on the connection between her and John as well? She'd forgotten about the other side of being surrounded by family and friends, and how they liked to pry into each other's personal lives. "Yeah, well, Haas recommended him—"

"You have *got* to bring him to the wedding as your date," Charlotte announced. "The women in this town deserve a chance to get to know him."

"My *date?*" Mari stared at her. "But I'm not dating

him—"

"You might as well be," Sally interrupted. "There's so much tension crackling between the two of you." She nodded conspiratorially toward Charlotte. "Can't you see all the electricity between them? That man is all over her."

"Is he?" Charlotte looked at John with renewed interest. "Really?"

At that moment, John chose to look over at them. He looked startled to see the three women staring at him, and for a fleeting moment, he had a look on his face like he wanted to bolt. It was gone so quickly she thought she'd imagined it, replaced by a steely expression. Without taking his eyes off them, he muttered something to Haas and walked directly over to them, his long, lean body striding mercilessly across the cement floor. He parked himself right next to Mari's shoulder, so close that his arm was brushing against hers. "May I help you, ladies?"

Sally beamed at him, and Charlotte grinned brightly. "Well, I invited Mari to my sister's wedding next weekend, and she doesn't have a date. We were brainstorming who she might take with her. She's new to town, so she doesn't know a lot of people." She blinked innocently. "I don't suppose you'd be available, would you?"

Holy crap. Really? Had she really just said that? Mari glared at her. "Charlotte," she warned, but got only an innocent smile back from her.

John visibly relaxed, his change in posture so extreme that Mari frowned, realizing he'd been on edge. Had he been worried about what the women were saying about him? What man worried about things like that? "Yeah, I'll take her." He looked again at Charlotte and Sally, who both looked delighted.

He had just agreed to be her date for the wedding? For a split second, excitement rushed through her, followed by raw fear. "No, no, no," she said quickly. "I'm not going. I don't need a date. I—"

There was a loud crack from above, and they all looked up just as a huge box slid off the shelf and catapulted right toward Mari's head.

"Get back!" John lunged for her, thrusting her to the side a split second before the box hit. It landed with an explosive crash and burst open, sending tile fragments all over the aisle. Mari jumped at the impact, her heart pounding in terror as she stared at the carnage. Sally and Charlotte started shouting and people started running toward them.

It would have killed her. If John hadn't pushed her out of the way, it would have *killed* her.

"You okay?" John's arm was still around her, his body between her and the shattered tiles as he pushed her back toward Haas, away from the crowd.

It had been too close. Too close. *Too close.* She gripped his arm as terror settled in her bones. The raw, cold fear that had gripped her so tightly for so long once again crushing her in its vise.

"Mari?" John gripped her shoulders, turning her toward him. "Are you okay?"

She couldn't take her eyes off the box. The straps of her purse were crushed under the edge, and she realized she must have dropped it when John grabbed her. That was how close it had been. Right where she'd been standing. A thousand pounds of ceramic. "That....that...that would have crushed me," she mumbled, starting to shake.

"It didn't hit you." John moved his body in front of her, blocking her view of the accident and forcing her to look at him. "Hey, Mari, stay with me."

She looked up at him, but she couldn't focus on his face. "My purse," she whispered. "It landed on my purse. Did you see that? It was like before. Almost like before. It almost happened again." She couldn't stop babbling, couldn't make the words stop.

His eyes narrowed, and he suddenly pulled her against him, tucking her under his arm. "Haas," he snapped. "Get her purse. I'm taking her out of here." He gave her no time to react or protest. He simply tucked her against him and guided her down the aisle, toward the front of the store. People were still hurrying past her toward the box, but she didn't turn around.

Her chest was too tight. She couldn't breathe.

"Hang on," John said. "We're almost outside."

The door opened and suddenly the cold air hit her, like a sharp slap of reality that cut through the tension in her lungs.

She sucked in the air gratefully, shuddering with relief as she looked around at the parking lot. They were outside. There was space. There was room. Nothing above her head. Plenty of places to run. To hide.

"Here." John opened the door to his truck and helped her into the passenger seat. He leaned into the truck, one hand on the dashboard and the other on the back of her seat, his shoulders looming wide, shielding her from the outside. "Look at me," he said. "Look at my face."

She wrenched her gaze toward him, staring into the intense green of his eyes. She could see the little line of contact lenses around his cornea. Contacts. *Contacts?* It made him seem so...human...so approachable...that a man who exuded such strength actually wore contact lenses. He was with her. He would keep her safe. She wasn't alone.

He smiled, a smile so lovely that it sliced through her terror and eased the grip that fear had on her. "That's right. It's me. I'll make sure you're safe, okay?"

She nodded, and lightly wrapped her fingers in the front of his jacket, needing to feel him, to touch him, to ground herself in him.

"Here you go." Haas leaned in past John, his wrinkled brow furrowed with concern as he held out her purse. "You okay, Mari? That was too damn close."

"I'm okay." *I'm okay. I'm okay. I'm okay.* She repeated the words in her head, using the same mantra that she'd used to bring herself back from the edge of panic so many times in the past. She hadn't had to use it since moving to Alaska and being gifted with the space of outdoors.

John's brow furrowed, and he glanced at Haas. "Hey, can you finish up here? I want to take Mari back to her house. She's a little freaked out by this." But even as he said it, Mari saw him look past Haas, scanning the parking lot carefully, as if he, too, were a little unnerved by what had just happened, as if he wanted to make sure no more boxes of tile were flying across the parking lot at them.

"You bet," Haas said. "I think I can fit it all in my truck, so I'll stop by with it later. Sound good?"

"Yeah, thanks." John turned his attention back to her.

"That okay with you, Mari?"

She nodded numbly, barely able to process the question. "What? Sure, I mean, thank you, yes, that would be great. All of it. Thank you, Haas."

He grinned at her, but his face was still concerned. "Yeah, no problem." He stepped back as John shut the door. "Don't leave her alone, Sully. She doesn't look good. The poor kid's more skittish than a horse in a thunderstorm."

"I'll stay with her," John assured him.

With a shuddering breath, she sagged against the seat, hugging herself as the men parted ways. John opened the driver's door, leaned across her, and grabbed a flashlight from the glove box. "Just give me a sec. I want to check something."

Mari frowned as he turned on the flashlight and then slid under the truck on his back, as if he were a mechanic checking things out. He was under for a few minutes, but instead of getting into the truck when he finished, he popped the hood and checked out the engine as well. By the time he completed his inspection and got back in, Mari was nervous again. "What were you looking for?"

John turned the ignition, and he seemed to relax when it roared right to life. "Thought it sounded a little dicey on the ride over, so I wanted to check a couple things." But he didn't look at her. Instead, he was watching the rearview mirror carefully as he pulled out of the parking lot.

Mari twisted around in her seat, trying to see what he was watching. There were a number of people walking through the parking lot, a few cars pulling in or out. A couple faces she recognized from her nights at O'Dell's, but most were unfamiliar. No one seemed to be watching them. She frowned and looked over at John again. He glanced at the road, and then looked again in his mirror.

She turned and saw that a red pickup truck was behind them, following them to the exit. It was too far away to see who was driving it. "Who is that? In the red truck?"

"Don't know." John turned left out of the parking lot.

"My house is to the right—"

"I know it is."

The truck turned left as well. Tension began to build in

Mari as she watched the red truck follow them. John's hands were tight around the steering wheel, and he took a sudden, sharp turn into the parking lot of the grocery store. He pulled into a spot, and they both watched the red truck continue onward down the main road, until it disappeared from sight.

"Well, that's good," John muttered as he backed out of the parking spot and headed out of the lot, this time heading toward her house. But as he drove, he still kept looking behind them.

Tension was hammering at Mari now, fear from the almost-accident at the store, along with increasing nervousness about John's actions. Did he think that someone was hunting them or something? Was he some paranoid freak? Some ex-military who thought the enemy was everywhere? She stared at him, her hands ice cold. "Who *are* you?" she asked. "I mean, really, who are you?"

He looked over at her, his face grim. "It's time we talked."

There was something dark and ominous in his tone, a violence that made cold slice through her belly. Whatever good humor John Sullivan had exhibited while hanging out with Haas was gone, replaced by a man with so much seething fury and violence in his eyes that she knew, without a doubt, that he was the nightmare she'd been so terrified of for so long. "What do we need to talk about?" she asked, as she slid her hand down toward the buckle of her seatbelt, and her other hand toward the handle of the door. It was still unlocked, she noted.

"Not here. At your house."

"At my house?" Where they would be alone and isolated? *No chance.* She jammed her thumb into the seatbelt button. The latch sprang free as she lunged for the door. It flew open, and she threw herself out the door as John swore and slammed on the brakes.

She stumbled as she hit the road, her hands scraping the asphalt as she fought to stay upright. Then she recovered, and sprinted toward the nearest building, a rambling farmhouse on the edge of the road. "Help," she screamed. "Someone help—"

John tackled her from behind, sending her sprawling to the ground, as he brought them down together, somehow twisting his body so he was beneath her, taking the brunt of the impact. "Let me go!" she screamed, struggling to get free, but his arms were like vices around her. Panic seized her, and she pummeled him with her fists and feet, fighting him off as she tried to slam her knee into his crotch—

"Mari!" He blocked her fists, but a grunt told her that she'd made contact with her knee. "My sister was murdered," he gritted out. "She met a guy, he died, and then two weeks later she was murdered. I don't think he's really dead. I think he killed her, and now he's after you!"

CHAPTER 5

Mari froze in his arms, her body going rigid. "What?" Her voice was stark with anguished horror, and her eyes were wide with shock. "What did you just say?"

He sat up, keeping his grip tight. Her face was ashen, her expression stark, which of course it would be. Crap. He hadn't wanted to tell her this way. Why the hell would she believe him? But he had to try. Everything depended on Mari believing him. "I think he's killed five women," he said, talking fast, knowing he had only seconds to convince her before someone came to assist her, responding to her screams for help. "My sister was the fifth. He finds women who have suffered an intense tragedy, and then he shows up, preying on their vulnerability. He wins them over, then fakes his death, and then murders them a few weeks later."

Mari started shaking her head, a desperate, frenzied denial. "No, no, no, you're insane." She scrambled back from him, holding her hands out as if she could ward him off. "You're crazy. Do you know? You need help—"

He pressed on relentlessly, not giving her the space she wanted. "When your family died, Mari, did you meet a guy? Did some man show up in your life to ease your struggle?"

Her eyes widened, and he saw the flash of fear on her face. "But—"

Her confirmation sent chills of fear down his spine. She'd already met the guy. "And where is he now, Mari? Is he dead? Or...is he still around? Are you still with him?" He stumbled over the last two questions, realizing he didn't even know the status of her relationship with the bastard. He didn't know what stage they were at.

Her face went pale. "He's dead," she whispered.

Dead. Adrenaline pounded through him. If the piece of shit was already "dead," the next step was to come after Mari. How much time did they have? Not much, he was sure of it. "Let me guess. He died in a car accident off a cliff into a body of water? No body found, but the car clearly identifiable, and plenty of witnesses saw him get into the car just before it went over, right?"

Her mouth fell open, and she stopped struggling against him. "But that's impossible. How would you know?"

"It's the same way my sister's husband died."

He could see the fear and denial raging in Mari's face, and regret bit at him for causing her distress, but at the same time, he didn't care what he had to do to keep her alive. "My sister called me right before he died," he continued, desperate to reach her before she called the cops and reported him as insane. Actually, it didn't matter what she told them. Just calling the cops would be enough to screw it all up. "She said she'd found all this stuff in his old apartment that freaked her out. We didn't have time to talk then, but when I asked her about afterwards, she wouldn't talk about it. Then, shortly after that, he turned up dead in the car accident. Two weeks after that, she was murdered in her own living room at two o'clock in the afternoon."

Mari started to shake, and John swore. "I'm so sorry, Mari," he said, softening his voice. "I didn't intend to tell you this way, but I can't let him kill someone else. I'm not going to let it happen, and I had to reach you before you ditched me."

She pulled back, scrambling to her feet, and he let her, rising swiftly to stand before her. "This makes no sense," she said, her voice shaking. "I mean, if it's true, where are the police? Why aren't they here? Besides, Joseph would never have killed anyone, and it's been over three months since he died. Nothing has happened to me, and he hasn't come back from the grave to kill me—"

"I had trouble finding you in Alaska," he said. "You'd moved. I expect he ran into trouble as well. It's taking time for him to find you." He realized she'd been vulnerable for three months. A cold sweat broke out on his brow. How close was she to being killed? Hours?

"Joseph wouldn't have done that," she shouted. "He wasn't a murderer! He was a nice guy who...who...who..." She stopped, staring at him.

"Who what, Mari?" He moved forward. "You broke up with him, didn't you? Because you knew there was something wrong with him? You *knew*, Mari, just like my sister. What the hell did you know? We have to find him before he does it again."

She stared at him, her eyes full of pain. "It was my fault he died," she whispered. "I broke up with him the night before our wedding. He was so angry, so devastated, and then he left. I never saw him again, and then he died, and it was my fault—"

"No!" Ben grabbed her shoulders, wanting to shake from her the same sentiments that he'd heard from his sister after her husband had died. "He didn't die. He's still alive, but I'm not going to let him hurt you. It ends here. It ends for him in Alaska, and I'm going to stop it."

Her hands went to his forearms, gripping tightly, as if she couldn't decide whether to push him away or hold tighter. "Joseph wasn't a murderer—"

"Why did you break up with him the night before your wedding? What did you sense? You had to know something. Trust your instincts, because they've kept you alive." The look of pain and guilt on Mari's face enraged him. How dare the manipulative bastard trick her like that? Just as he'd done to his sister. "Why did you break up with him, Mari?"

She stared at him, and suddenly the fight seemed to leave her. "He scared me," she admitted quietly. "He was so nice to me when I needed it—" She blinked, as if realizing that she was confirming what Ben had said. "But there was something about him that seemed...evil...I don't have another word for it. I had dreams that he killed me." She looked at him, searching his face. "I thought I was losing my mind because of all I'd been through. He was so angry when I broke up with him. I thought...I thought he was going to kill me right then, for a split second. But then he left and got in the car accident. I felt so guilty..."

Ben closed his eyes, gripping her shoulders just a little

tighter. How close had she come that night to pushing the bastard beyond his limits? "If you absolve yourself of the guilt of causing his death," he said quietly, opening his eyes to study her expression. "If you stop worrying about all the emotional burdens you were carrying, and if you give yourself credit for being clear-headed, do you really think that you were wrong to break up with him?"

Mari pressed her lips together, searching his face for the answers, for the truth that she already knew. "I—"

"What's wrong?" The door to the farmhouse swung open, and an older man stepped out. "Who was screaming? You okay, miss?"

Ben stiffened, studying Mari's expression as she whipped around to look at the man. He watched her carefully for any indication of what she was going to do. He wouldn't stop her, but if she turned on him, he had no choice but to get the hell out of there. No choice. Her hands tightened by her side, her mouth pursed, and her eyes darted back and forth between them.

The man moved down the stairs toward them, his gaze riveted suspiciously on Ben. "You were screaming," he said, and Ben saw one hand was out of view behind his back. What was he carrying? A gun? Shit.

Slowly, Ben dropped his hands from Mari and shifted his weight, glancing at his truck to see how far away it was. If the guy had a gun, he'd never make it. Shit. His heart started to pound as he looked back at Mari. Her skin was still ashen, and her pulse was hammering in her neck. Snow still caked her back from when he'd knocked her down, and he swore. Why would she trust him? *Why?* He'd told her stories that had no proof, at least not in this moment.

She looked at her rescuer. "Do you know Haas Carter?" she asked.

He frowned. "Yeah, sure, everyone knows Haas."

"Has he ever been wrong about anyone?"

The man narrowed his eyes as he looked again at Ben. He was only about ten feet away now, getting too close. "No, he hasn't. The man can spot shit from a continent away, and smell roses in a pile of manure six stories high and ten miles wide." He glanced again at Mari, and then back at Ben. "He used to work for some secret government shit back in the day. You don't mess with Haas. Why?"

Mari met Ben's gaze, then her attention slithered away, back to the other man. "This is John Sullivan," she said, her voice strong, despite the trembling beneath the surface. "He's new to town, but Haas thinks he's a good man. He trusts him."

The farmer followed her glance, and Ben stiffened. He wanted to bolt, like he'd done so many times in the last six months, but something made him stay this time. And he knew that something was Mari. The pain she carried, the strength she called upon to forge forward despite the traumas she had faced, that moment of understanding they'd shared on her front steps. Against his instincts, he took his gaze off the man, the one who was the threat, and looked at Mari. The other male might be the one who could take him down, but Mari was the one who could save him, in more than one way.

Her gaze flickered toward him, and then their gazes locked.

"Did he hurt you?" the man asked, his voice a low and lethal tone. "'Cause Haas is getting old, and one of these days, he's going to lose his edge. One of these days, he's going to make a mistake about who to trust."

"No," she replied, still looking at Ben. "He didn't hurt me."

"He scare you?"

"Yes." Her answer was a whisper.

Suddenly, there was a click, and a rifle was pointed at Ben's face. Ben froze, his adrenaline whipping into a frenzy as he fought not to react. One quick move, and he could wrest the rifle from the old man, but he didn't dare move. He needed Mari to make the choice.

Mari yelped. "No, no, no! Don't shoot him!" She started to leap toward the gun, and Ben swore and shoved her backward.

"Not in front of the gun," he commanded.

"No!" She lunged forward and flung herself at Ben, wrapping her arms around his chest.

The man swore and averted the gun, while Ben swung them both around so his body was between her and the gun. "Don't ever do that—"

"Okay," she interrupted, staring up at him.

Something tightened in his gut, and he became viscerally aware of her body pressed up against his. "Okay, what?" he asked.

"Okay, take me home. Tell me the rest." She searched his face, those brown eyes so intense and pure that they seemed to carve right through all the blood on his soul. "I believe you."

I believe you. The words plunged right into his gut, and for a moment, he felt as if the entire world had shifted beneath his feet. *She believed him.* It was surreal, the depth of emotion swirling through him at her words. People didn't believe in him. No one had, in his whole life, except for Mack. No one, with the exception of Mack, had believed his story, that he was the good guy. But Mari, who had so much shit in her past, so many reasons to be afraid, believed him.

Without a word, he tightened his arms around her and pulled her close, crushing her small frame against his, as if he could enfold her against him and shield her from what would be coming for her, and for them.

She melted into his embrace, no longer resisting, as if she were simply too drained to fight anymore.

"Damn lovers' spat," the farmer grunted. "Don't be screaming like that again if you don't mean it."

Ben couldn't help but grin as he turned his head. He wasn't going to argue the lovers' spat label. "Sorry to disturb you."

The man glared at him. "Good thing Haas likes you, or I might have shot you just for interrupting my coffee. Take your woman home and stop scaring her. Hear?" He waved his rifle. "Or it won't matter if Haas tattoos himself to your ass. I'll shoot you anyway. Got it?"

Ben grinned as he slung his arm around Mari's shoulder, tucking her against him, ridiculously pleased by her acquiescence as she let him anchor her against his side. She wasn't fighting him anymore. Trust was beginning to build between them, tenuously, he was sure, but it was a start. He'd made it past the first hurdle. "Let's go home," he said as he turned her back toward the truck.

"My home," she corrected, glancing at him. "It's not your home."

"Yeah, sure." But he saw the farmer glance at them, his

eyes narrowed. Yeah, the man had heard his comment, laying claim to Mari's space. He knew he'd be checking in with Haas, and that was the way it should be. The groundwork was being laid.

And now, it was time to get serious.

⌘⌘⌘

"This is what I found in my sister's desk." John sat beside Mari on the couch, a somewhat battered large manila envelope in his hand.

She was still shaken by what John had told her, but there was no way for her to deny the ring of truth in his words. Too much made sense, and too much seemed to clarify what she'd been through with Joseph. John had the missing information that she'd needed in order to understand what she'd been through and why she'd reacted to Joseph the way she had. But at the same time, it was impossible to fathom that the man she'd almost married was a serial killer. "What is that?"

"His stash." John shook the contents onto her coffee table. Newspaper clippings spilled out, along with pages torn from a notebook with scrawls on them. They were divided into six sets, each paper-clipped together. On the top of each stack was a newspaper article accompanied by a photograph of a woman. "Six women," he said. "Each of them was the subject of a newspaper article that detailed a trauma that they'd gone through." He held up one, an image of a tearful woman clutching a small dog. "My sister, Holly, interviewed after the school she taught at burned down, killing several of the children in her classroom."

Mari sucked in her breath as she took the stack. "Holly Forsett," she read. Even though the image was black and white, the tears on Holly's cheeks were glistening, and her dark eyes were shadowed with grief.

"The image got nationwide attention as the symbol of the school tragedy," John said. "I think he saw it, and then came after her." He set another stack in her hand. "Bev Smith's family was killed by a drunk driver who had just been released from prison due to overcrowded conditions." And another. "Julie Timmins lost her father, brother, and fiancé in Iraq all within two days of each other."

Tears began to burn in Mari's eyes for all the trauma these women had faced.

"And you." He set an article in her hand, and she saw her own eyes staring back at her. Beneath her face was the screaming headline, "Mass Murder in a Small Town." She jerked her gaze off it, unwilling to read the sensationalized version of the tragedy that had stolen her family from her. Instead, she focused on John, anger simmering inside her. "So, you knew my family had died that day when you asked me why I was crying. You *knew*, and you made me tell you."

Regret flickered across John's handsome face. "Yeah, I knew about your family, but I didn't know that's why you were crying. I was trying to figure out if Abraham had found you yet."

"Abraham?" she echoed, trying to follow his logic. "Who's Abraham?"

"That was the name he used when my sister married him." Grief filled his eyes, and he turned his head away.

His visible grief plunged past the anger that had been building inside Mari, and she sighed. "I can't blame you for all this," she said. "It's not your fault." She tossed the clippings on the table and leaned back against the tattered couch, the one she'd found in the living room when she'd moved in and decided to keep.

Yes, it was old, and it showed years of wear, but there was something about the faded blue plaid that reminded her of her mother's homemade clothes she'd insisted they all wear growing up. It felt comfortable to her, so she'd kept it. "Tell me the rest. Tell me how you found me." As awful as it was, she had to hear the entire story. No more secrets.

CHAPTER 6

John shifted so he was facing her, one arm resting above her head along the back of the couch, and the other on his knee, which was resting lightly against her hip. She stared at his knee, her heart starting to pound at the feel of him against her. She should move away. She knew she should. But she didn't want to. There was something about the touch of another person, of a man, of *John*, that felt good. She'd been isolated too long. As John leaned toward her, his muscled shoulders straining against his flannel shirt, his hair curling on his collar, she felt safe, like she was going to finally start to get answers about the hell that she'd been struggling with for the last year.

"After my sister died, and I found the stack of pictures, I did a little checking." He ran his hand through his hair, raking it back from his face. She saw a faint scar above his right eye, a mark from long ago. He was a man who had never lived a completely safe existence. She noticed that he had a hole from an old ear piercing in his right ear as well. "By the time I tracked them down, the first five women were all dead, supposedly murdered by someone close to them. A brother, an uncle, an ex-boyfriend. Always a male, always someone they knew." Intellect flared in his eyes. "Just like my sister."

She blinked. "Who murdered her?"

He didn't hesitate. "Abraham did."

"But you just said they were all murdered by someone close to them—"

"He always sets it up so it *looks* like they were killed

by someone they knew. Since Abraham has already faked his death, no one looks at him. How could he do it if he's dead? It's the perfect cover." His face looked so drawn and exhausted, but at the same time, there was a fire burning in his eyes and a fierce set to his jaw, a man ignited with determination. "After my sister died, I tracked down every single one of those women. Same story, every time. According to friends and family, every woman had faced a trauma that had been covered in the press. A guy showed up to rescue her, but no one really knew much about him. Eventually, he died in a car wreck, and then a couple weeks later, she was dead, murdered by a man close to her. Same pattern, *every single time.*" He leaned back, clasping his hand on top of his head. "He names himself after the old testament. David. Abraham. Joseph. Emmanuel. Matthew. A angel of mercy to save these women and then kill them. My sister was his fifth victim." He looked at her. "You're the only one in that stack who's still alive, but you've already completed two-thirds of his profile. The next step in his game is your death."

A cold chill settled in her bones and she looked out the window. The vast Alaskan wilderness that had seemed so safe after what had happened to her family in that crowd, suddenly seemed terrifyingly isolated. "What's his real name?"

"I don't know. His description changes every time. I don't know what he looks like. What his accent is. His real name. He's a master of blending in and hiding who he truly is." He shoved himself off the couch and strode across the room to the picture window. He braced his palms on the frame, peering out into the wilderness. "But he's out there, somewhere, and he can't let you live. He has to kill you."

Mari swallowed, her head pounding against the stress. "Why? Why does he have to kill me?"

John looked back at her. "Because that's what he does. Who knows why the hell he's doing it? But it's what he does. Do the women reject him, and he has to punish them? Does he find a new woman?" He met her gaze. "The article about you was dated three weeks before my sister was murdered. He already had you in mind when he killed her. I think he decided it was time to move on and save another woman."

Mari felt sick, so utterly nauseous at the thought of

what Joseph had done, her mind instantly jumping to all the times that Joseph had made her uncomfortable. How many times had she'd seen that flash of coldness on his face that had been chased away before she could digest it? She'd been fooled by him, tricked into trusting him and ignoring her instincts. "I almost married him," she whispered, feeling so stupid. "I almost *married* him. I'm so stupid—"

"No." John strode across the room and crouched in front of her, gazing at her intently. "You need to understand that this guy is an expert at what he does. The reason he selects the women he does is because they're vulnerable. They'd just had their world completely blown up, and they need something, *anything*, to hold onto so they don't drown." He grabbed her hand, forcing her to look at him. "You had no chance to resist him, Mari, but you managed to get out in time. You didn't marry him, did you? My sister did. All the other women did. But *you didn't.*"

She stared at him, gripping his hand. "I didn't," she agreed, her throat raspy and raw. "I couldn't do it." She held onto his words, desperately trying to find a way to believe she was stronger than Joseph, than the man who was planning to kill her.

"Because you knew." He touched her cheek gently. "Despite all the burdens you were carrying, and your need for someone to carry you through hell, your instincts sensed something and you got out." He smiled softly, and there was no mistaking the pride in his eyes. "You did good, Mari. Really good. Be proud, not ashamed."

She nodded, and let out her breath, but her hands were still shaking. "Okay, so then, let's just pretend that I'm smarter and tougher than he is, okay?"

John grinned. "The fact that you're sitting here on this couch, alive and unharmed three months after you ditched him says that you are. No need to pretend."

Mari nodded, but it wasn't as if she could shake the fear that had settled permanently in her spine. "So, then, what next? He has to set someone up for my death, right? But I don't know anyone up here. I haven't really made friends, and I haven't dated anyone. And my family... is dead." *Dead. Dead. Dead.* She looked at John, a sudden fear congealing in her belly. "He didn't...he didn't *kill* my family, did he? He didn't make that happen so he could rescue me, did he?"

John started to shake his head, but then stopped. "Shit, Mari. I never thought of that, but I don't know. I guess it's possible. But how would he have found you? You were living in coastal Oregon, and my sister was in southern Maine."

She realized how tightly she was gripping John's hands, and she immediately let go. Here she was, doing the same thing she'd done with Joseph, falling into John's strong arms to help her cope.

A sudden thought made fear congeal in her chest. What if John was Joseph? Was Joseph that good at changing his appearance that he could fool even her? What if *this* moment was Joseph's next move? She looked sharply at John, searching his face. He was taller than Joseph and broader, but those things could be altered with heel inserts in his shoes or a padded jacket. She looked at his eyes, at his bright green eyes, and went cold. "Are those colored contacts?"

John went still, so still that her heart started to pound. "Why?"

Why? Not a denial. *Why?* Dear God, was it him? Nervously, she glanced around, but there was no way to defend herself. If John *were* Joseph, she'd be a fool to expose him while she was alone here with him and force him to act. Her heart pounding, she shook her head, her voice stuck in her throat.

John stared at her, his green eyes so intense as he watched her, then he swore under his breath and rocked back so he was sitting on the floor instead of crouching. He draped his arms over his knees and watched her. "You think I could be him."

"What?" she gasped, trying to instill shock in her voice. "How could you be him? I dated him for six months. I would know—" But she cut herself off. If Joseph was really that good, *would* she really know? "But you know, I think it would make sense to call the police, right? I mean so we can catch him and stuff?" She started to reach for her purse, which she'd set on the table, but John set his hand on top of it, locking it in place.

She froze, her hand still extended. "Um—"

"You can't call the police," he said quietly.

"Why not?" She blurted out the question before she

meant to. She didn't want to corner him into making a move before she could devise a plan—

He waited a long, interminable moment before answering. When he did, he kept his gaze locked on her face. "Because they'll arrest me."

Her hands became ice cold and sweat trickled down her back. "You?" she whispered. "Why?"

Again, another long pause while he searched her face. "The police think I'm the one who murdered my sister. My name's not John Sullivan. It's Ben Forsett, and there's a manhunt searching for me right now, to throw me in prison for the murder of Holly Forsett. If you make the call, the police will arrest me, and no one will be looking for the man who really killed Holly, the one who's coming after you."

<hr/>

The expression of shock and horror on Mari's face made Ben's stomach turn. He knew it had been too soon to tell her the truth, but he'd had no choice. She was too intelligent, and he needed her trust.

Her mouth opened and closed in silence, her face ashen. She looked so small and fragile on that huge couch, making him want to haul himself off the floor and sweep her up in his arms and protect her, and take away her pain. His body actually shook with the need to stop the hell of his life from pouring into this room, but he knew that he had no choice. No matter how badly he wanted all of this to be nothing more than a bad dream, it wasn't. It was a living nightmare that wouldn't let any of them go.

He hadn't protected his sister, but he would not fail Mari.

"Holly called me two months before she died," he said, gritting his teeth against the guilt, and the anguish of reliving the story that he'd replayed again and again in his mind, trying to find ways to make it unfold differently. "She told me that she and Abraham had eloped and gotten married. I hadn't even met the bastard yet, and I wasn't as happy for her as she had wished. I asked questions about him that she couldn't answer. She got angry that I couldn't be happy for her, and she hung up on me."

Mari stared at him. "Joseph wanted to elope," she whispered. "None of my friends ever met him. He kept me away from everyone."

A cold chill settled in Ben's bones. How close had Mari come? "I didn't talk to her for six weeks. Not a single communication," he said, unable to keep the regret from his voice. "I was too damn busy to worry about it, and still pissed that she'd gotten married to some guy I hadn't met. Then, she called one night, at two in the morning. I was still at work, but she left a message saying that maybe I was right, that she found something about Abraham that she wanted me to look at." The guilt seemed to crush him again, never abating even in the ten months since she'd died. "I was in the middle of a trial. I didn't call her back."

Mari was watching him, and her eyes were shiny with unshed tears. "What happened?" she whispered.

"He died in a car accident two days later. My sister was so freaked out that she wouldn't tell me what she had found. She wouldn't talk about any of it. She just kept saying it was her fault that he'd died."

Mari's face paled, and he recalled how she'd said almost the exact same words about Joseph. "Then what?"

"I got a text from her a couple weeks later at ten in the morning. She said she'd meet me at home and that she was going to tell everyone the truth." The truth. The whole truth. The truth that had damned him. "Her text felt off, and I knew something was wrong. I left my office that instant. I just dropped my shit and walked out." The one day he'd finally gotten his priorities right, and it had burned him.

"What truth?"

He met Mari's gaze. "That's the irony, Mari. I thought she was going to tell me what had really happened with Abraham, but I was wrong. It wasn't her texting me. It was him. He had her phone and he'd texted me to get me out of the office by ten in the morning."

Mari frowned. "Why did he want you out of the office?"

"So I had no alibi for the next four hours."

Her face paled. "What?"

It was so clear now, but at the time, he'd been a stupid

pawn. "She and I always referred to our mom's place in northern Maine as home, so that's where I went. It's a six-hour drive. I'd been on the road for four hours when I got a call from an unlisted number. I always answer them because I get a lot of calls in my job. It was some guy, saying that he was Holly's neighbor and he'd heard shouts from her house." Shouts. His own sister's screams for someone to help her.

Mari was leaning forward, listening intently, and Ben focused on her, trying to ground himself in the present instead of letting the past consume him. "I called my mom, but she said Holly wasn't there and she hadn't heard from her all day. So I turned around and hauled ass back to her house. I got there at four and..." He swore. "The door was locked. I used my key to get in, and when I walked in, the place was trashed and Holly..." He couldn't keep his voice steady, the grief just as strong as the day it had happened. "She was on the floor in the living room, a knife sticking out of her chest."

Mari sucked in her breath. "Was she still alive?"

"Yeah, yeah, she was. I could hear her breath rattling in her chest. It sounded like she was drowning, like blood was in her lungs." He could still remember the acrid smell of blood, the roar of his own voice as he lunged for her, and he could still feel the cold, slick handle as he'd grabbed the dagger. "I ran across the room as I dialed 9-1-1. I don't even know what I yelled into the phone, and then I threw my phone aside and grabbed her. She was reaching for me, her hand—" In his mind, he could still see her hand stretching for him. "She was trying to talk, but she couldn't. Just gasps, these horrific sounds of death." He'd heard those sounds twice before when he was a kid, but nothing had prepared him for having it be his little sister. "I grabbed the knife to pull it out, and she screamed, so I didn't. I didn't know whether to remove it or not, you know?"

He was on his feet suddenly, pacing the small room, unable to contain his energy, his tension. "So I just ripped off my shirt and pressed it to her chest, trying to stem the flow of blood, but there was so much. It was this bright red, coming out of my sister—"

He ran his hands through his hair, still pacing, still walking, still trying to outrun the memories. "I started to pull her into my arms, but she grabbed my hand. She kept pulling at it, trying to talk. I realized... I realized she was putting my fingers on her wedding ring." He stopped then, looking at Mari, whose face was pale. "She wanted me to notice her wedding ring, Mari. It took me a second to process it, and then I looked at her, and I asked her if Abraham did it. It made no sense, because he was dead, but something made me ask." He looked at Mari, desperate for her to understand, to know, to believe him. "She nodded," he whispered. "I asked if Abraham did it, *and she nodded*. And then I said but he was dead, and she shook her head. It was him, that bastard killed my sister."

And Holly had tried to warn him. She'd tried to ask him for help two weeks earlier. And he hadn't done it.

"What happened next?" Mari asked, her voice a trembling whisper.

"The police came. The ambulance. They took her." Ben ran his hands through his hair, surprised to see they were shaking. "She died in the ambulance without saying another word. I told them what she'd said, and I thought they'd hunt for Abraham, but a week later, they arrested me. The text that she had apparently sent me, saying that she was at home and was going to tell the truth was what buried me. They thought that she was going to tell my law firm the truth about me, and that I'd killed her to save my job. My job, Mari, my worthless job. Those stupid people actually thought I'd kill my own sister for a *job*." He looked at her. "And you know what? Every single person at my firm told the police that they thought I was capable of murdering her. Everyone had a story about me, to make the police believe I was that guy."

Mari was frozen on the couch, staring at him as tears rolled down her cheeks.

Ben had nothing more to say. That was it. That was his story. That was all he had to offer to make Mari believe in him.

But instead of telling him she believed him, Mari just stared at him, her face still stricken. Ominous silence began to build in the small, rough living room.

Ben felt the tension begin to thicken. Why had he thought Mari would believe him? People he'd worked with for fifteen years had sold him out. Why would this woman who had no reason to trust the world, let alone him, see through the shit and see the truth? His fist bunched at his side. "I don't give a shit if you believe I didn't kill her," he said. "I don't give a crap if you report me to the police. But I will tell you right now, that I'm not going to prison until that bastard is done pulling his shit, and until I know that you're not going to be the next one in line."

He grabbed his keys off the coffee table. "You won't see me, but I'll be around, and I'll be watching. I'll stop him. I promise." Without another word, he spun around and strode across the room. The agony and grief over reliving Holly's death was gone, replaced by the cold, hard visage of war that he'd been living for the last year. He reached the door and his fingers closed around the cold, metal knob—

"Ben."

He froze, his senses leaping into high awareness. He didn't turn, but he went on alert, listening for the telltale sign of a cell phone dialing, or the swish of a text message being sent. For any indication that she was about to tell the world where Ben Forsett was hiding.

But he didn't hear any electronics. He just heard the creak of the floorboards, the soft tread of her feet as she walked up behind him. He went rigid, not turning, just waiting.

And then he felt the soft slide of her hand over the back of his shoulder. He sucked in his breath, his adrenaline jacking at the contact, waiting for her touch to change. For her fingers to dig in. For her to grab his shoulder and spin him toward her, accusation flashing in her eyes for lying to her, for not saving his sister, for being a scum-sucking pig who let Holly die.

Her fingers did tighten, but it was so slight that it was almost imperceptible. "Ben," she whispered. "I'm so sorry. I'm so incredibly sorry."

Stunned, he turned his head enough to look at her. There were still tears glistening on her cheeks, and her eyelashes were wet. She met his gaze, and there was nothing in her face except empathy and sadness. No accusation. No recrimination. No anger. Not even fear. Just emotions so deep and so raw that they seemed to plunge straight into his gut. Slowly, in disbelief, he let his hand slide off the knob as he turned to face her. "I didn't kill her," he said gruffly.

To his numb shock, she nodded. "I know."

"You do? You believe me?" He didn't understand. "Why?"

She set her hand over his heart then, a touch so soft and gentle that he didn't even know how to react to it. "Because you showed me your pain." She smiled sadly. "I know that kind of pain, Ben, and I know that it's real in you. In me. I wish I didn't know how to recognize it, but I do."

Her words seemed to lift a thousand tons of weight from his shoulders. The room actually seemed brighter, as if a thick cloud had rolled away from the sun. Fresh energy surged through him, reigniting his commitment and determination. "I didn't get there in time," he said. "I failed her. I won't fail her again by letting this guy get away, or by letting him kill someone else." He raised his hand to her face, to the incredibly soft skin on her cheek. "I won't let him hurt you," he said, unable to keep the fierceness out of his voice. "I won't."

"I know." She laid her hand over his, pressing his palm to her face. "And I'll be honest with you in return. I have to tell you something."

"What is it?" He slid his hand to the back of her neck, tangling his fingers in her hair. She felt so real, so alive, so beautiful, a respite from the hellhole that had become his life since he'd walked into Holly's house ten months ago.

"When my family died," she said. "I didn't know how to keep going. They were my world. Then when Joseph died, I felt like it was too much. It had been my fault they were killed, and my fault Joseph had died—" She managed a small smile. "—though now, I know that part wasn't my fault. That morning when I got the call that Joseph was dead, I made the decision to keep on living, to find a way to go on. That's why I moved here. Because it was the only way I could survive."

The strength and bravery in her voice touched him, and he nodded. "Yeah, I get it."

Her fingers wrapped in the front of his jacket, which he was still wearing. "My point is, Ben, that I'm scared to death, but at the same time, I'm not ready to die. I'll help you fight him. We'll do it together. For Holly. For all those poor women he killed, and for the ones next in line."

There was such fierceness in her voice that he had to smile. Gone was the fear he'd seen earlier, replaced by the burning strength that told him exactly how indomitable she was. He knew now why she had been able to extricate herself from Joseph, when none of the other women had. Mari might be carrying the shadows of a terrible past, but there was a fire and a courage in her that shone like a bright flame in a hurricane, a breath of hope in the spiral that his life had become, in the hell he'd lived for so long.

Suddenly, she wasn't simply the next victim on a psycho's list. She wasn't just the woman he needed on his side to stop a serial killer. She was more than that, so much more. She was Mari Walsh, a passionate, vibrant woman who seemed to breathe the life into him that he'd been without for so long. She was a survivor, a beautiful woman who carried no airs or judgment, who bled with her heart and spoke the truth with her words. She was everything, a gift, a breath, and freedom.

Her cheeks flushed, and her breath became ragged. "Why are you looking at me like that?"

"Because," he paused as he tangled his fingers deeper into her hair and slid his other hand down her side to her hip, "you're getting to me."

She swallowed, and her hands tightened on his jacket. "I'm a total emotional mess," she whispered. "I'm in no place to get involved."

"I'm an escaped murderer on the run, skating through each day on a dozen different identities," he said, dropping his head so his mouth was hovering just above hers. "Not the kind of guy any girl should have fantasies about."

Her brown gaze was riveted on his. "Who said I have fantasies about you? I'm afraid of men now."

"I'm not a man," he said, tightening his grip on her. "I don't exist. I'm a ghost." And then, well aware that it was probably the worst choice he could have made in that moment, he kissed her.

CHAPTER 7

Ben's kiss was pure heat, a decadent temptation that promised seduction, passion, and raw, untamed sex.

But it was also more than that. It was him offering her his strength. It was the formation of an unshakeable bond with a man who understood the nightmares that chased her and had endured the same loss that she had. Ben was a survivor who had braved a hell as bad as hers to fight for the ending he wanted. He made her feel like there was hope, that it was right not to give up, and that it was okay to want to reclaim living after everyone she'd loved had died.

His whiskers prickled as he kissed her, his tongue sliding in a seductive caress that ignited emotions and longings that she hadn't felt in so long. With a low growl, he locked one arm around her waist and anchored her against him, the kiss getting more intense, more possessive, and more desperate, as if he needed the connection as much as she did.

She knew her need for him wasn't logical or smart. She knew that she should step back, stay focused, and protect herself, but with the heat of his body pouring into her, she wanted nothing more than to let herself tumble into his seduction. She needed him to envelop her in his raw strength, in his relentless courage, and in the depths of the grief she understood so well.

Releasing his jacket, she slid her hand over his chest. She could feel the steady, strong beat of his heart beneath her palm, and it felt incredible. There was life, passion, and fire burning in this man, all the things she had been struggling to find since her world had fallen apart.

He whispered her name as he pulled her closer, sliding his kisses down her neck. Chills raced through her, and she closed her eyes, astounded by how incredible it was to experience such sensual gentleness. His seduction was like a call to her very soul, luring it to reawaken and start living again. He pulled back and stared at her, his green eyes blazing with so much intensity that her body leapt in response.

They both moved at the same moment, coming together in a kiss that shredded all their defenses. Hot. Fiery. Intense. Desperate. He trapped her hand against his chest with his palm, and his other hand went to her lower back, then he slid it lower, dragging her against him until her breasts were crushed against his chest. Her nipples ached, ignited by the feel of his hard body against them. She tangled her fingers in his hair, desperate to have him closer, to kiss him more deeply, to—

A car door slammed outside, making them both jump. Ben released her instantly, leaping to the window in a single, effortless move as he held out his hand to tell her to stay back.

Of course she wasn't going to move. She couldn't even think, not with the heated passion of his kiss still pulsing through her. She blinked, trying to bring herself back. "Who is it?"

"Haas. He's unloading the truck." Ben turned back to her, and his eyes went right to her mouth.

Silence swelled between them, and her heart started to pound again.

"Sorry." He didn't take his gaze off her. "That wasn't my plan."

She managed a small smile. "Mine either."

Again, silence.

She cleared her throat, uncomfortably aware of the intensity of his stare. What was he thinking? She didn't want to know. She really didn't. "What now?" she asked.

One eyebrow went up, and his gaze went right to her mouth again.

Dammit. He thought she was talking about the sex? *What now?* Really? What kind of question was that? That was lame and weak, and made her sound needy. She'd been needy when Joseph had showed up in her life, and it was pretty damn clear that needy was not a good state of mind. Needy led to poor, desperate choices. It was better to be strong and independent, powerful enough not to be sucked into the temptation of being saved. She could only be with someone who wanted her to be strong, not weak and dependent. She raised her chin. "I meant, what's the plan with the Joseph situation. I wasn't talking about the kissing thing..." Ugh. She sounded like such a klutz.

But Ben gave her a break and didn't comment on her stumbling awkwardness. "Who matters to you?"

She blinked at the question. "What?"

"Who matters?" He walked over to her, and she couldn't suppress the surge of anticipation as he neared. She went still, her heart pounding as he gently pushed a strand of hair back from her face. She'd figured his comment that he hadn't meant to kiss her had been designed to set their relationship back to where it had been, reverting them to strangers bonding over a psychotic madman. But his touch was more than that. His caress felt amazing, and it was too intimate to ignore. "Joseph will need to set someone up for your death," he said. "Someone who is close to you. I need a list of names—"

"There's no one." She could hear Haas whistling outside, and a part of her wanted him to go away and let them finish what they'd started. But at the same time, she knew his arrival had been a gift. She didn't want to sleep with Ben. She didn't want to get involved with anyone. Not now. Not ever, maybe. And not with the man who was her only chance of staying alive. "I haven't kept in touch with anyone from Oregon. I needed a break from the memories, and I haven't gotten to know anyone here. There's no one." As she said the words, she realized how pathetic they sounded. She was a grown woman, without a single person in her life who was close enough to set up for her murder...hmm...well...that was not exactly the way to look at it, she supposed.

But instead of looking like she was some pathetic wuss, a triumphant gleam appeared in Ben's eyes. "Excellent."

"Excellent? Why?"

"Because there's no one for him to pick. It limits his options."

Mari's stomach churned at the topic. Were they really

discussing who might get set up for her murder? It felt so horrifically surreal, and she could barely comprehend that this was actually happening. "Are you sure we can't call the police in on this? I mean—"

"All the evidence points to me killing Holly. You'll have to tell the police that the man you think will come after you is presumed dead, and there's absolutely no evidence at all connecting him to the other women. Your only proof would be my claim that I found all those files in my sister's house, and that she said her dead husband did it. Since I'm accused of killing her, I don't make the most convincing witness." He shook his head. "We've got nothing to go on, Mari. Nothing. Not yet, at least, but that will change." He gave her a grim look. "Right now, all they care about is putting me in prison. Nothing else. They have their guy, and it's me. My prints were on the knife because I tried to pull it from her chest. There were no other ones on that knife. Just mine."

Her chest tightened at the grim look on his face, and she knew he spoke the truth. It made sense, she knew it did, but it wasn't exactly comforting. "Well, if there's no one for Joseph to select as my murderer, do you think he'll just...kill me and make it look like an accident?" Oh, God. That sentence just sounded so awful saying it aloud. "I can't believe I just asked that question. And to think I thought my life sucked when my family died."

Ben smiled gently and tugged lightly on a strand of her hair, a casual intimacy that eased just a fraction of her stress. "I think he has a pattern, and he'll do it the same way."

She frowned. "What makes you so sure? Are you an expert on murderers?" Because although that would certainly be handy if he was, she was also not sure that was a positive attribute.

He shrugged. "I've been around."

She blinked. "You've 'been around?' What does that mean?"

"It doesn't matter. I'm sure I've been fired from my job by now. Having a suspected murderer on staff isn't good for business." The bitterness in his voice was evident, and his fingers tightened ever so slightly in her hair. "Joseph needs to find someone to pin it on, someone in your life," he said, clearly not interested in further discussion about who he was, or how he knew so much about murderers. Hello, *murderers?* What kind of trivia was that to have in your head? How about making brownies? Wasn't that a *better* thing to know about?

"Mari?"

"Yes, I'm listening." She shook her head, trying to focus on the issue at hand, the one that was much more important than what Ben did for a living. "There's no one in my life that I'm close to. There's no one he could pin it on."

"There will be." Ben turned to face her, his eyes so intent, she knew what he was going to say before he said it. "Me," he said quietly. "We're going to set me up. The ball is already rolling, because the guy at the farmhouse who tried to rescue you from me will be calling up Haas and checking out our relationship. We're already getting connected, and Joseph will hear about it."

A cold chill rippled over her, a deep fear of setting him up. Ben was the one man on her side, and they were going to risk him? Especially when he was already in trouble for another murder? "Oh, no. I don't think that's a good—" Her phone rang suddenly, startling her. It never rang anymore. Her friends had given up calling her, and there was no family left to call.

Ben's eyes narrowed as he looked over at the table where her purse was sitting. "Were you expecting a call?"

"No. I don't get calls much these days—"

He swore under his breath, strode past her, and grabbed her purse off the table, holding it out to her. "See who it is."

Something in the grim set to his jaw made chills ripple down her spine. "He wouldn't," she whispered as she took the purse.

"He might."

The phone buzzed again as she dug her hand into her purse, and she found it at once. She pulled it out, glanced down at the display, and then froze when she saw the name come up. "Oh, my God," she whispered, as the phone slid out of her hand.

Ben caught it before it hit the floor and turned it over. He read the display, then raised his eyes to hers. "Joseph Daniels?" he asked. "Is that him?"

"I didn't take his number out of my phone." The words stuck in her throat, and she couldn't take her gaze off the phone gripped in Ben's hand. He was dead, he'd been dead to her for three months, and to see his name on her phone. "He wouldn't... he's supposed to be dead..."

"Answer it." He hit speakerphone and held it out to her with a nod.

Slowly, agonizingly, Mari took the phone from Ben and held it out so he could hear the caller as well. Her hand shaking, she cleared her throat. "Hello?" she whispered.

A woman's shrill voice seemed to shatter the tension. "Elizabeth? Where are you? I'm down here waiting."

Mari jerked her gaze to Ben, relief rushing through her. His phone number must have been reassigned. "I'm sorry, I think you have the wrong number."

"Isn't this Elizabeth Montgomery?" the woman asked.

"No, sorry."

"Wait a minute." The woman rattled off a phone number that was one digit off from Mari's. "Is that the number I dialed?"

"No, it's not."

"Well, sorry then," the woman said, before abruptly hanging up.

Mari's hand fell limply to her side, relief rushing through her. "His phone number must have been reassigned."

Ben already had his own phone out. He hit one button, and then put it to his ear. "I need you to track this call," he said without preamble into the phone. "Tell me where the cell phone is located that called this number." He looked at Mari. "What's your phone number?" As she rattled it off, he repeated it into the phone, twice for clarity, then hung up without further discussion.

The chill settled deeper in her bones. "Who was that?"

"Mack Connor, a crazy bastard I grew up with."

"He believes you're innocent?"

"Yeah." He said no more, but Mari heard the depth of emotion in his voice, and she knew that this man, whoever it was, meant a lot to him. It made her smile, because she knew what it was like to have someone who stood by you. Ben might be intense and somewhat ragged-looking, but there was so much more to him than what he carried on the surface. "That call wasn't a coincidence, Mari. It was our man."

She stiffened. "It was a wrong number—"

"I don't think so." Ben was already walking back toward the table, shuffling through the papers he'd set there. "You think it's a fluke that the person who got his phone number happened to call *you* by mistake? Of all the numbers she could have misdialed, you think it's likely that yours is the one she hit, calling from the phone number of the man you were engaged to?"

Mari swallowed. She didn't want to hear this. She didn't want to go down this road. "I have a new phone number. I got it when I moved here. I wanted a new start. He wouldn't know what it was."

"No? Here." Ben held out a newspaper article. "Read this. This is one of the articles I found at my sister's place. The third woman to marry a random stranger who died shortly thereafter, and then she was murdered a week or two later. The third woman on his list."

Mari took it. It was a photograph of a young woman, not much older than twenty, who was standing on the edge of the road. Her face was stark with terror, and she was holding a small dog in her arms. Behind her a crowd was milling, along with a number of police officers. "After a massive tornado devastates a small town, one woman had to watch as police pulled her twin daughters from a destroyed school. Elizabeth Montgomery, 24, watches as—" She froze, rereading the name, then looked at Ben, a deep cold settling in her bones. "Elizabeth Montgomery? Isn't that the name that the woman who just called me was looking for?"

Ben nodded grimly. "His phone hasn't been reassigned, Mari. He's back, and he's found you. Using the name of one of the women he's murdered was his idea of a private joke."

Her legs started to shake, and her hands involuntarily crushed the article. "He's hunting me, isn't he?"

"Looks like it. It probably took him a few months to track you down, but yeah...he's here, and it looks like he wants to play around with you before he makes his move." Swearing, he ran his hand through his hair. "He's toying with you," he said softly. "He wants to have fun with this."

"Fun?" She felt sick, nauseous, like the room was spinning. Had that really been Joseph on the phone, disguising himself as a woman? Or had he paid some random woman to make the call? Had he really found her? "I don't understand how this is happening..." But even as she said it, she knew she was lying. After she'd broken up with Joseph, she'd had nightmares that he was hunting her. More than once, she'd woken up in the middle of the night, drenched in sweat, terrified of a noise that she couldn't place.

She'd known the truth even back then, before she'd had any concrete reason to distrust him. She'd been such a mess after her family's deaths that she'd been desperate for help to keep from drowning, but it still hadn't taken long for her to start feeling like something was wrong...that something about Joseph was off. Her relief when he'd died had been extreme, which had forged even greater guilt, and doubt about whether she'd imagined the threat she'd felt from him. He'd scared her, and even in her grief about her family, she'd seen it. But too late, too late, *too late*. She couldn't believe this was happening. She just couldn't.

"A year ago," she whispered. "I was helping my parents and sister run our family gourmet cheese shop. I did all the decor and staging. I grew up in that store, and I knew everyone in town. My grandparents had owned the business before us. It was my world. And now, I have none of that, and there's a serial killer hunting me." She stared at Ben. "So much death. Murderers. I don't understand. It's just...this doesn't make sense. How can all this be a part of my life?"

"Hey, hey, hey," Ben said softly as he walked over to her and set his hands on her shoulders, squeezing gently. "It's going to be okay, Mari. You're going to make it through this."

She gripped his wrists, not wanting him to let go. Yes, he'd swept into her life bringing terrible news, but he had also offered strength and empathy. For a year, she'd kept her grief to herself. There was simply no way to explain the murder of your family to strangers, to people who lived regular lives. But Ben got it, because he'd faced the same thing. Somehow, he seemed to lessen the burden, because he carried it too. "How do you do it?" she asked. "How do you stop having the nightmares of all the blood?"

He hesitated, then shook his head. "I don't know, but eventually, it just goes away."

"Has it gone away for you yet?"

"With Holly?" He shook his head. "No." His voice had hardened, as if the last thing he would allow would be for the memory of his sister's death to leave his mind. "It's not going to go away until the bastard who killed her is done."

The bastard who'd killed his sister. The man who was hunting Mari even now. Fear rippled through her, not the nameless, faceless paranoia that had gripped her so ruthlessly for the past year, but true, grounded terror for the fate she was hurtling toward.

"No," Ben said. "Don't panic. You've got the leverage here, Mari. He has no idea you know what's going on, or that you have me in your corner. I'm ready for him, and so are you. He's not going to hurt you, okay? He's not that good. He just takes advantage of the fact that no one expects a dead man to come back from the grave to kill them. But we know. Even a ghost can't sneak up if you're looking for him."

"Yeah, okay." She swallowed, her mouth dry and pasty with fear. She'd seen death. It had haunted her for so long. To have to face it again—

"Mari," he said quietly, drawing her attention to him. His green eyes were penetrating and focused. "The game has started. You ready for this?"

CHAPTER 8

Was she ready? Mari wanted to scream that she would never be ready, grab her car keys, and then drive away as fast as she could until everything was gone, until her life was swallowed up in a place where there was no pain, no fear, and no death. But she'd tried that when she'd left her life and moved to Alaska, and it hadn't helped, had it? Was there really a question about whether she was ready? No, there wasn't, because she had to be. It was time to stop hiding.

She took a deep breath, then raised her chin, meeting Ben's steady gaze. The feel of his hands on her shoulders felt good, easing away some of the terror that had been building. "Who are you, Ben? Why in God's name do you feel like you can beat this guy?" She needed him to give her a reason to believe in him. Something concrete. Something to make her laugh smugly whenever Joseph called her and tried to scare her.

Ben shrugged evasively, and a steely glint flashed in his eyes. "Trust me, Mari. I'm not the nice, clean-cut guy I appear to be."

She surveyed his ragged, collar-length hair, his rough whiskers, and the heavy sweatshirt exposed by the unzipped parka. "Clean-cut?"

He looked down at himself, then grimaced, as if surprised to see what he was wearing. He looked back at her. "I grew up on the streets. I saw my best friend gunned down on his twelfth birthday. My mom had the last rites said for me on two different occasions. I saw shit before age ten that no one should ever see."

She was startled by his confession. He looked rough, yeah, but he looked outdoorsy rough, not street gangs and handguns rough. "Really?"

"Yes, really." His eyes were glittering defensively, as if he expected her to judge him. "After I was arrested for Holly's murder, the judge denied bail because I was too dangerous and a potential flight risk, based on the testimony of my friends and colleagues. I was in prison for good, but I got myself out. Remember that call I just made? I have access to the kind of help I need to do things like get out from behind locked bars. So, yeah, this bastard may think he's tough shit, but I'm more than he's used to dealing with. I've been tracking him for months, and he has no idea I'm after him. He thinks it's just you, and that you have no clue." He met her gaze. "He's *wrong*. He's underestimated you, and he's underestimated me."

The depth of emotion pulsing through his words was riveting, bursting over her like a white-hot inferno of strength, galvanizing her. For the first time since her family had died, she didn't feel like a victim. She didn't feel afraid. She felt like she could take her life back, and it felt amazing beyond words. She needed that strength. She needed that kind of passion. She needed that kind of fire. She needed *him*, and it was time to take control of her life. Ben was what she'd been searching for. "So, what do we do?" Because she was, finally, *ready*.

"We start tonight at your work. He's not going to make a move until he has someone to pin your murder on, so for now, you're safe. The control is ours." His voice was low and determined, brimming with the intensity of a man who would not be diverted from his mission. "We need to show him that we have a personal connection, and then tempt him into using me."

For the first time since her life had fallen apart, standing there in Ben's shadow, she felt hope again, like she had a chance to reclaim her life. She nodded. "Okay, but promise me one thing?"

He raised his dark brows. "What's that?"

"Try not to get murdered in front of me. I really can't handle more of that."

He grinned. "I have a hero complex, Mari. You need to

feed it better than that. Being worried that I'm going to get my ass kicked doesn't represent a lot of faith in me."

His smile was riveting, so bright that it made her heart leap. God, when was the last time she'd noticed anyone's smile? "You're making jokes?"

"Shit, yeah." Respect gleamed in his eyes as he eased down onto one knee. He took her hand and pressed it to his chest, gazing up at her. "I swear on my sister's soul, that I will not let this bastard kill you. If I have to go back to prison to keep you safe, I'll do it."

Her throat tightened at the honesty in his promise, at the depth of passion in his words, even as the smallest hint of disappointment pulsed through her. She realized that when Ben looked at her, he didn't see *her*. He saw his sister, and a chance to keep Holly from dying a second time. That was great, of course, from the perspective that it gave him a strong motivation to keep her alive, but at the same time, after so much loss in her life, it had felt good to connect with him, to *matter*. The kiss had been more than a kiss to her. It had been a recognition that she was alive, that she was breathing, that life moved forward. It had made her want more from her life, from him, and from herself. She didn't want to be in the shadow of his sister. She wanted him to see *her*.

A loud knock sounded on the door, and then Haas's cheery greeting rang out. Ben didn't get off his knee, staring up at her. "You ready?"

She looked at her phone, the one that Joseph had already tracked her to. He would find her. He would make her suffer for the fact she had rejected him. He would make her pay.

Slowly, she eased down to her knees, so she was level with Ben. "I've been running away since the moment I watched that madman spray bullets all over our store and gun down the only people I loved. I hid in the safety net Joseph offered me, and then I ran away to Alaska. It didn't help, and I'm tired of running." She met his gaze. "Hiding doesn't keep the pain away," she said softly. "I've been scared since that day, terrified of violence, of some deadly lunatic showing up and stripping my life from me. I can't sleep. I can't be in crowds. I can't even get in my car without checking the back seat. I can't live like that anymore, Ben. I don't want to be afraid anymore. I can't hide anymore. I have to fight."

He smiled then, a beautiful, heartwarming smile that seemed to lift all the darkness from the room for one glorious moment. Without a word, without a warning, without asking permission, he locked one hand behind her head, tangling his fingers in her hair, and kissed her.

It was a kiss of fire and heat, a kiss of raw, untamed determination, an infusion of strength and solidarity that ignited flames within her that had been extinguished on that terrible day. She wasn't alone now. They both had so little left to lose. Ben had already lost his sister and would always carry the guilt that he hadn't protected her. She had lost everyone she loved. They had nothing left to lose, nothing except the nightmares that haunted them both.

As she fell into the kiss, seeking refuge in the passion he offered her, she realized that she'd been wrong. Ben didn't see her as his sister. He saw her as his chance at redemption. His soul depended on keeping her alive, but her own soul depended on finding a reason to live again, to trust, and to summon the courage to believe. She wasn't afraid of dying. She was afraid she would die even while she continued to live, which would be the biggest failure of all, and the ultimate betrayal of the fact that she had been the one to survive that day.

He deepened the kiss, and desire began to lick through her. The kiss became about her as a woman, and Ben as a man, about two souls so broken that their fragments were held together by nothing more than the thinnest of filaments. It became about a need and desire burning and pulsating through them, about shields being stripped, and the vulnerable truth exposed.

His hand went to her hip, then slid around to her rear end, yanking her against his hard erection. The kiss changed to a dominating, carnal assault, driven by the primal instinct of a man about to bury himself in a woman, of a woman desperate to find salvation in the strength of a man. He slid his hand beneath the edge of her shirt, and she gasped at the heat of his palm on her flesh. It had been so long since she'd been touched, since she'd felt the warmth of another against her body. Longing burned through her, a need for more, for what he could give her—

"Are you guys going to open up? Bunch of indecent activity going on in there or what?" Haas thudded the door again, and Mari jumped, pulling back.

But Ben didn't release her. There was something so haunted in his face as he looked at her, his arms locked around her. She held her breath, her heart hammering, tensing. What was he going to say?

Haas thudded the door again. "Mari! You okay? Open the damned door!"

"Coming," Ben called back, his voice vibrating with tension. With a low curse, he released her, and waves of disappointment cascaded through her as he stood, holding out his hand to pull her to her feet. She set her hand in his and he swung her up easily, so she was standing right in front of him, so close that one deep breath could bring them together.

Ben touched her hair briefly, his eyes haunted. "You're too innocent for this hell," he said softly.

Her throat tightened at the gentleness in his eyes. How long had it been since anyone had looked at her with tenderness, since she'd felt the beauty of that kind of intimacy? Of a look and a moment, just for her? She managed a smile. "I think everyone is too innocent for the hell they have to face, on some level."

He cocked his head, as if considering her words. "I was never innocent," he said. "I'm the good guy, Mari, but never, ever delude yourself into thinking that I'm a nice guy. There's a difference. There's nothing soft in me. There's just the endless nightmare of my sister's blood all over my hands, and a thousand lifetimes of regret that I didn't save her." Then he dropped her hand and turned away, striding back toward the front door to where Haas was waiting.

As he opened the door and stepped outside to follow Haas to the truck, Mari couldn't help but touch her mouth, which was still burning from his kisses. She'd felt the absolute conviction in Ben's words, his true belief that he wasn't the nice guy, that there was no redemption for him. She sensed in his words a darkness far beyond what she'd ever felt in anyone...but it was a darkness she recognized because it was a part of her now.

She didn't think she could ever go back to where she

had once been, an innocent woman in a small Oregon town. Ben Forsett, with his tormented past, and his guilt, and his seductive, ravaging kisses, was calling to her more desperately than anything she'd ever felt before.

He was dangerous. His kisses were lethal. And a madman was closing in on them.

But God knew, Ben made her want to live for the first time a very long time.

She wasn't going to walk away from that, no matter what the risk. It just felt too good to care about someone, anyone again.

※◎※◎※

Ben couldn't concentrate.

He couldn't concentrate at all, and it was driving him mad.

And endangering them both.

All Ben could focus on was Mari. All he wanted to do was watch Mari as she tended bar, her brown hair tumbling out of her ponytail as if he'd torn it free himself. She was wearing a short-sleeved black top that didn't seem to match the biting autumn wind outside, but she was working hard and the press of bodies was raising the temperature in the joint. He couldn't get the kiss out of his mind. No, not the kiss. The *kisses*.

What the hell had he been doing kissing her? He hadn't kissed a woman like that in a long time. Too damn long. Yeah, he'd noticed women from time to time, but he'd never kissed them like that. It wasn't as if those women had mattered. It wasn't as if they'd cared whether he thought they mattered. They hadn't mattered to him, and they hadn't cared about him either, a mutual lack of admiration. They'd wanted him because they liked the size of his bank account. They'd craved his power. They'd coveted his presence. He knew it, and he didn't give a shit about the emptiness of what he'd had with them. He hadn't even thought about it...not until he'd seen Mari staring up at him with those blazing eyes so full of vulnerability. He would never forget that moment when she'd touched his shoulder and used his name, his real name, and he realized that she'd seen his truth and believed in him.

Son of a bitch. To have a woman look at him like that? Like she knew who he really was, and thought he was the most beautiful thing she'd ever seen? It had felt incredible. Way too incredible.

Ben scowled and folded his arms over his chest, sinking further down into the seat he'd snagged at a table by the back wall. He had no time to notice her like that. He had one job, one mission, and that was it. Getting involved with Mari was the fast track toward making a mistake, the kind of distracted mistake that would get them both screwed, and not in the good way.

He hadn't paid attention to details with Holly, and she'd died. If he started thinking about getting Mari naked, he'd be looking into those incredible eyes instead of at the truck slowing down, or the shadows moving in the woods. He had to see *around* her, not focus *on* her.

Gritting his teeth, he forced his gaze off the bead of sweat on her upper lip and scanned the bar again. The place was getting crowded, more crowded than it had been the previous night. He didn't like it. He didn't like all the bodies, all the faces he didn't know, and all the holes he couldn't plug. A tall, muscular man eased down to a seat at the bar, wearing a black skull cap and flight goggles perched on top of his head, making it difficult to see his face clearly.

Ben sat up and narrowed his eyes as the pilot beckoned Mari. He watched her face intently as she looked over at the customer, waiting to see her reaction. A small smile of recognition flared in her eyes, and she hurried over to him, clearly seeing him as a friend, not an enemy. Instantly, Ben's caution morphed into a dark, foreboding jealousy as the man touched her arm and said something that made her laugh.

"Your underwear too tight, or you park your ass on a splinter?"

Ben looked up as Haas pulled out the chair beside him. The older man had helped them most of the day, and they'd managed to get the plywood secured over the hole in Mari's house. It wouldn't hold against anyone who was determined to get in, but Ben still felt a hell of a lot better. "Who's that guy Mari is talking to? You know him?"

Haas glanced over at the bar, and nodded. "Cort

McClaine. Flies out of a town near here, but often stops in. If he's here, most likely his partner will be in before long, along with their wives. Cort and Luke are a couple of the best pilots around."

"Wives?" Feeling suddenly like an overly jealous jackass, Ben leaned back in his seat, clasping his hands behind his head. See? Noticing that Mari was a woman, and not just a potential victim of Joseph, was a bad idea.

"Yeah, wives." Haas eyed him. "You got the hots for Mari already? You watch yourself, Sully. She's a sweet kid, but she's carrying a load of pain. You don't play with a girl like that. You mean it, or you stay away. Build her house and sleep in your own bed at night."

"I don't have a bed." He studied another man who had just walked in. He looked late thirties, but had an air of authority about him. He was a man who owned the space he walked in. Ben's skin prickled in warning as he watched the man work his way around the room, greeting everyone, but not really looking at anyone, his gaze constantly on the alert, scanning the room. His hat was pulled low, making it difficult to see his face, but his bulky coat made it look like he was well-built and stocky. "What about him? You know him?"

"Trey Harper. New state trooper assigned to this area. Decent chap."

"State trooper?" Swearing, Ben sank lower into his seat, pulling the jacket of his collar up higher. He shook his head, letting his hair fall into his eyes as he shoved his chair back against the wall, retreating into the shadows.

"Yeah, state trooper." Haas eyed him, his old eyes too sharp. "Sleep in your truck. In an alley. In the damned river. Just not in her bedroom."

"I don't plan to sleep for a while," he muttered. "No time."

"If you don't sleep, you get slow. I don't think you can afford to get slow right now, can you?"

Ben glanced at Haas, and for a split second, he almost considered confiding in the old man. Haas knew this territory, and he didn't seem fazed by what he'd managed to figure out about Ben so far. He needed an ally—

The door swung open, and another crowd walked in. This group was younger, early twenties, again buried under layers of outdoor gear. "What's with all the people?"

"The Tanner wedding is this weekend. Apparently, the groom has a lot of family and friends that he's bringing in for the entire week." Haas took a slug of the beer that the waitress had plunked in front of him without even asking what his order was.

Ben swore under his breath as more strangers came in, to the sound of loud greetings and stomping feet. There were too many to track, even for Haas. He glanced over at the bar and saw that the trooper had taken a seat near Mari. For a split second, he felt relief that the law would be near her, then a cold chill settled over him as he watched Mari walk over to him. The trooper took off his jacket, and he saw Mari's gaze land on his badge. Her gaze swiveled toward Ben, and for a moment, they simply looked at each other.

He shook his head once, slowly, and then to his great aggravation, she shook her head right back at him. "Son of a bitch," he muttered. "She's going to ask him for help." He started to get up, but was stayed by a gnarled hand on his arm.

"Sit your ass down, boy." Haas's words were unyielding, his gaze hard.

Ben sank back into his seat, but he didn't take his gaze off the bar. Mari had moved away, but he knew she was going to ask the trooper for help. Son of a bitch. How much was she going to give away?

"You got demons on your ass," Haas said. "And you're bringing Mari into it. No man can pull shit off alone, not out here, not in this wilderness. You need help, and I'm offering. What the hell's going on? And don't lie to me anymore."

Ben finally looked at him, and he saw in those blazing eyes the badass Haas Carter had once been. Swearing, he shook his head. "You don't want to know."

"Don't tell me what I want. I'm too damn old for that shit." Haas leaned forward. "I got legs too, my boy, and I'm just as capable as Mari of marching over there and telling Trey that he needs to take a second look at you. Tell me the truth, Sully. You talk, or I walk. I vouched for you, and I can pull that veil of protection off you faster than you can blink."

Slowly, Ben turned his head. "Is that a threat?"

"Yeah." Haas grinned. "It's a good one, too, isn't it?"

"If I tell you, you'll be mixed up in it."

"Good." Haas leaned in closer. "I like to get dirty."

Ben almost laughed at the old man's excitement. He reminded Ben of his next door neighbor when he was a kid, the one who used to tell him what a stupid ass he was for all the shit he used to pull. The old man who Ben had gone to for advice when his own father had pulled the disappearing act. "You have kids?" he asked Haas. "A sister?"

Haas nodded. "Got a little sister down in Florida. I visit her every January. A little boring, but the sunshine sure feels good. She turned a lot nicer when she hit seventy. I might even start to like her by the time she's eighty."

His words were tough, but even Ben could see the softening of his expression as he talked about his sister. Haas got it. Grimly, Ben leaned back in his seat so he could watch Mari. "My sister was murdered a year ago," he said quietly, the words coming more easily now that he'd told Mari. "They want to hang me for it, but I'm going to find the real bastard who did it before I let them take me."

Haas said nothing.

Ben watched the bar, but his adrenaline was humming. Why wasn't Haas reacting? It wasn't like he'd just told him that he needed a new haircut. The man couldn't be that low key.

"Where does Mari come in?" Haas asked.

"She's next on his list. He's going to try to kill her." Ben glanced over at him, still waiting for a reaction from the old man.

Haas let out a low whistle. "You're sure?"

"Yeah."

"Well, shit, man. What's your plan?"

"Make him come after me instead." He looked at Haas. "I'll be ready. He doesn't know I'm here."

"Doesn't he?" Haas eyed him as he fished a piece of paper out of his pocket and slammed it on the table. "I found this on your windshield at Mari's house. I decided to take it."

"What is it?" Ben looked down at the paper. It was a photograph of him in shackles, being led into the courtroom for

his arraignment for Holly's murder, with the caption and story intact. He went cold, ice cold, staring at it. The bastard already knew he was there, he knew who he was, and he knew where Mari lived.

CHAPTER 9

Mari set the burger down in front of the state trooper, who was scanning the crowd with purpose. He looked to be in his late thirties, with lines on his face that hinted at maybe a little older, or else some tough experiences. She didn't dare look at Ben, and her heart was pounding. "Excuse me," she said. "May I speak with you for a moment?"

He swiveled his head to look at her, flashing her a grin as he gave her a typically masculine once-over that failed in its subtlety. "Of course. My name's Trey Harper. I'm off duty, so just Trey."

"Well, Trey," she paused, her heart starting to hammer as she considered how to say it. "My name's Mari Walsh. I... think I'm being stalked. Hunted. Whatever."

Trey's eyes darkened, and he focused on her with rigid intensity. Gone was the seductive leer, replaced by the all-business visage of a protector. "By who?"

"My former fiancé." She quickly launched into a hurried explanation of what had happened with Joseph, including the call from his phone earlier, but as she talked, she saw the skepticism growing on his face, and her words faded. Without being able to reveal that Ben had found the names of all those women in Holly's house, her story sounded so weak and lame. In fact, she realized grimly, even if she'd added in Ben's part, it still sounded far-fetched. She had no evidence at all that it was anything more than inauspicious creativity.

Silence fell for a moment. Then Trey said, "You think

your former fiancé faked his death and is now coming after you? Have you seen him since he supposedly died?"

She cleared her throat. "No."

"Spoken to him?"

"No, unless that was him calling, disguised as a woman."

Trey arched an eyebrow. "Has anyone you know seen him or spoken to him since he supposedly died?"

"No. No one...no one really met him while I was dating him." For four months, she'd dated him, and he'd somehow always managed to avoid meeting a single one of her friends.

Trey studied her. "Do you have a picture of him?"

She bit her lip, knowing full well that she didn't. She'd tried to find one after he'd died, and she'd realized she didn't have one. He'd never let her take his picture. Not once. "No."

Trey leaned forward. "So, there's this guy you dated for a while, who no one you know ever met, or even saw, right?"

She nodded. "Yes, but—"

"He then died in a car accident, but no one ever found his body, or anyone else's, in the car, which I am guessing was registered to you, so there isn't even a paper trail that he existed. And now you think he's tracked you to Alaska and is planning to harm you? Yet, you haven't seen him, talked to him, or heard from him since he supposedly died, and you don't have even a single photograph to prove he even existed in the first place?"

A cold chill settled down upon her as the reality of his questions sank in. Joseph had played it perfectly. *Perfectly.* He could stalk her all he wanted, and even if she called in the police, there was nothing for them to act on, nothing for them to believe. With a grim sense of foreboding, she began to understand how he could have set up Ben so cleanly for his sister's murder. The man was a ghost. He didn't exist. She and Ben were on their own. She glanced over at Ben, and saw he was staring down at something in his hand, an expression of shock on his face.

Fear rippled over her, and she willed him to look up, but he didn't.

"Ms. Walsh," Trey said, drawing her attention back to her. "Is this all a lie?"

She jerked her gaze toward him, outrage building inside her. "No, it's not. If I wind up dead, remember this conversation.

Find him. Don't let him do it again. His name was Joseph Daniels when I knew him, but I don't think that's his real name. Someone has to know him. It will be on your shoulders if you walk in here someday and discover I was found stabbed to death in my living room."

Trey's eyes narrowed. "Don't threaten me, Ms. Walsh. I am more than capable of doing my job. I don't know you well enough to know whether you would lie about this, or whether you really believe it, but there's not a damn thing I can do with what you told me, and you know it. Get me evidence. Get me proof. If it's real, give me something to go on. If it's not, then find a better way to get attention."

Heat flamed in her cheeks. "I'm not making it up," she snapped.

"Good." Trey reached into his pocket and pulled out a business card. He tossed it on the bar. "Then, when you have more, call me."

She took the card, desperate to try one last time. "Isn't there *anything* you can do?"

"Trust me, Ms. Walsh, I have no interest in having your murder be my next case, but I have a lot of shit going on, and I don't have time to chase shadows that don't exist. If they do, show me. Otherwise—" He gave her a skeptical look. "I can't help you." He then picked up his burger and began to eat, ending the conversation.

Mari gripped the card as she walked away, so much emotion burning through her. She was angry at Trey, but at the same time, she understood him. She'd offered him nothing but stories. Joseph was good. Too good. That's why there were five dead women, and five innocent men in prison for their deaths.

Or four, because the fifth one was sitting ten feet away from her, a posse on his tail. Instinctively, she glanced back at Ben's table—

He wasn't there. The table was empty. Haas was gone, too.

Frantic, she scanned the restaurant, but she couldn't see him. Fear began to beat at her. Ben wouldn't leave her unprotected. Not even for a minute. Where was he? What had he been looking at in his hand that had shocked him so badly?

Numbly, she fought her way past the tables to the front door, where Charlotte was hostessing. "Charlotte! Have you seen Ben? Did he leave?"

Charlotte's brow furrowed. "Ben? Ben who?"

She bit her lip at her slip and quickly corrected herself. "John, I mean John Sullivan. The guy who's working on my house? Did you see where he went?"

"Oh..." Charlotte grinned. "The hot guy you're taking to my sister's wedding?"

She was so not going to deal with the wedding issue right now. "Yes, did you see him? He was just here."

Charlotte shook her head. "I didn't see him, and I would have noticed. Maybe he's in the bathroom?"

"Bathroom?" she echoed blankly. Of course, bathroom. Even men like Ben were human, right? She whirled around and shoved her way through the crowd again. Ben and Haas's table had been taken over by a group of gray-haired men who all looked to be Haas's age, but Ben and Haas weren't with them.

She reached the bathroom door and shoved it open a crack. "Be—" She cut herself off, horrified by her second slip in less than a minute. "John! Haas! Are you in there—" The door opened and she jumped back as another man Haas's age stepped out. She thought he looked vaguely familiar. Had he been one of the men at Haas's table some night? Haas always seemed to have a posse with him. "Excuse me," she asked. "Do you know Haas Carter?"

The man glanced her way, and she saw that he had the same fiery intelligent eyes that Haas did. Despite his hunched shoulders and age-worn skin, he was a man who was still burning and alive, just like Haas. Was that what Alaska did? Kept people vibrant long after their bodies began to fade? God, she wanted to be like that. Burning with life again. She'd felt old for so long, ever since that night when her family had died.

"Yeah, I know Haas," he said. "Why? Is he giving you trouble?"

If she weren't so worried about Ben's disappearance, the man's question would have made her laugh. Haas had to be in his eighties, and he still had a reputation for giving people trouble? She loved it. "No, I'm looking for him, and his friend

John Sullivan. Did you notice whether they were in there?"

"No one in there but me," the man said. He leaned his hip against the door and backed it open. "Feel free to check. I'll guard for you." He gave her a little wink that said Haas wasn't the only gray-haired man who still had a reputation.

"Um, thanks." She edged past him and ducked into the restroom that she'd cleaned more than once after hours. The two stalls were empty, and no one was in there. Dammit. Where was he? She turned around, and saw Haas's friend was still leaning against the door, almost blocking the doorway. Suddenly, a wave of trepidation went through her. What had she done, walking in here by herself? The door locked from the inside, and it would be so easy for him to block the door. A cold chill rippled over her as she realized how easy it would be for Joseph to get to her, even in a crowded bar.

The old man met her gaze, then moved, making her jump. But all he did was sweep his stocking cap off his head and bow. "My name is Max Cady, at your service." His voice was gravelly, as if he'd smoked too many cigars in his life, matching the wrinkling of his skin and the trembling of his hand as he held this hat.

She relaxed, realizing that this time, at least, she was safe. But she also realized that old Max would not be able to help her if Joseph showed up, no matter how gallant he wanted to be. "Thanks, Max. I appreciate it, but I really need to get back to work." Still feeling the need to get out of the small room and back to the protection of the crowded restaurant, she hurried past him, almost running back down the hall. She reached the entrance, once again scanning Haas and Ben's table, but they weren't there.

Trey was gone from the bar, his burger only half-eaten.

The place was crowded and noisy, no one noticing her—

A hand clamped around her arm and yanked her backward into the shadows of the hallway. She shrieked and tried to get free, but her call for help dissolved in the loud hum of conversation, and her frantic struggle was hidden by the shadows. It took only a split second, and then she was out of sight, in the corner, in the shadows, blocked from any safety, shielded from the sight of anyone, *anyone*, who could help her.

A large, broad-shouldered male blocked the light, framing himself in shadows Mari couldn't penetrate. "Where have you been?" he demanded.

The deep tenor was an infusion of the most incredible relief that she'd ever felt in her life. "Ben?" she whispered, unable to keep the incredulity out of her voice.

"Yeah, it's me. Where did you go— Oomph." He finished the question in a grunt as she flung herself at him, wrapping her arms around his neck. For a brief second, he staggered under her unexpected assault, then his arms went around her, hauling her tight against his body.

He swore under his breath, looking past her down the hall to make sure no one had followed them. "You okay?"

She nodded. Her arms were still tight around him, and he could feel her body trembling against his. Swearing, he pulled her closer, easing her deeper into the shadows until it was just them, until no one would be able to see what they were doing. "Mari," he said softly. "What's wrong?"

She pulled back, gripping the front of his jacket. "You *left.* I turned around, and you were *gone.* Where did you go? Why didn't you tell me?"

Her vulnerability touched him, and he leaned into her, wedging her up against the wall and shielding her with his body. If someone came down the hall, they would see only his back, and her hands around his neck. No one would be able to tell it was them. "Sorry. I had to check something outside."

"*Something?* What something? Why didn't you tell me?" Sharp intelligence dissipated the fear as she studied him. "What happened?"

Ben heard footsteps and glanced over his shoulder. It was two of the women in the Tanner party, giggling as they headed toward the bathroom. One glanced his way, and he moved closer to Mari, ducking his head so his mouth was a whisper from her ear. "He knows I'm here," he said quietly. "He knows my real name. He's ahead of us, Mari. He's already ahead of us."

Her fingers tightened in his jacket, and she sagged back against the wall, staring at him in disbelief. "What? How do you know?"

"Long story." He looked up and down past her, checking the hallway each way. "He's not going to turn me in to the police, though, I don't think. If he were, he'd have told the cops where I was, instead of just telling me he knows."

Her mouth dropped open. "Tell you? Did you see him?"

"No." He set the newspaper article in her hand, pausing just long enough for her to see what it was, not wanting her to read all the details of his arrest.

Mari looked up at him, her eyes wide. "Where did this come from? What if he decides to tell the police where you are?" She gripped his arm. "If they put you in jail, then—"

"He's not going to hand me over to the cops. If he does, he loses me as a fall guy. He's just playing with me, letting me know that he's onto me. It's part of his game." He was certain of his words, but at the same time, there hung the very real danger that at any time, Joseph would decide to expose him. Any second, any moment, Ben could turn around to find a state trooper pointing a gun at his face...and then it would be over for all of them: Holly, Mari, and himself. Any chance at securing justice for his sister's murder would be gone.

"Where did you find this? How do you know it was meant for you?" Mari was grasping at straws, but he liked the fact that she accepted nothing at face value, that she allowed no unfounded assumptions.

"Haas found this on my truck at your house."

"At my house?" she echoed, and he knew she was putting the pieces together.

"Yeah. On my windshield beneath the wiper." He hesitated, not wanting to scare her, but at the same time, he knew he had to be honest. She had to know what they were up against. She had to know to be careful. "It wasn't on there when we were driving back from the store, which means he put it there *after* I was parked at your place."

She made a small noise of fear. Or was it protest? Disbelief? "He was *outside* my house while we were in there?"

"I think so."

"Oh, God." She started to slide down the wall, as if her legs were suddenly giving out.

"Hey, hey, it's okay." Ben wrapped his arm around her waist, and pulled her against him, supporting her. "Here's the thing," he said softly. "As we both know, he is very, very good."

She gripped his arms, managing a small laugh of irony. "Right, that's true, so yeah, it's all okay, then, because he's really *good* at what he does. That's really reassuring, so thanks for that."

He chuckled. "The thing is, he won't make a move until he's absolutely certain that he has his fall guy set up perfectly, with no room for error. He never makes a mistake with setting up the innocent person for the murder. He doesn't have that in place yet. You have no history here, and even though he knows who I am, it doesn't help him yet. No one knows me, and I have no connection to you. If he sets me up for it, there's no motive. The police always want a motive. He's not going to do it yet. It needs to be irrefutable. So, we're still good. We have time."

"Time. Okay, great. We have time until he tries to murder me. I feel better now." But she took a deep breath, and he could tell she was focusing, which was good, but he had to admit, he didn't like the situation.

It had been one thing when he'd simply been hunting Joseph, but now that he knew Mari, and realized what danger she was in, it changed everything. It was too risky. Too personal. What if he slipped up? What if somehow, someway, Joseph got past him? A cold chill sliced through him, and he asked the question he'd been thinking about ever since he'd seen the state trooper sit down at the bar near her. "Did you talk to the trooper? What did he say? Did he believe you?" Maybe it would be different in Alaska. Maybe in Alaska the police were smarter and more willing to see the truth that wasn't written on the surface—

But she was shaking her head. "No, he thought I was making it up. There's no proof of anything, Ben. Nothing. Even if I could tell him about the articles you found, what would it do? You're hardly a convincing witness."

"I know." He ground his jaw. "That's what I discovered." Even though he'd expected it, it was still a blow to know that they were truly on their own...and with Mari's life at stake. At this point, he didn't even give a shit what happened to him, as long as he brought justice to Holly's death and kept Mari alive.

The stakes were getting higher by the minute. Joseph was weaving the trap even as they stood there, and the repercussions of failure were rapidly increasing. He looked down into Mari's brown eyes, noticed the determined set to her trembling jaw, and he knew that he couldn't fail her. It was about more than Holly now. It was about Mari, who, in the last twenty-four hours, had become a real woman to him, not just a nameless, faceless way to try to find the bastard he'd been hunting. This woman who had already been through so much...how could she endure more?

A loud male shout made him turn sharply, and he saw two men slouch down the hallway toward the restroom. One of them glanced over and stopped short, staring down the passageway toward Ben and Mari. The other one stopped beside him. "What's going on there?"

"You okay, miss?" The stockier one called out. "Is he bothering you?"

Ben swore and turned his back, not wanting his face to be seen. "Tell them you're fine," he muttered, planting his hands on either side of her head, using his body to isolate them.

Mari looked at him in surprise. "I thought you wanted them to see us together. That you wanted to give Joseph a reason to pick you."

"He's already chosen me, but I need to give us time. Until the rest of the world sees us together, he can't pin it on me."

"Hey!" The stockier guy moved closer. "You okay or what?"

"Yes, fine," Mari called out, her trusting gaze fixed on Ben.

"You sure?"

Ben swore. "They don't buy it." He met her gaze. "Kiss me, babe, so they know you're cool."

Resolution darkened her eyes, and she didn't hesitate. She tightened her grip around his neck and dragged his head down toward her. A surge of anticipation that had nothing to do with Joseph rushed him, and when her lips touched his, Ben knew he was a dead man.

The first time he'd kissed her had been good.

The second time had been intense.

CHAPTER 10

Mari's mouth was like silken fire against his, an irresistible siren call that he could never resist. He leaned closer, letting his body make contact with hers, pinning her up against the wall, even as he fought to keep his palms braced on the wood beside her head. He couldn't take her the way he wanted. Not here. Not now. He didn't dare touch her with his hands, certain that if he so much as brushed his palms over her body, his need for her would doom him.

But she didn't hold back. His control slithered ruthlessly out of his grasp as Mari hugged him more tightly around his neck, as she welcomed the press of his body against hers. Her breasts were full and soft against his chest, an unreal temptation even through his jacket, like searing heat burning his flesh. He deepened the kiss, needing more, wanting more, desperate for *more*, and she gave it to him. Every kiss, every touch, and every fantasy he'd ever had about what it could be like to kiss a woman who actually *mattered*...she brought them all to life.

With a low growl, he dragged his right hand off the wall to her hip, cupping her curves as he pulled her even tighter against him. Her belly was flush against his cock, a temptation so incredible that he had to use every bit of control not to drag her out of there and make love to her right then, right there, to sink himself into her and—

"Mari! What are you doing— Oooh. *That's* what you're doing. *Nice.*"

With a curse, Ben broke the kiss, turning his head to see

the hostess standing a few feet away, a brilliant grin on her face. "Charlotte," he muttered, struggling to recall her name.

"That's me." She grinned wider, looking past him to Mari, who had released him, but one of her hands was still on his side, resting lightly, as if she were as unwilling as he was to break contact. "So, Mari, your customers are getting antsy. You think you could break away to serve them?"

"Oh, yeah, right." Mari stepped away reluctantly, glancing at Ben. "Um...so..."

"I'll be around." He kept it casual, but knew that their gig was up. The rumors would start, faster than they could control, which meant that their man would start building ammunition. They needed a plan, a better plan than his, and fast.

Mari nodded and ducked under his arm. "Okay, then." She started to walk away with Charlotte, her small frame dwarfed by the taller woman, who wasn't even that tall. Dammit. She looked so vulnerable. "Charlotte," he interrupted.

Both women turned around. "Yes?"

"Mari and I want to keep this quiet right now, for personal reasons. You think you could go with that?"

Charlotte glanced at Mari, then back at him. He saw something flicker in her eyes, an understanding? "It won't stay quiet long, you know. People notice things," she said. "But I'll try."

He grinned. "Thanks."

Mari added a smile. "We appreciate it, Charlotte."

"Girlfriend," Charlotte said, as she tucked her arm through Mari's and herded her back toward the restaurant. "John is one of the hottest strangers to walk into this bar full of old men in a long time, and you're this huge mystery that no one has been able to figure out in the two months you've been here. There's no chance people won't be watching, so you'd better get ready for it. With him working on your house and watching you every night like he wants to have you for dessert, I'm guessing you have a day, maybe two at most, before everyone assumes you guys are getting naked every single night. By the time you two show up at my sister's wedding, people will already be asking if you're pregnant yet."

Mari's cheeks turned red, and she glanced back at him

as they turned the corner, as if checking to see if he'd heard the comment. He couldn't help but smile at her discomfiture, and he gave her a small salute that made her laugh. She disappeared out of sight, and he moved quickly to the doorway to watch her progress across the crowded floor. As he watched her and Charlotte navigate the room, his amusement faded as he considered Charlotte's comment.

The wedding.

They could skip it, or they could use it to shift the tide in their favor....somehow. It was soon, sooner than he'd planned, but he knew the timetable had just moved up. Somewhere out there, Joseph was watching her. Watching him. Putting them together.

As Mari settled in behind the bar again, Ben scanned the room carefully, inspecting every male in the place. Was one of them Joseph? Was he in there even now? The place was packed with males of all different types: old geezers, brazen twenty-somethings, red hair, brown hair, ancient gray hair. Some were clean cut with their damned preppy sweaters, and others looked like they hadn't bothered with a shower since last spring. But even as he looked around, he knew he'd never know if one of them was the man he sought, not by looking at him. Each time Joseph had wooed a woman, the description had been different. The man was a chameleon, changing his appearance so completely Ben wasn't even sure whether Mari would recognize him—

His gaze jerked back to Mari, who was once again moving efficiently behind the bar, making drinks and serving food to those eating. She glanced over at him. Though she gave no outward smile of recognition, the heat of her stare seemed to burn through him. One of the men at the bar turned around and caught his eye, and Ben knew that Charlotte was right.

There was no way to hide that they were connected.

Joseph would have his fall guy by the end of the week, because there was no way in hell that Ben was going to be anywhere but by Mari's side.

"Hey." Haas walked up beside him, snow dusting his jacket and hat. "Here's the rest of them. I finished up when you came in." He handed Ben a piece of paper with several dozen license plate numbers scrawled in a shaky hand, along with their states of registration.

Ben grinned. "Damn man, you're good." Once he'd gotten the article from Haas, he'd hauled ass outside to try to identify what Joseph was driving, certain that he'd been following him. There'd been too many cars to search, and too many people, but he and Haas had started recording license plates before he'd gotten too restless and had needed to check on Mari...who *hadn't been there.*

A cold chill stole down Ben's spine at the memory of that moment of raw terror when he'd walked back into O'Dell's and discovered that Mari was gone. *Gone.* He'd been scared shitless. There had simply been no other word for it. And when he'd sprinted into the back hall and seen her alive and unharmed, his entire world had seemed to explode around him. All he wanted to do was touch her and hold her, proving to himself that she was there, that she was alive, and that he hadn't lost her. He needed to *know* that Joseph hadn't killed someone he cared about *again.*

Haas shrugged, but there was a pleased smile on his face. "This shit's fun. I forgot what it's like to have some bad guys causing trouble. You need help getting those tracked?"

"No, I have a contact." Ben gripped the paper. He needed to get a visual of the man. He needed to have some idea what to look for. He needed *something* to ground himself. Right now, he felt like he and Mari were exposed raw, with no defenses. He glanced at their table, which was still occupied with a bunch of old-timers. "I need a table."

Haas shrugged and headed right back to where they'd been sitting. With a few loud guffaws and the scrape of chairs moving, there were suddenly two spots at the table, both of them with their backs to the wall and facing the room. Ben nodded his thanks and eased into his seat, pushing his chair back from the others to keep his space. Haas did some quick intros, once again introducing Ben as John Sullivan, a man down on his luck, but this time, he added flair to the story. "So, boys, here's the thing. That ex-wife of his? The man she married is a right bastard, and he's been hunting our boy Sully here, harassing him. So, if you see anyone riding on Sully, you let me or him know. We gotta stick up for our man."

The table was full of resounding curses for bastard

second-course wife stealers, and Ben was surprised at their vehemence. Most of the old-timers weren't wearing wedding rings, but their outrage on his behalf almost made him laugh... which was dangerous. Everyone he came in contact with, everyone he cared about, was at risk. "Listen," he said, leaning close to the table. "I appreciate the effort, but the guy's an ex-Navy SEAL. He's a serious bastard, and I don't want anyone getting hurt. I can take care of myself, so just stay out of it." He looked at Haas. "You, too."

"Shit no," Haas said. "This is fun, ain't it, guys?"

There was another resounding round of support from the table, and a deep tension began to build inside Ben. There were too many innocents getting tangled in the net. Ben knew he had to break free from them. With a muttered excuse, he got up and moved to an empty seat at the end of the bar. He didn't make eye contact with Mari, but he sensed her sharp intake of breath. He bent low over his phone, letting his hair shield his face as he both scanned the room and began to enter the license plate numbers into an email.

He'd just finished when the door opened, and the state trooper from before walked in, accompanied by another one. Swearing, Ben turned his back to them, studying the mirror above the bar to keep track of them. They were walking slowly through the room, scanning faces with purpose and intent. Son of a bitch. They were looking for someone. He was sure of it. Was it him? Had Joseph played that card?

They moved closer and closer, and Ben caught Mari's eyes. He jerked his chin toward the troopers, and she looked over at them just as they neared the bar. The one he hadn't seen before was holding a small photo in his hand, and both men were continually checking the photo and looking around.

Ben glanced at the kitchen door as the troopers moved up right beside him, so close that Ben had to shift to keep his shoulder from bumping them. He kept his head down and averted, watching them in the mirror, his body tensed and ready to bolt. His car was parked by the front door, not the kitchen door, so he'd have to sprint around the building. Shit. That was too far. They were so close—

"Ms. Walsh," one of the troopers said. "May I have a

word?"

Mari didn't even look at Ben as she walked over and leaned on the bar. "Yes?" She looked right at them, not trying to hide.

"Do you know this man?" He held out a picture.

Ben ducked his head slightly to see what they were showing, and froze when he saw it. It was his headshot from his law firm website.

Mari looked at it, and then laughed softly. "Trey, that kind of man doesn't come around here."

Ben knew what she was looking at. In that photo, he was wearing a custom Italian suit. His hair was light brown, cut so short it was almost military length, and his eyes were dark, almost black. He was clean-shaven, and the photographer had even digitally altered the image to make him look like he couldn't have grown a beard even if he wanted to. He was a good thirty pounds heavier, and he'd been looking at the camera as if he hated every minute of the photo shoot.

Which he had.

"You haven't seen him?" the trooper asked again, watching Mari closely.

She met his gaze. "A man like that wouldn't be able to blend in here," she said. "If he's around, we'll know." She raised her eyebrows. "Why? What's he done?"

"Just thought it might be the guy you were asking about."

"My ex?" Mari leaned forward, studying the image more closely. "No, no, it's not him. But why would you think that?"

"Got a tip," Trey said, his voice relaxing. "This image was dropped off at the office with a note that you might know him. He's some hotshot lawyer apparently wanted for some shit back in the Lower 48. Don't know why they thought he was here."

Mari eyed him as Trey sat down beside Ben. "So, you believe me about my ex?"

Trey tossed the picture on the counter as the other trooper leaned on the bar, still scanning the room. With so many people from the Tanner wedding in attendance, there were actually a few men with the clean-cut look in the image, and

Ben could tell that the other trooper was studying each of them carefully. "I got a tip to ask you about this guy," Trey said. "That's all I know."

The other trooper nudged Trey. "I want to talk to those two in the corner."

Ben surreptitiously followed his glance and saw a couple of preppies shooting darts. The troopers moved off, leaving Ben and Mari behind.

For a long moment, neither of them spoke. As Mari quickly wiped down the counter beside him, Ben looked over and saw her hand was shaking. Swearing, he moved his arm enough to brush against her hand. "There's a reason I have green eyes," he said quietly. "People notice the green, and they see nothing else. It makes the rest of me invisible."

She looked at him, her eyes wide. "You're about as invisible as an elephant at a Saturday night bingo game," she hissed. "Every damn woman in this place is lusting after you."

He almost grinned. "They see a rough Alaskan with green eyes," he said. "That's what they want, and that's what they see. In other states, my eyes were blue. Or light brown. Or silver. Never boring brown, because that's what they really are."

As he spoke, he continued to watch the progress of the troopers around the room. Not one person looked his way, not even when the troopers stopped at Haas's table. The old-timers let out with a litany of insults against the uptight lawyer in the picture, and the troopers had to give up. The green eyes went against logic, which said he should be as non-descript as possible, and he should never have selected a feature to stand out. In his experience, however, a man who was too invisible aroused suspicion. His green eyes invited attention, and they made the rest of him dissolve, since the police were looking for a clean-cut prick, not a ragged piece of shit bold enough to have eyes that no one would forget. "Joseph knows no one will recognize me from that photo," he muttered. "He knew that picture wouldn't lead them to me."

"Then why did he give them my name?" she whispered.

"To control us. To limit our options. To taunt us that he's in control." He looked at her. "What time do you get off?"

"Eleven."

Five hours. He looked at her. "Can you promise not to leave this bar until I get back?"

"Not to leave—" Her eyes widened. "Where are you going?"

"To your house. I want to set some things up. Can I have your keys?"

She shook her head. "I don't think—" Then she stopped, looking right at him. Her eyes were clear and intelligent, and he saw too much awareness of what they were facing, a realization that they had to act before they had no more choices. "What if you don't come back?"

"I'll tell Haas and the boys to stay. He'll take care of you."

She blinked. "He's eighty."

"He's got some skills." But Ben was already planning his instructions to Haas: just to watch her. Not to interact on any level. He didn't want Haas to get linked to Mari. Any liaisons were too dangerous right now. "You just have to stay in sight. Don't go into the bathroom or the kitchen. Stay in plain sight in the crowd. Got it?" His adrenaline was screaming with the wrongness of leaving her behind, but he knew she was safer in a crowd, at least right now.

Slowly, she nodded. "Okay."

"Okay." He hesitated, then jotted down his phone number on a napkin. "This is a secure, untraceable line. If you need me, use it. If you're okay, don't call. I don't want your phone bill to record this number unless absolutely necessary."

She took the napkin, read it carefully as if she were committing it to memory, and then slid it into her pocket. "Okay."

He nodded. "Okay."

For a long moment, neither of them moved. They simply looked at each other. Ben was consumed by a sudden, almost uncontrollable urge to reach across that bar and kiss her, to stake his claim on her, and make damn sure the entire world knew that she was under his protection.

But to do so would be a public statement that they were connected, which was what Joseph was looking for. He would not give it to him. Not yet. "Stay safe."

She nodded. "You, too. Try not to get set up for any murders, okay?"

He grinned. "I'll do my best." He slid off the stool. "I'll be back."

Her eyes glittered. "You better not break that promise, Sully."

"No chance." Then, without another word, before he could succumb to the burning need to toss her over his shoulder and bail before anything could happen to her, he turned away, striding across the room toward the back door. He jerked his chin at Haas, and saw the older man rise to his feet to follow Ben into the hallway for a private chat.

As he reached the door, he turned back to look at the bar. Mari was chatting with a young couple, her smile captivating and engaging. His heart actually stuttered for a moment, stunned by how young and carefree she looked. She was riveting, and he suspected that was how she used to look, how she used to be. When she turned away to fill their drinks, her smile dropped off her face and the same haunted look filled her eyes. The change in her demeanor was dramatic, and it filled him with a dark anger that her light could have been stripped like that.

Fierce determination rushed through him, a resolve to bring that smile back to her face. Holly would never smile again, but Mari could. He realized that he didn't just want to keep her alive, but he also wanted to help her reclaim a normal life. He wanted to hear her laugh. He wanted to see her with a smile that meant something. He wanted her to have the second chance that Holly never had, and he knew that he was her only chance.

Which sucked for her, because he had a track record from hell.

CHAPTER 11

Never had the clock moved so slowly. Never had Mari been more aware of the movement of every man in the bar. Never had she searched people's faces so carefully for recognition.

Mari still couldn't believe that the man in the picture was Ben. He looked so different, like a ruthlessly wealthy, powerful lawyer who would crush a child under his heel if it meant he got what he wanted. The photograph was nothing like the man she'd met, the man she'd kissed, the man who had spoken of his sister with such emotion that her own heart had bled. Which was the real Ben? A man like the one in the picture? His expression had been so hard, so fierce, and so empty of humanity that she could almost believe he would kill his own sister to get what he wanted.

"Mari!" Charlotte bounded up beside her. "Did you hear? Some crazy ex-lawyer from Boston might be in town. Isn't that wild?"

Mari almost dropped the glass she'd been filling. "Yeah, I saw the picture." She slanted a look at Charlotte. "Did he look familiar?"

"I would totally remember seeing a man like that. Gorgeous, but chilling. Did you see his eyes?" Charlotte shivered. "They were evil, weren't they? Heaven forbid I ever see those eyes in real life."

Mari swallowed and nodded. "Yeah, I know what you mean." She hesitated, and then looked at the hostess. "Hey, so, I used to date this guy back in Oregon—"

"You did?" Charlotte's gaze sharpened at the first bit

of personal information that Mari had ever shared with her. "Really? What happened?"

"I broke up with him, but he's turned into a bit of a stalker. I'm afraid he may have tracked me up here. If you see anyone watching me...or John, will you let me know?" If Joseph was around, someone had to have seen him. Charlotte was there all the time, and knew all the locals.

"Is he dangerous? Do you think he's going to hurt you?" Charlotte looked worried. "What does he look like?"

"He makes me nervous," Mari said evasively. "Last time I saw him, he was about five ten, with short brown hair and brown eyes, but..." She paused. "I think he might change his appearance. He's...an actor...and he's good with makeup. If he knows John and I have something going, it might set him off."

"No kidding? That's why you wanted it quiet?" Charlotte whistled gently and looked around the room. "I'll be honest, most guys in here watch you. You're new and attractive. I wouldn't know where to start." She nodded at a table in the corner, where two men were sitting still with their heavy jackets and hats on. "Like them. They've been watching you all night, and I don't know who they are. Do you?"

Mari followed her gaze. The man facing her had gaunt shadows under his eyes, and hunched shoulders, but he didn't look away when he saw her watching her. "I don't recognize him."

"Well, good, right? I mean you'd recognize the guy if you saw him, wouldn't you?"

Mari thought of how different Ben had looked in his photograph. Would she have recognized him if she hadn't seen his name beneath his image? She had a feeling she wouldn't have. "I don't know," she said quietly. "It depends on what he's done to his appearance."

Charlotte's eyes widened. "Girlfriend, that's not good. You need to tell the police."

"I told Trey, but without any evidence, he can't do anything."

"Did he say that? Really?" Charlotte set her hands on her hips. "Well, I'm just going to have a little chat with that man. Seriously. Men just don't understand what a threat bastard ex's can be for women, do they?" Her eyes were flashing with a grim understanding that caught Mari's attention.

"Were you...do you have a bad ex?"

Charlotte rolled her eyes, but her face became tense. "What woman doesn't? Yes, I have a bad ex, but I haven't seen him in a couple years, so hopefully it's over now, right? They do move on at some point."

"Maybe."

"Yeah, maybe." Charlotte lowered her voice and leaned forward, her gaze intense. "Do you have a gun?"

Mari stared at her, and an involuntary chill raced down her spine. "No guns," she said. "I won't touch them."

"Then get a really big, mean dog," Charlotte said, not taking her gaze off Mari. "Do you lie awake at night, afraid?"

Mari stared at her. "Yes."

"A dog helps." Charlotte managed a smile. "I have a gun, too, but I pretend it's for hunting. Next time we walk out together, I'll introduce you to my boyfriend, who is always in the car with me. His name is Bear, and he's a one hundred and twenty-five pound shepherd. Sleeps with me. Drives with me. And I've trained him *never* to eat any food unless I've approved it. No one can get to him, and no one can get to me."

"You're scared," Mari realized.

"I'm not scared, because I've taken control." Charlotte squeezed her arm. "But you're still scared. It's a terrible way to live. Don't let one bastard ruin it for you, right?"

Mari clenched her fist. "You're right."

"I know I am." Then Charlotte winked. "But until you find a big shepherd to live with you, you should hire John for the task. He certainly seems tough enough and from the way he looks at you, I'm pretty sure he's not going to let some crackpot ex-boyfriend near you."

Mari's heart began to pound. "How does he look at me?"

Charlotte grinned. "Like he didn't know what it meant to be alive until he met you."

"Oh, shut up." Mari turned away, her cheeks flaming.

"I swear. I know because I'd give anything to have a good man look at me like that."

Mari glanced over at the hostess, remembering what Charlotte had said about Ben's work picture, and how he'd looked almost evil. "You think he's a good man?"

"I do." Charlotte shrugged. "But you're the one who knows him best. You have to make the call." She patted Mari's shoulder. "I need to get back to work, but if you need help, let me know. I will see you and John at the wedding, right? I want to live vicariously through you. The few men I find to date can't compare with how he looks at you, and that's an understatement." With a quick wink, Charlotte turned and hurried back to the front of the restaurant.

As she watched Charlotte, a warm feeling settled in her. It felt good to confide in Charlotte, and it was nice to have someone looking out for her. The start of a friendship? God, it had been too long. She sensed that Charlotte might actually understand about her past, and not freak out if Mari told her that her family had been gunned down in front of her by some crazy bastard. After all, the woman packed a gun and had a killer canine as a lap dog.

As she watched Charlotte flash her smile at the latest customers to walk in the door, Mari felt a tug of camaraderie with the brunette, a connection bound by having seen the darker side of life. As she watched, a man came in, tall with heavy shoulders under an overcoat. Mari couldn't see his face, but he turned to talk to Charlotte, his bulk swallowing her up.

For a split second, Mari couldn't see Charlotte at all, and a cold fear raced through her. Then the man moved, and she could see the hostess still standing at the desk, writing something down. Everything was okay. *It was okay.* But even as she thought it, a sinking sense of fear settled in her. Anyone Mari was close to was in danger. Had Joseph ever set up a woman for the murder? Did she have to worry about Charlotte? What if she was cast as a jealous friend who wanted the same man as Mari, a desperate lover who would do anything to claim her man? Joseph could kill both her and Ben, and have Charlotte take the fall. A gun and a shepherd would be no protection against a man who played in strategy and intelligence, who out-thought others before they could even act.

Mari drew back against the wall of the bar, her shoulders

brushing against the bottles. Everyone she connected with was at risk, she realized. Everyone who reached out to her was a potential target. Who would Joseph choose? What if it was someone they didn't expect? Haas? Charlotte? Even the shopping cart lady at the store who'd prompted Charlotte to invite Ben to escort her to the wedding? What if Joseph saw something he could work with even in that short conversation? After all, the box of tile in the home supply store had crashed down to the floor right at that moment. Maybe he'd been there. Maybe he'd been watching the whole thing. Maybe he'd made sure that the tiles cracked loudly before they fell, so she would have time to get away, so he could start to mess with her...

Who would he select to take the fall? Would he choose someone who he could pin two deaths on, both hers and Ben's? What if she and Ben didn't see him coming until it was too late?

It had been her fault that her family had died.

She couldn't let anyone else be hurt because of her. Not Charlotte. Or Haas. Or Ben.

Her mind flew to Ben as he'd sat at her counter tonight, his broad shoulders hunched as he'd turned his head away from the troopers who had been holding his photograph. She thought of how he'd kissed her in the hallway, touching a chord deep inside her with his tenderness and his pain. Joseph had defeated him once, and he was already pulling strings that they weren't ready for. What chance did she and Ben have against a man who was already manipulating them with such ease?

Suddenly, she wanted nothing more than for Ben to walk in the door, flashing her that grin, teasing her with those green eyes. Alone, she had no chance. Alone, he'd already lost once. Alone, each of the women who had loved Joseph had lost the battle. Alone, everyone fell to him. But together, would it be different? Together, could they do it?

She thought of Charlotte's concern, of Haas's jovial humor, of her own family, buried after a life that was too short, and knew that she could not allow more death and destruction into her life. She and Ben had to succeed. *They had to find a way.* But how? Their opponent was an expert, already lining things up, and all they had was each other.

***

Hours later, but still with time to spare before Mari got off work, Ben eased the old truck up to the kitchen door of O'Dell's. The faded blue of his newly acquired vehicle looked like a dying gray in the weak light in the back alley, but the engine was smooth, the tires were new, and the license plate was an untraceable fake. Beside him on the bench seat were two large duffel bags, and everything else was in the bed of the truck, which he had intentionally left uncovered so he could see if anyone was trying to catch a ride back there.

He pulled the black stocking cap down over his head, and jerked up the collar on his borrowed flight jacket. Three silver skulls hung from the holes in his left ear, and his jeans were old and faded, tucked into knee-high insulated boots that were ready for trekking.

He left the truck parked by the back door, and quietly strode around to the front of the building, using his phone to take pictures of all the cars in the lot. He hadn't heard back from his friend Mack Logan about the plates, and he sent the new pictures to him.

At the front door, he paused, scanning the lot. The wind was cold and biting, and there were snowflakes streaking horizontally across the parking lot, swirling like miniature white funnel clouds preparing to savage the asphalt. The dimly lit parking lot was full of shadows, but all was still. There were only six cars left, belonging to a few stragglers and the staff who were closing. There was a slight movement by one of the vans in the back, and he stared at it, narrowing his eyes.

Nothing moved.

He waited.

Still no movement.

Scowling, he slid his hand into his jacket pocket, his finger wrapping about the cool metal of the gun that was too much like the one he'd had when he was fourteen. Determined to cut himself free from the life he'd had as a teenager, he'd gone decades without holding a gun, until Holly's death had spurred him into armed pursuit of Joseph. When'd he'd finally picked one up, however, he'd been grimly aware that the smooth metal had been hauntingly familiar and felt like an extension of who he was. He'd never left behind who he had once been, and he knew now that he never would.

He saw a shadow flinch, and adrenaline leapt through him. Hunching his shoulders against the wind, he broke into a sprint, streaking across the parking lot toward the car he'd been watching. There was a sudden movement, and then a man dressed in black exploded from behind the van, hauling ass across the parking lot into the woods behind the bar.

Anticipation burst through Ben, and he ran harder, flying across the asphalt, the only sound the thudding of his boots, and the pounding of the other man's. For an instant, they were suspended in time, two dark shadows in the swirling snow. Ben was gaining on him, getting closer—

The man broke to the right, bolting into the thick trees. Ben adjusted his angle, sprinting to cut him off. He could see the man's shadow streaking past the tree trunks, fading fast from sight. Swearing, Ben ran harder, reaching the trees a split second later. He broke into the woods, and then stopped almost immediately as the forest closed in upon him.

He went utterly still, surrounded by darkness and trees, visibility almost nothing between the night, the snow, and the forest. There was no sound, just the wailing of the wind and the silence of the falling slow. He whirled around, ready, waiting for someone to leap out at him. Shit. He had no defense in here. No visibility. No chance to see the enemy coming.

Turning sharply again, he strained to discern the sound of footsteps, but there were none. He glanced down at the ground to see if he could see footprints, but the snow wasn't deep enough. Just a dusting across the dirt, swirling in mocking laughter that he could not track his quarry.

With a muttered curse, he quickly retreated to the edge of the woods, knowing that following the man through such dense foliage was foolish. He paused on the perimeter, listening for an indication that his target had returned, but he heard nothing. Had it been Joseph? Or some hoodlum kid who had been switching license plates in the parking lot?

Keeping an eye on the woods, Ben jogged back to the place where the man had come from. He'd been hiding between two cars. One was an old van, rusted with plates so filthy they weren't even readable. Ben quickly took a few pictures of the plate and the VIN, emailing them to Mack. He tried the doors, but they were locked. Shielding his eyes, he peered in through the driver's window. There was nothing of interest visible in the interior.

The other car was a rental, and there were tourist maps on the front dash. Part of the Tanner party? He took pictures and sent them to Mack, but had a feeling that the cars weren't going to lead him anywhere. Joseph was just smarter than that.

But as he headed back into the bar, the skin on the back of his neck began to tingle. He whipped around, searching the woods. Nothing. Then a movement caught his eye across the street. He turned sharply, and he saw an old pickup truck was idling on the other side of the street. The driver's window was down, and the driver was watching him, his face in shadows and a hat pulled low over his head.

Adrenaline raced through Ben, and he eased his hand into his jacket pocket again. The truck was too far away for Ben to see the driver clearly, and way too far for him to run it down. For a long moment, they simply stared at each other, the silence thick and heavy in the night.

Then the driver eased his foot off the brake and the truck began to roll slowly down the road. Ben took a step closer, and the driver hit the gas. The vehicle leapt forward, its rear tires fishtailing, and then he was gone, nothing more than two red taillights mocking him in the darkness.

Ben waited until the truck was gone. Then he waited some more.

When he was finally convinced it was gone, he spun around and sprinted back toward the restaurant. There was no doubt in his mind. Joseph was back, he knew all the players involved, and he was on his game.

※※※

Ben flung open the front door and strode inside, not even bothering to stomp the snow off his boots. He just barged past the hostess stand, his gaze riveted to the bar. His gut went cold when he didn't see Mari there. "Mari!" he shouted, not even bothering to hold back. The place was almost empty. All that was left were Haas and two of his old-timer friends, and a few of the staff clearing the tables. "Mari!"

She stood up from behind the bar, a tray of glasses in her hands. The moment he saw her, relief rushed through him, the most relief he'd ever felt in his damn life. He couldn't take his gaze off her familiar face, her slightly askew ponytail, and her vibrant brown eyes. His body actually shuddered from the hit of emotion that cascaded through him at the realization that she was *safe*.

Her eyes widened with welcome, and then her shoulders sagged with visible exhaustion, as if she had suddenly stopped holding on so hard when she'd seen him. "You said you'd be back at eleven," she said. "It's ten past. I thought you were dead."

"Sorry." He knew she meant it, and he regretted having made her worry. He moved swiftly through the room, sidestepping tables, not taking his gaze off her. He reached the bar and leaned forward, lowering his voice. "You okay?" He couldn't stop thinking about the man from the parking lot. Had he been inside? Had he been watching Mari all night?

"Yes, fine." She set the glasses down, and he could see the strain in the corners of her mouth. "I'm beat though. Can we go?"

"Yeah, you bet." He took her arm as she exited from behind the bar, shouting good night to the others. She began to head toward the front door, but he redirected her. "We're going out through the kitchen."

"The kitchen? Why?"

"Because I want to stay low profile." He passed by Haas's table, and saw that the old man had been joined by Donny, and another old-timer Ben vaguely recognized from earlier, a man who had come out of the back hall at the same time he'd found Mari there earlier. "Thanks, man." He shook Haas's hand. "Appreciate it."

"Any time." Haas raised his brows. "See you at Mari's house tomorrow morning to do some work on it? I want that place secure."

Ben laughed softly. "You and me both, but no, we won't be there."

Mari looked sharply at him. "We won't? Where will we be?"

He glanced at her. "Somewhere else," he said evasively. He looked at Haas. "I'll be in touch, okay?" He'd gotten Haas's phone number earlier, and had given Haas the number for his voicemail system. Not the phone number because that was too vulnerable.

Haas nodded. "You bet, Sully."

Eager to get away from the joint, Ben wasted no time herding Mari through the kitchen to the back door. He paused just inside the door and handed her another jacket, a heavy one, large enough to go on over hers. "Put this on."

She didn't argue, hoisting it over her shoulders, along with a red and black checked hunter's cap. He quickly helped her tuck her hair under it, then pulled up the collar. "There," he said, with a grin. "You look like a hunter who had a stunted growth spurt. It's not much, but it's something." He then donned his own similar outfit. "I picked up a new truck. It's parked right next to the back door. Don't go around it. Just go straight in through the driver's side."

She nodded, her face determined as he reached past her and shoved the door open. Swirling snowflakes fluttered inside, but he held her back as he leaned out the door and inspected the area. It was dark and silent, no cars or movement. He did a quick inspection of the bed of the truck and the interior of the cab. Satisfied they had no stowaways, he gestured her inside. She vaulted easily into the truck, and he climbed in after her, locking the door and starting the engine with one efficient move.

In less than a second, the tires were rolling and they were moving out. "Go low," he said.

Mari didn't argue, scooting down toward the floor. "You think he's watching us?"

"He was. I chased him off. I don't know if he's back yet." But as Ben pulled out onto the main road, he saw no headlights, or lurking vehicles. He drove in silence for twenty minutes, and saw nothing to arouse suspicion and finally relaxed his hands on the wheel. "I think we're good."

"Really? Because I was getting pretty comfy down here." Mari pulled herself back onto the seat. Her cheeks were flushed from the heat, and she began to peel off the layers as she glanced out the window. She frowned immediately. "Where are we? I don't recognize this."

"We're not going to your place."

She glanced at him. "Where are we going?"

"The wedding is the place for us to take control," he said, "but I don't want to give him access to us before then, or to expose anyone else. So, we're going to lay low until then." He'd thought about it from a thousand different angles, and he'd concluded that the only possible option was to take the control back, and that meant controlling the information, and controlling their exposure.

She peeled the jacket off and tossed it beside her, eying him over the two duffel bags still on the seat between them. "So, where are we going then?"

"A hotel."

There was no mistaking the sudden tension in the cab of the truck at his words. "A hotel," she repeated. "Us? Together?"

"Damn right together. There's no chance in hell you're sleeping alone. Not until this is over."

CHAPTER 12

Mari stopped in the doorway to the hotel room she was about to share with Ben, staring at the rustic four-poster king-sized bed in the middle of their suite. "One bed?" She looked around for a doorway that would indicate they had a suite, but there wasn't one. One bed. She and Ben sleeping together... Heat seemed to jump into her belly, and she swallowed, her heart suddenly pounding.

"Yeah." Ben didn't even pretend to apologize as he walked past her, dumping the massive load of bags onto the couch on the opposite side of the room. "I wanted their most secure suite, and this was the best they had." Apparently oblivious to any sexual implications of them sharing a bed, Ben walked across the room and slid the curtain aside. "It looks out onto the river. No houses or any structures back there, just an open field. We can see anyone approaching from that angle. We're on the third floor, so no one can climb up, and since the roof is another two stories up, no one's coming down."

Mari sighed at the disappointment that settled like a stone in her belly at his reaction to the sleeping arrangements. Of course, it was not about sex or seduction. It was about security. She chastised herself for being so uptight, even as she nervously watched him stride across the room, checking out the kitchenette. "This is good enough," he said, opening the fridge. "We have enough food and space. We won't need to leave until the wedding."

Not leave for five days? She tensed. "Wait, at all? But

my job—"

"You're going to get food poisoning tonight," he said, glancing over at her. "You can't make it to work for a few days." He stood up, his green eyes still scanning the room as he walked over to the bathroom and peered inside.

"What?" She set her hands on her hips. "I need that job—"

"You need to stay alive." He walked over to the door, turned the deadbolt, and hung the chain with an ominous click.

Mari's heart began to pound as he turned toward her. She was really locked in with him for five days? "Ben—"

"We're secure." His gaze went to hers, and the protest died in her throat. His eyes were haunted, and she noticed the dark shadows beneath them. Suddenly, he didn't look like the ruthless mercenary ready to confront the enemy. He looked like a man who was too tired to take another step. A man who had fought until he had no reserves left.

She studied him carefully, her growing tension dissolving in the face of her concern for the man she was depending on so much. "Are you okay?"

Her question seemed to shake him from his weariness. He pulled back his shoulders and nodded, striding across the floor. "I went to your place and grabbed everything I could find that you might need." He lifted two of the duffel bags onto the couch. "Including a couple fancier outfits for the wedding, and pretty much all the toiletries in your bathroom. You didn't have much, so I figured you needed it all."

Heat flamed her cheeks at the idea of him rummaging through her personal belongings. It felt so intimate to know he'd taken that liberty, and a sudden longing surged through her, a yearning for the kind of intimacy that would make something like that normal and okay, even under regular circumstances. "Um... thanks."

"Sorry if it bothers you, but I didn't want you going back there tonight. I felt it was too risky." He wouldn't look at her as he hauled more bags to the kitchen and began to unpack them. Milk. Coffee. Ground beef. Chicken. Vegetables. Fruit. Eggs. He moved with ruthless efficiency, a man who wasted no effort.

Slowly, she sank down on the bed watching him. Weariness began to steal over her, but he didn't slow, relentlessly unpacking his things and setting them up. Two computers. Several smaller zippered packs. Maps of Alaska. Files about Joseph. Within minutes, the table looked like the workstation of a man who'd spent years at it.

As his computers booted up, he leaned back in the chair and clasped his hands behind his head, but his leg was bouncing restlessly, and his gaze was still methodically searching the room. He was so restless that he made her tense just watching him. "Ben?"

"Yeah?"

"Have you been living like this since your sister died?" When he looked at her blankly, she gestured around the room. "Living in hotels with your computer. Paying for the rooms by cash. Ditching your old car and buying new ones every few days. Buying enough groceries that you don't have to go out in public for days."

He looked surprised, then shrugged. "I guess so. Why?"

"Do you even sleep?"

"Not much."

She understood that, at least. She didn't either. "It's kind of an awful way to live."

His face darkened. "Not as bad as rotting in prison knowing the man who killed your sister is out there killing other women."

Point taken. "I know, I was so happy when the man who killed my family was shot by police—" She cut herself off, almost embarrassed by how bloodthirsty that sounded. Shouldn't she have wanted justice? But she hadn't. She'd just wanted him gone. Forever. Never to hurt anyone again.

"I get it," Ben said quietly, his voice low, rumbling through her like a warm, understanding hug. "It's okay."

She looked at him. "I can't imagine how it must feel to be living with Holly's death, knowing the man who killed her is still free."

He studied her, then some of the tension that he'd been holding so tightly seemed to slither off his shoulders. He dropped his head to his hands, and his whole body seemed to shudder.

"Ben? I'm sorry, I didn't mean to—"

"No." He stood up suddenly, walked across the room, and went down on his knees in front of her, kneeling almost between her feet, which were dangling off the bed. He put his hands on either side of her hips, staring at her with such stark emotion that she wanted to hug him. "I never said thank you," he said roughly.

"Thank you? For what?" His hair was tousled and messy, dangling over his right eye. She wanted to fix it, but the move felt too intimate.

"For believing my story." He searched her face, his fingers gripping the comforter by her hips. "For getting in my truck tonight, and letting me pack you off to some hotel. For looking at the picture the troopers showed you, and then not pointing your finger at me." His voice was raw and rough, thick with emotion.

"Ben," she said softly, her heart aching for his pain. This time, she didn't resist the urge to brush his hair back from his face, the dark strands softer than she would have thought. "How could I not believe you?"

"How could you trust me? After all you've been through? I don't get it." He was still studying her, almost desperately needing answers. "I don't understand why you're sitting on that bed in front of me, and not running for the door screaming. You don't even know me. I'm on the run for murder. I...I don't get it." His hands suddenly went to her hips, digging in. "I need to know why you trust me when I don't deserve it."

Her heart broke for the vulnerability in his eyes. Here was a man who had achieved it all, at least according to his work photograph, and yet he was on his knees, haunted by the loss of his sister, and unable to understand how anyone could stand by his side. "Because I feel the pain of your loss, and I know it's real, because I feel the same thing."

He smiled, a smile that didn't reach his eyes. "I'm sorry to hear that," he said softly. "I'm sorry you've suffered in that way."

"Me, too." She managed a small smile, trailing her fingers through his hair. In this quiet moment between them, she suddenly wanted to talk about the morning that she'd never revisited since the day it had happened. She'd been unable to cope with the reactions of other people when they heard what had happened to her family. She hated the looks of horror on their faces, the way they'd stared at her as if she were some foreign, cursed creature. Part of coming to Alaska had been about surrounding herself with people who didn't see the death that haunted her. But Ben would understand what she'd been through. He would know it all, without her having to relive each detail.

"It was a Sunday," she said quietly. The moment she said the words, a feeling of relief cascaded through her, as if the dark veil around her heart had suddenly thinned, letting in the first ray of light in so long. "A beautiful Sunday morning. We never opened our store on Sundays. The Walsh Cheese Shop had been in that spot for forty-two years, founded by my grandparents. Never once had it been open on a Sunday."

Ben's eyes narrowed, his expression becoming intent as he listened. He didn't ask any questions, and didn't try to figure out why she was telling him the story. He just listened, because she wanted to tell him.

She tangled her fingers in his hair, happy that he wasn't pushing her away. She needed this contact with him as she talked. She needed his strength to ground her as she allowed images long buried to come to life in her mind again. "That Sunday was a local festival for the town. It happened every year, but this time, the organizers had managed to secure several high profile bands for a benefit concert. The stage was going to be set up on Main Street, less than thirty feet from our store. I wanted to open the store. I thought it would be wonderful for business, and would help us establish connections with non-resident customers to help our internet sales, you know?"

Ben nodded. "Makes sense."

"I thought it did." Guilt coursed at her, horrible, insurmountable guilt, a lead weight in her belly, but she kept going, needing desperately to purge what had been eating at her for so long. But Ben would understand, and she needed that. "Everyone in my family wanted to go to the concert, but I convinced them to open the store instead. How else would we continue to grow and thrive, right? My parents said they were happy with the size of our business, but I..." She swallowed, hating herself for the words she'd thrust at her family to make them do it. "I made them open it that morning."

"You wanted to evolve," Ben said softly. "Take things further. Breathe more. Live more."

"Yes!" She couldn't believe he understood that part of the story. "I'd worked in that store since I was five years old. My sister had, too. We never went on vacation because we were open six days a week. It was the same, always the same." Even as she said the words, guilt rushed through her. "I mean, I loved it," she said quickly. "I loved my family. It meant everything to me. I just—" She stopped, unsure how to articulate it.

"—wanted it to be all that it could," he finished, somehow knowing exactly what she had been trying to say. He reached up, and brushed her hair back from her face, just as she had done to him. "That's a good thing, Mari."

"No," she whispered, clasping his wrist, needing to ground herself in the present, in his understanding. "No, because I made them open that store on Sunday. There were so many crowds. So many people. Our shop was packed, with people in and out constantly. It was everything I'd told them that it could be. I thought it was perfect."

He rested his palms on her thighs, moving closer, invading her space as if he could sense her need for it. "No?"

"No," she whispered. "After an hour and a half, my mother walked over to the door and flipped the sign to closed. She turned back to me, to all of us, and she said that this wasn't what the store was about. It wasn't about strangers who had been drinking too much and listening to rowdy bands. It was about intimacy and community." Tears began to burn. "I told her she was wrong and then—"

He rose up on his knees so he was level with her and clasped her face in his palms, his face searching hers. "And then what, sweetheart?"

Tears streamed down her cheeks as she looked at him. "The door opened behind her, and a man walked in. He...he was young...maybe in his early twenties...drunk...angry...and—" She started to cry. "He was yelling. I don't even know what he was yelling about...he was just so mad and angry. He pushed my mom out of the way, and she fell against the shelves. My dad shouted at him and raced toward him— And then— And then—"

She couldn't breathe. Couldn't get any air. She could still see it, the way he turned so slowly toward her father as he ran at him. "I didn't even see the gun. I just...there was this loud crack and then my dad just...just...just flew backwards against the wall. My mother screamed and then he spun around and shot her, and then he killed my sister as she was lunging toward the back room to hide...and then he turned the gun toward me."

She could still remember it. That moment was frozen in time. The gun that had been aimed at her. His black eyes fixated on her.

"Hey, sweetheart." Ben lightly kissed her, not a kiss of seduction, a kiss of comfort, of protection, a kiss to remind her that she was sitting on a bed with him, safe and protected in his presence. "You don't have to go there again. It's okay. I know—"

"I have to tell you." She'd never talked about it. Never. She had to tell him. "I was standing there, standing against the bread wall, frozen. I had nowhere to go. Nowhere to hide. I was trapped, and his gun was aimed right at me. My sister was gasping, my mom and dad weren't moving, and there was blood everywhere, this bright, red blood. I knew I was going to die. All I could do was stand there, waiting, because there was nowhere to go. Then there were all these shouts and people started running and screaming, and the police were outside yelling at him, and it was just us. Alone in that store. His gun pointing at me, my family dying. All the noise outside didn't matter. They would never stop him in time. It was over—" She cringed, holding her hands over her ears, as if she was trying to block out the screaming again. The blood. All the blood.

"Hey, hey, hey," Ben whispered, stroking her hair. "It's okay, it's over. He didn't get you. You're safe now. I'm here. I've got you, okay?"

You're safe now. I'm here. I've got you. She repeated his words in her head, clinging desperately to the resonant baritone of his voice, drawing it deep into her, using it to ease the grip of terror. She swallowed, searching his face, needing to see him, but barely able to focus through the tears that wouldn't stop. "He raised his gun to shoot me, and then the glass of our front door shattered. His forehead exploded in blood, and he fell to the ground. A police officer had shot him, and it was over." She started to shake again, remembering that moment when he'd fallen, when she'd looked around the store and seen everyone she loved dead, when she'd realized that the world was not safe, that she would never feel safe again.

"Hey, sweetheart, I know. I really know." He kissed her again, lightly, brushing his lips over her cheek, her forehead, her lips, a steady caress that made her want to tumble off the bed and into his arms, to let him simply take away the pain.

"No one would have been there if I hadn't made them open the store," she whispered, squeezing her eyes shut so she could concentrate on each of Ben's kisses. "Ben, it's my fault. All I wanted was to do something for them, to give my family the success they deserved, and they all died. Every time a door opens now, especially in a crowded place, I cringe, waiting for it to happen again, for everything to happen again. I'm scared of crowds. I'm scared of doors that open suddenly. I'm scared of being trapped and not being able to get away. I'm haunted every minute of every day by the fact that they would not have been in the store if I hadn't made them do it."

There it was, laid out for him to judge. The entire story. The carnage. The guilt. The trauma. How completely messed up she was over the whole thing. Every bit of it. No more pretending to be charming and witty, the gal from out of town who always knew the right thing to cheer up a customer. She was flawed, imperfect, and a complete mess. She waited for the recrimination, for the blame, for him to agree, but he didn't. He just eased up beside her on the bed, wrapped his arms around her, and pulled her against his chest, holding her, hugging her.

She stiffened, waiting for the words she would have to defend against...but they never came. Just the quiet brush of his lips over her temple, and his low voice in her ear. "It's not your fault, sweetheart. It's the bastard who pulled the trigger. Not yours."

Overwhelmed by his kindness, tears trickled down her cheeks, new tears, no longer reflecting guilt or anguish, but something different. They were rivulets of hope that he could hear her story and know what she'd done, but not condemn her, like maybe, just maybe, it was okay to be who she was. "But—"

"No." He wiped his thumbs over her cheeks, brushing away the evidence of her overwhelming emotions. "Look at me. It's not your fault. You went to work. That's all. *It's not your fault.*"

She stared at him, searching his face for pretense, for deceit, for some sign that he was lying, but there was nothing but stark, raw honesty in his face. "But they wouldn't have been there—"

"They were in the same place they'd been in six days a week for almost half a century," he said. "They were living their life. Some bastard took that away, but that's his fault, not yours." He pressed a kiss to her forehead, a kiss so gentle, so sweet, and so affirming that tears of true heartache threatened to overwhelm her.

Numbly, she closed her eyes, trying to contain how moved she was by his embrace, by his kindness, by the gentleness of his kiss, and by his forgiveness of what she'd done. "But you said that it was your fault that Holly's dead. Because you hadn't protected her. It's the same."

Ben's lips went still against her forehead, and for a long moment, he didn't move. Then he leaned his forehead against hers, his arms still strong and protective around her. "I think," he said softly, "that's different because she asked me for help, and I was too busy with work to give her my attention. If I had listened, I would have known something was wrong. I had time to help her, and I chose not to. Violence was hunting her, she asked for my help, and I should have known it. You...you just wanted to sell cheese."

"I wanted to sell cheese." His words seemed so trite, so silly, and so ludicrous, that she laughed, an anguished, sobbing laugh, but a laugh nonetheless. "That sounds so ridiculous. I wanted to sell cheese, and my family got murdered instead. It's like a bad movie."

He pulled back to look at her, and he, too, had a small smile playing at the corners of his mouth. "The day that a hunk of cheese can be blamed for a mass murder is a day that has not yet arrived, sweetheart. It was a terrible, terrible tragedy. It was wrong." He set his palm over her heart, his touch so solid and warm it seemed to fill her. "It will haunt you forever, but no matter how much you torment yourself, it will never change what happened, and it will never bring them back."

Fresh tears flooded. "I know that—"

"Do you? Or do you think that if you torment yourself enough, it will change the past?" He caught her face in his hands, searching her. "Mari, you have to forgive yourself. What you did was okay. It really was. *It really was.*"

The genuineness of his compassion was so honest and real that it flooded her, breaking the dams that had held her emotions under tight wraps for so long. With a low whisper of comfort, he pulled her into his arms and held her as she cried, as she finally, mercifully, released the burden that had kept her captive for so long.

Within his arms, cradled in his embrace, and protected by the shield of his warmth and his body, she finally felt safe again, safe enough to cry, safe enough to mourn the loss of her family, and maybe, just maybe, even safe enough to begin to stop hating herself so much for what she had done.

CHAPTER 13

This moment was perfection.

Ben hadn't thought that there could ever be such perfection in his life, not with how many layers of filth and scum had been woven into his existence. Yet as he lay in the bed with Mari asleep on his chest, the fresh scent of her shampoo wafting gently in the air, he felt the first sense of peace he'd had in a very long time, perhaps ever.

He looked down at her as the orange rays of dawn cast a faint glow on her face. Her eyelashes were dark, swept across her cheeks. Her arm was wrapped around his torso, as if she was afraid she would lose him while she slept. Her breathing was rhythmic and even, finally settled after hours of crying and anguish. She was still wearing the same clothes she'd been wearing last night, crying herself to sleep in his arms.

Once she'd fallen asleep, she hadn't moved again. It had been deep and peaceful, but even in her sleep, she had held tight to him all night, never releasing him, as if he were the reason she had finally found solace.

With a soft sigh, he ran his hands through her hair, gently untangling the matted curls. Her story last night had been devastating. He'd felt her grief and guilt with every word she'd spoken, but at the same time, he'd felt her relief at finally being able to share her burden. He was glad he'd been there for her. He understood what she was dealing with, and she knew that he got it. Knowing about her past made him understand why she'd believed in him, and why she was lying in this bed, trusting him to keep her safe while she slept.

Mari believed in him because she had been victimized by the worst of humanity, and Ben's grisly history was nothing compared to the evil that she'd faced. She'd looked into the eyes of a murderer and seen him pull the trigger. It had changed her forever, as it had changed him when he was a kid. It had taught her to see beyond the surface, to see who he really was. His chest tightened, and he bent his head to brush his lips over her temple.

She moved slightly, snuggling deeper against him, and he smiled...and then he frowned. What was he doing? Swearing, he let his head fall back against the headboard. He was getting too involved. How could he possibly stay focused if he was scared shitless that Joseph would hurt her?

"Ben?" Her voice was muffled against his chest.

"Yeah, sweetheart. I'm here." He scooted lower on the bed, so his face was level with her. "You okay?"

Her eyes flickered open, the sleepy half-mast of early morning. "Sorry I fell apart on you last night."

He shook his head. "No, it was good. A guy likes to feel like a man sometimes, and the best way to do it is to help a woman through a rough spot. So, I owe you."

She laughed softly, snuggling her head against the pillow as she watched him. "I feel better. Better than I've felt in a long time."

"Good."

"Did you sleep at all?"

He was surprised by the question. What did it matter if he slept? "No, I don't sleep much. I don't need to."

She studied him. "You held me all night, but never slept?"

"Yeah." He brushed his fingers over her cheek, still marveling at how soft her skin was. Even first thing in the morning, she still looked as beautiful as she had the night before. Her beauty didn't come from heavy layers of makeup that was gone by morning. It was all natural, simply a woman living each day with her heart. "Beautiful," he whispered.

Her cheeks turned red, but she smiled, brushing her fingers through her hair as if she were trying to make it neat. "You must be blind."

He caught her hand, stilling it, not wanting her to change anything. "Nah, just seen too much crap in my life. I know real beauty when I see it, and it's you." His gaze settled on her mouth, and he became all too aware of the fact that their legs were tangled beneath the covers. Her bare foot was warm against his ankle, her thigh wedged between his. Sudden desire lurched through him, and an entire night of innocent holding vanished, replaced by a pulsating awareness of the intimacy of their position. How long had it been since he'd shared a bed with a woman?

He couldn't even remember the last time.

Mari rolled onto her back, stretching her arms above her head in a cat-like move that made desire pulse even more thickly between them. He was riveted by the curve of her neck, by her breasts pushing against her shirt as she arched. Swearing, he jerked his gaze back to her face. What was he doing? He had to focus, not ogle her...or worse. That was it. He was getting out of bed. Now. He grabbed the sheets to jerk them back—

"You know what?" she said suddenly. "I'm sorry you lost your old life."

He paused, one hand on the sheet he'd been about to toss back. "What?"

"Your life," she said, rolling onto her side again to look at him. She tucked her hands under her head, looking so damned innocent that his cock went hard again. "In your photograph, you looked so..." Her cheeks flushed. "Handsome. Clean."

He raised his brows. "Clean?"

She grimaced. "Well, yes, like clean-cut, I mean, like you know, you got to shower and get a haircut and stuff."

He couldn't help but grin at her discomfiture. "You think I smell now? Is that what you're saying? That I should shower and clean up? Get my hair cut again?"

"No, God. No. I think you're much better-looking with the longer hair." She slanted a glance at him. "More approachable. You looked a little harsh in that photo."

"Harsh?" He was surprised by that. Harsh was not a word he'd ever associated with himself. For a moment, he considered asking her, but then realized that delving deep into personal discussions was not conducive to keeping his distance.

"So, better looking now, but you still think I smell?" he teased, trying to shift the topic to something that didn't matter. "Because I noticed you avoided that question."

"No, of course not!" She grabbed a pillow and smacked him with it. "I didn't mean that you smell or anything, because you don't. Well, I mean, you do, but it's like this really sensual, masculine scent that curls through a woman, not like that aftershave that guys slop on that is supposed to be attractive. It's more subtle, like when I'm close to you and I breathe, it wraps around me and makes me feel—" Her cheeks turned pink, and she cut herself off, her fingers over her mouth. "Oh, sorry, I didn't mean to go on like that. God, I'm such a—"

"No." He moved forward, dark, hot temptations building inside him as he caught her wrist. All amusement was gone, replaced by a stark awareness of her as a woman. "No woman has ever talked to me like that before." His voice was low and rough, and her eyes widened as he slid one leg over her hips, pinning her to the bed. "They want my money. They want my power." He moved suddenly, sliding on top of her, his hips sinking down against hers. "They would never, *ever*, notice anything like what you just said."

Mari's eyes were wide, her hands resting beside her head on the pillow. She was flat on her back, defenseless, but there was no fear in her eyes. Just desire that struck right in his gut. "I didn't mean to. I just meant that you looked like you had everything before, and now, you're stuck in a hotel room hiding from a murderer, spending your nights wiping the tears of a woman you just met. I just meant that I was sorry you lost that life." Her gaze flicked to his mouth, and then jerked back to his eyes. "I wasn't trying to seduce you," she whispered.

"I know. That's why it's working." He bent his head, his mouth hovering over hers. He knew he shouldn't do this. He knew it. This wasn't the time. It wasn't the place. It wasn't the situation. "I'm tainted," he growled, trying to convince her to kick his ass off the bed. "I could wind up in prison tomorrow. No matter what happens, I know my job and my career are toast. No firm would touch an attorney who has as much bad press as I do, even if I turn up innocent. You don't want me, Mari." But hell, her body felt so good beneath him. He was barely touching her, supporting himself above her, except at their hips and their legs. His chest wasn't even touching hers, and his triceps were beginning to burn with the effort of keeping himself from lowering himself on top of her, inch by inch, until there was no space between them. Just flesh. Just bodies. Just them.

Her eyes were wide, her breath rapid. "I know."

"Which part?" Unable to resist, just needing the tiniest touch, he bent his head and grazed his teeth over her earlobe. "Which part do you know, Mari?" he whispered against her ear, biting ever so gently.

She jumped, and suddenly, her hands were on his chest, clenching his shirt. "I know you could be in prison tomorrow," she whispered, her voice shaky.

"And the other part?" He trailed his mouth down the side of her neck. "What about the part where you tell me you don't want me? Just say it, Mari. Say it now." He needed to hear it. He wasn't a saint. Not by a long shot. There was no way he could be the gentleman he was supposed to be, not with her beneath him, telling him how his scent wrapped around her. "Tell me you don't want me."

There was silence, and he pulled back, searching her face. "Mari?"

For a long moment, she said nothing, then she gave the tiniest shrug of her shoulders. "I can't help it," she said.

"You can't help it?" He blinked. "You have to help it."

But she didn't help it. She simply set her hands on his cheeks, framing his face just as he'd done to her. Her touch was so soft, so innocent, so beautiful. Son of a bitch. "I can't do this," he gritted out. "I can't have you in this bed, looking at me like that, and not touch you."

She fastened her gaze on him. "Ben," she said quietly. "I lost my family. You lost your sister. We both could be dead tomorrow, or you could be on your way to prison. We both know all too well the unpredictability of life. There's so much unknown, so much to lose, so much that could be yanked out from under us without any warning. For months, I've been walking around, half-dead, barely functioning. But you changed that. You've given me something back. Security? Safety? Hope?" She touched his jaw. "Physical connection with another person?

I don't want to miss out on this moment. I don't want to be a martyr and say no, when this might be it, my one chance to feel this good, to be held, to be...connected with another person. A person I'm not scared of."

Her words hung in the air, so poignant, so beautiful, it was as if they had bled hope into his own, blackened heart.

Without another word, words that he couldn't have articulated anyway, he bent his head and kissed her.

She was ready for him, and her lips met his with equal fervor. Desire crashed through him, months and months of tension and grief were unleashed into the kiss. He lowered himself onto her, almost groaning at the feel of her body beneath his, her breasts crushed against his chest. Her lips were frantic, and warm, a temptation so silky it seemed to caress his very soul like a sensual seduction.

He shifted his weight to the side, bracing himself on his left arm so he could tug her shirt up. He palmed her belly, and she sucked in her breath, her muscles quivering at his touch. "So smooth," he whispered, sliding his hand across her stomach and over her ribs. He couldn't believe how soft her skin was, how pure, how intoxicating. "I need to kiss it," he whispered, scooting down to press a kiss to her belly button.

"God, Ben, that feels so good." Her fingers were in his hair now, clenching as he kissed his way across her belly, down toward the waistband of the jeans she'd slept in. He braced one arm across her belly and then slowly, ever so slowly, unbuttoned the top of her jeans.

She bit her lower lip and propped herself up on her elbows to watch him. Her eyes were dark, darker than he'd ever seen them, and her cheeks were flushed. There was no agenda in her eyes, just the raw need of a woman for the man she was with. A sudden need to possess her roared through him, and he crawled up her body, a slow, predatory crawl of domination. Her eyes widened, and her gaze flashed to his mouth.

"Yes," he whispered. "Want me, Mari." Then he caught her mouth in his, a kiss that was on fire. Desperate. Hot. Passionate. Intense. Searing with need. The kiss became about more than a physical connection. It became about losing himself in her. It became about waking her soul. It became about stoking the fires between them until the inferno consumed him.

With desperate need building within him for her, for more skin, and for more intimacy, he dragged her shirt over her head in one rough move, then slowed to a sensual crawl as he slid his hands back down her arms, over the bare flesh. Her breasts were small but perfect, cradled by a simple gray bra with just a hint of lace around the edges. Sexy as hell with its understated femininity, and blood pulsed in his cock. "So beautiful," he whispered.

He cupped her breast and bent his head, trailing kisses across the rounded swell, then pulled the lace aside to expose her nipple. He drew it into his mouth, and she gasped, gripping his shoulders as she shifted restlessly beneath him. Her uninhibited response was like a spark that shredded what little control he had left. He jerked back and ripped his shirt off over his head, awareness pulsing through him as she watched him unabashedly.

He rolled off her and yanked his jeans off, tossing them on the floor, quickly followed by his boxers. With ruthless aggression, he grabbed her calves and swung her around to face him as he dropped to his knees in front of her. Without taking his gaze off her face, he wedged himself between her knees and ran his hand up her thigh, over the denim. Mari propped herself up on her elbows, desire flushing her cheeks, her breasts spilling out of the bra that he'd dislodged. Her dark curls were tumbling over her shoulders and across her breasts, as if they were caressing the flesh he'd just been kissing.

He slid his hands up to her hips, then rose to his feet, leaning over her to take her in another bold kiss of lips and tongue and raw possession. Her response was instant fire, a kiss that went straight to his cock. Just as she was reaching for him, he pulled back, retreating to his knees again, his hands still on her hips, but sliding oh-so-slowly toward the junction of her thighs.

Mari's eyes were bright with anticipation and lust, and he craved more of that. It felt incredible to watch her respond to him, to know that she was completely into him, and only him. There was no agenda in the room with them right now. No furtive peeks into his closet to see how many custom suits he had, no compliments about his expensive rug. Just a woman who had been stripped bare by life, putting her entire being into his safekeeping. He knew this wasn't simply about sex. It was more. Deeper. A connection between two souls who had both been through more loss and more hell than most people would ever comprehend. But they both did. They both knew what it was like. They had both seen the blood of those they love spilled ruthlessly across the ground. They'd both lost it all, and were surviving only by their fingernails, by sheer, raw instinct.

With a low growl of desire, he unzipped her fly, yanking it down with restless impatience. He needed more of her. He needed to cement this connection. He needed to ground himself in this woman who got it, who got him, who saw the shit in him and didn't care.

Once again, he moved over her, kissing her fiercely and relentlessly, using his kisses to push her down onto her back even as he grabbed her jeans and yanked them down over her hips, taking her underwear with them. They hit the floor with a soft swish, and then he locked his arm around her and dragged her farther up the bed onto the pillows, never breaking the kiss, needing, for some reason, to be the one in control, to show her his strength, to prove that he could be the man for her, not the man who had let his sister down, but the man who could protect her and be her strength.

Mari slid her hands around his neck, holding him closer, kissing him back just as fiercely, surrendering to his strength and his need to be in control. With a low groan of intense pleasure, he lowered himself on top of her, skin to skin along the length of their bodies. He peeled her hands off his neck and stretched them above her head, pinning them against the headboard as he kissed her more fiercely. His grip was tight, trapping her, but he was attuned to every nuance of her body, prepared to release her the moment he sensed any fear from her.

But there was none. Just a mounting desire in her kisses, and in the restless movement of her hips beneath his. He realized suddenly that she *trusted* him. How was that possible? How could she trust *anyone* after what had happened to her with her family and then with Joseph? But she did. He could tell. Her body was relaxed, her kisses just as intense as his, and she was making no effort to shield her body from his or free herself from his grip.

The magnitude of her trust shuddered through him, igniting a roar of lust so intense he almost bellowed with need. Instead, he shoved his knee between hers, forcing her legs apart, his hips pinning her down to the bed. He was twice her size, his weight insurmountable, trapping her ruthlessly and putting her at his mercy for whatever he wanted to do with her. And again, *again,* she allowed him to control her, not resisting, not fearing, but fully surrendering to him, trusting him not to hurt her.

He didn't get it. She'd seen the darkest sides of him. She knew he wasn't that lily-pure pretty boy in the picture, and yet here she was, opening herself to him in the most vulnerable way possible. The enormity of her trust swelled through him, driving him to more frenzied kisses, more burning need, an all-consuming need to protect her at all costs, no matter what, for all time.

He wanted to ask. He wanted to beg permission. He wanted to hear her say yes, but at the same time, he needed to just do it, he needed to feel her offer herself to him without having to hear the words that so many women wanted, as if that made them true. So, instead of speaking, he broke the kiss and pulled back.

Her eyes opened, her gaze meeting his. Her eyes were burning with desire and emotion, shiny with...unshed tears? For a second, horror pulsed through him, and he froze, then he saw the corners of her mouth curve up in a private smile just for him, and he understood. The tears were for the fact that she was trusting him, and he realized that she, too, was in awe of the fact she wasn't scared. Just as she'd given him a gift by trusting him, he'd done the same for her, by somehow giving her back the ability to feel safe. In his arms, trapped beneath him, at his mercy, she felt safe.

He grinned back at her, pressed a quick kiss to the tip of her nose, and then buried himself in her in one ruthless stroke.

CHAPTER 14

She gasped and arched back as he held his position. He loved the play of emotions cascading across her face as her body adjusted to his. Wonder. Awe. Desire. Need. She was slick and wet, and his penetration had been an easy, effortless move, both of them so ready for what had been building between them.

Slowly, ever so slowly, he withdrew, grinning as she gripped his shoulders and stiffened. "You're just mean," she gasped.

"I know." Then he plunged again, burying himself even deeper as her fingernails dug into his shoulders. Her legs were wrapped around his hips, locking him against her as she shifted restlessly. "I want more, Mari. *More.*"

Pulling out once again, he grabbed her ankles and shoved her legs upward toward her shoulders, trapping her again, exposing her to him. Totally defenseless. Totally at his mercy. Her eyes were lidded, watching him in sensual anticipation as he nudged his cock against her entrance.

No words were spoken, but the emotions were so thick in the air, mingling with the scent of their lovemaking. His gaze riveted to hers, he eased inside her, groaning at the sensation of her body taking him in. He went all the way, so deep at this angle that his balls smacked against her body. She gasped, trying to move her hips in response, but he held her still, not letting her move as he withdrew and then thrust again. Again and again, he tormented them both, always watching her intently, always primed for any hint that she was feeling scared or pressured, but there was none. Just rising ardor, her body slick with need for him, her gasps coming faster and louder with each of his thrusts.

She wanted him this way, he realized. She *liked* putting herself at his mercy. She *liked* feeling his strength and power as they made love. This woman, this courageous, brave woman somehow, someway, believed in him. Him. *Him.* Suddenly, it became too much. The intensity of what was happening between them. The impact of her trust, of her giving herself to him. He lost himself to the need for her, thrusting deeper and deeper, faster, more frantically, until he forgot to hold her down and fell into her, kissing her frantically as he drove into her.

She came first, her body convulsing beneath him as the orgasm ripped through her. He could feel the tremors in every muscle, her utter capitulation to it, and it tore the last vestige of his self-control from his tenuous grasp. He shouted her name as the orgasm exploded through him, an endless, ruthless vortex of need that ricocheted through him again and again, until all he could do was hold onto the woman in his arms and whisper her name again and again, and again, anchoring himself in her, using her to find his way back.

※※※

Mari bolted upright, her heart pounding frantically. Terror ripped through her like a knife jammed into her chest. She barely stifled a scream as she leapt back against the headboard, her hands up to protect herself. She frantically scanned the room, searching for the threat that had jerked her from her sleep. It was too dark to see, shadows cascading over the room like a veil of doom closing in on her. And then she saw it, the blue glow of a computer screen by the window. A man was bent over the table, talking in a low tone, his voice angry and rough. There was an earphone dangling from his right ear, and he had pulled the microphone close to his mouth while he talked low and fast. She yelped in terror—then cut off the scream when she realized she recognized the familiar slope of his shoulders. It was Ben. Not Joseph. *Ben.* The man who had held her through her tears. The man who was there to keep her safe.

Relief shuddered through her, an agonizing release from the debilitating fear trying to consume her. She bowed her head, clutching her knees to her chest as she tried to control her racing heartbeat. Her dream had been so real. She'd been sleeping at her house and woken up to find Joseph on top of her, his gun pointing at her forehead, screaming at her so violently that spittle sprayed from his mouth, coating her with his filth. Charlotte's mangled body had been sprawled across the bed, while Ben had been on the floor in the corner. A slow, deadly bloodstain had been spreading across his shirt as he shouted at her to run and save herself, even as he collapsed, succumbing to the wounds Joseph had inflicted upon him.

As the visceral memories rooted themselves in her conscious mind, renewed fear tried to grab her again. "No, it's not real," she said aloud, fighting against the tremors shaking her so violently. She hugged herself, rocking back and forth, trying to clear her head. "It was a dream. It was a dream. Nothing but my imagination." But it had been so real, so real—

"Mari? What's wrong?"

She looked up, and saw Ben looking at her, holding his hand over the microphone. His green eyes seemed to glow even in the dim light, and her throat tightened at the concern on his face. She wasn't alone. Even in the aftermath of her nightmare, *she wasn't alone.* The realization was staggering, a surreal relief after so long of fighting the nightmares by herself. Tears swam in her eyes as she felt her body begin to uncoil under his attention. "I had a dream—"

Then she saw he was holding a gleaming handgun. For a moment, she was frozen in sheer terror, her gaze riveted by the gun that looked just like the one that had taken down her family. She couldn't move. Couldn't speak. All she could do was stare at the gun, horror spreading through her—

Ben immediately set the gun down, and held up his hands. "It's okay, sweetheart. I'm not holding it anymore. You're safe."

She scrambled back against the headboard in sudden panic. "Put it away. Put it away! *Put it away!*"

"I'll call you back," Ben said into the phone. Then he ripped off the headset and jumped up, coming toward her. "It's okay, Mari. It's—"

"No!" She held up her hands, unable to take her gaze off

the gun. It was right there on the tabletop. Ten feet away. All he had to do was grab it, point it, and then pull the trigger. Then it would all be the same as before. Blood. Screaming. Death. "Stay back!" she commanded.

Swearing, Ben grabbed his jacket and threw it over the gun, hiding it from sight. His move broke the gun's hold on her, and she flinched as she was jerked back to reality.

"Mari," Ben said softly. "You're safe. You're in a hotel. That gun can't hurt you. *It can't hurt you.*"

She couldn't drag her gaze off his jacket, away from the table where she knew the gun still rested. "Get it out of here," she whispered. "You have to get it out of this room."

"I can't." He continued to move toward her, ever so slowly, his voice a low caress. "I need it to protect us against Joseph."

"No, no, no." She shook her head, hugging herself. "You can't have a gun in here. It's too dangerous—"

"I need to have one with me." He reached the bed and eased down next to her, his eyes haunted. "Mari. Look at me."

She shook her head, unable to pry her attention off his jacket, almost waiting for the gun to emerge on its own. She had to know where it was. Had to watch it. Had to—

"Mari!" Ben's voice was sharp now.

She tried to see past him toward the table, but he moved into her line of sight, using his shoulders to block her view.

"Look at me," he commanded sharply, his deep voice finally seemed to reach something inside her, the rational side of her.

She looked at him, and this time she actually saw him. She noticed his green eyes, and the mouth that had kissed her so beautifully such a short time ago. "Ben?" she whispered.

"Yeah, it's me." He took her hand, gripping firmly, a small smile flickering across his face. "Can you listen to me for a sec?"

She touched his face, needing to reassure herself that it was him. His skin was warm and soft. His hand was reassuring and strong where he held hers. He was real. He was kind. He was strong. This was the man who had made love to her, who had promised to keep her safe. "Okay." She swallowed, her mouth dry with fear as she stared at him, waiting for him to say more, for him to somehow pull her out of the panic that was trying to overwhelm her.

"Okay." He scooped a heavy gray sweatshirt off the floor and wrapped it around her shoulders. The soft fleece was much too big for her, but it smelled like him. The familiar, comforting scent enveloped her, easing the tension gripping her so ruthlessly. He sat next to her, facing her. He braced one hand on the other side of her hips and leaned across her, inserting himself into her space. "Do you believe I'm a murderer?"

"What?" She stared at him, still trying to focus. "No, no, of course not."

He nodded. "Then is there a reason to fear a gun in my hands?"

She took a shuddering breath, and shook her head. "No, but what if he took it from you—"

Ben didn't give her a chance to finish her thought. "Is he here now?"

She looked around again, even though she knew that, of course, Joseph wasn't anywhere in the room. "No."

"So, can anyone use that gun right now, except me?"

She stared at him, his calm logic finally severing the panic gripping her. "No," she admitted. "No, they can't."

"So, is there a reason to fear it?"

"No." With another shuddering breath, she leaned back against the headboard, and shook her head. "I understand that logically, but it's still a gun, Ben. A gun killed my family. To say that I'm terrified of guns doesn't even begin to explain how I feel about them. Seeing a handgun so close to me, in my room, makes it almost impossible for me to think logically about it."

"I know, sweetheart." He took her hands in his, and pressed his lips to each knuckle. "But a gun is merely a product of the person carrying it, and I have it only to protect us."

She glanced at the desk again, at his black jacket sprawled across the rustic wood. "Why do you even have one? Do you know how to shoot it?"

He laughed softly. "Yes, I do."

She looked back at him. "How? You're a lawyer. Lawyers in big Boston firms don't wear handguns under their suits, do they?"

For a long moment, he just looked at her. Then he stood up and walked across the room, putting distance between them. He sat back down in his chair and turned to face her, spinning restlessly as he braced his forearms on his thighs and studied her with a hooded look. "I told you I grew up on the streets, right?"

She hugged herself, pulling the blankets tighter around her, suddenly not sure she wanted to hear what he was about to tell her. "Yes," she said cautiously.

"I was in a gang by the time I was ten. I was carrying a loaded handgun by the time I was eleven."

She shivered, staring at him. With his grim face, and his dark hair hanging in his eyes, he looked every bit the dangerous predator.

"I learned to react first and ask questions later. I was nine the first time I saw someone shot and killed. My cousin, Daniel. He was so close to me that his blood spattered on my sneakers. He was eleven."

Her mouth dropped open. "Oh, my God," she whispered. "You were both so young." Not that there was such a thing as being old enough to be killed in cold blood, or to watch someone being gunned down in front of you. No one should ever have to experience that. Ever.

He shrugged, a careless gesture that belied the tension radiating through his shoulders. "You learn to survive in that situation, Mari. You survive or you die. I wanted to survive, so I got tougher than the rest of them. I got faster. I became a better shot. I got smarter." He jerked back his sleeve, and she saw a dark tattoo of a snake on the underside of his forearm. "This was our mark. We protected anyone with this tattoo, and defended against anyone who didn't like it."

She stared at him, cold dread settling in her stomach as she stared at what she knew must be a gang symbol emblazoned on his flesh. Ben had been in a gang. He and his friends had shot people, and been targets.

No, that was impossible. The man she was counting on to keep her safe from Joseph could not possibly be a killer. But still, she asked the question. She had to know. "Did you, have you...did you ever shoot someone? And kill them?"

He jerked his sleeve down. "I survived, Mari. That's what I did."

Fear clamped in her belly. Had Ben murdered someone? Was he just like the man who'd killed her family? The one who had killed his sister? "When you find Joseph, are you..." She could barely ask the words. "Are you going to kill him? Or just catch him?"

He met her gaze. "I was in juvie for six months when I was fourteen," he said grimly. "And I was in prison until Mack got me out this time. I know how bad it is to be locked up. There's no way I want to go to prison. If I kill Joseph, I could end up right back behind bars."

Relief rushed through her. "So—"

"But," he interrupted, still watching her intently. "Avenging Holly's death and making sure the bastard doesn't kill anyone else is more important than where I spend the rest of my life. So, yeah, I'll do what I have to do, if it comes to that."

She saw the conviction in his eyes, his absolute willingness to fight whatever battle needed to be fought. This, she realized, was the real Ben. Not the Italian suit pretty-boy with an attitude, which had been his work photograph. Not the cutthroat attorney. Not the man who'd held her and made her feel cherished while he'd made love to her. This was who he was. Raw, real, and fearless...and not afraid of violence. It was all in the name of honor, she knew that, but at the same time, as she looked into his eyes, she realized that his past, including the violence and the deaths, would always be with him, always haunting him, always on the periphery.

As long as she was in his presence, she couldn't lie to herself that life was rosy and safe, and that the future was bright. He would always remind her of what she'd lost. Suddenly, all the warmth and hope she'd felt during their lovemaking slithered away, leaving her with a cold isolation. This man could not be her salvation. He would not make the nightmares end. He would bring them closer, a constant reminder of the terror she'd been working so hard to leave behind.

Ben's eyes darkened. Strained anticipation lined his face, and his jaw hardened. He was waiting for judgment, she realized. Judgment by her that his shadowed past made him unworthy.

"You're a good man," she managed to say, meeting his gaze.

Anger fermented in his eyes. "Don't lie to me," he said quietly, his voice steely. "I'm tired of lies. I can see you withdrawing already. You're judging me as a piece of shit who grew up on the street." There was so much anger in his eyes, far more than the situation warranted. "Yes, Mari, I've taken a human life before. It was in self-defense, but yeah, I've done it. Twice. I'm soiled goods, babe. Not worth your time."

"Hey! I'm not judging you!" Answering anger fumed through her and she stood up, furious that this great man would cut himself down like that. "Don't be angry at me because I'm afraid of guns," she snapped. "My parents were murdered and now some crazy psychopath is hunting me. Hunting us. *Hunting*, Ben. *Hunting!* Every time I turn around, he could be there with a gun aimed at my heart, so forgive me for being a little freaked out by learning that the man I'm sharing a hotel room with has that same capacity to kill people! I don't think you're crazy. I don't think you're bad, and you're a complete idiot for calling yourself soiled goods and for seeing me as the kind of person who would judge you for your past, but for God's sake, Ben, I'm scared!"

Her outburst echoed across the room, and then fragmented into heavy, ominous silence. For a long moment, the only sound was her heavy breathing, and the steady howl of wind outside.

Then, with a heavy sigh, Ben dropped his head to his hands, his shoulders bunched.

He didn't say anything, and neither did she.

Awkwardness grew thicker, and his phone rang.

He didn't move to pick it up. He didn't move at all.

It stopped ringing.

Finally, he raised his head to look at her, but there was an emptiness to his eyes that hadn't been there before. "I'm sorry."

"Me, too." She sat back down on the bed, suddenly exhausted. "I didn't mean to yell."

He looked at her. "I'm scared, too," he said tonelessly.

She stared at him, not wanting to hear the words he'd just uttered. If Ben was scared, what chance did they have? He was supposed to be the strength she was relying on. "What?"

"He defeated me once, and my sister's dead. If I fail again, you die. The stakes are too high. The price of a single mistake is too high." He dropped his head again, running his hands through his hair. "He's good, Mari. He's really good. Better than I am."

Oh, no. This wasn't right. She didn't want to hear this. Ben was her defense against all the darkness coming for her. If he wasn't confident, she would freak out. She needed his strength in order to find her own. He was her rock. "No, he can't be better than you."

He raised his head to look at her. "He knows I'm in Alaska. He knows who I am. He was outside O'Dell's tonight. He's been at your house. He's been everywhere we've been, but he's like a ghost slithering just out of our sight. We don't know who he is or how he's tracked us. He's toying with us, Mari. He's using us to amuse himself until he gets bored, and I don't know how to stop him, so yeah, I'm scared, too."

She inched to the edge of the bed so she could be nearer to him. "There has to be a way, Ben. We can't let him win."

"I know that." He leaned back in his chair, his body tense. "That's why I brought us here. It gives us time to figure what the hell to do, because I don't have the answer right now." He met her gaze. "There's a reason why he's killed five women and set up five innocent men, but no one except you and me has figured it out. He's really good at it, Mari. I can save my ass if a gunfight erupts in the middle of a street, but I have no experience with this cat and mouse shit. I'm running blind, and he's got night vision goggles."

The weight of his words was like a heavy blanket in the room. Suddenly, Mari didn't want to be in the bed anymore. She wanted to be dressed, prepared, and ready to do whatever it took to defeat Joseph. Restlessly, she climbed off the bed and grabbed her jeans, which were still on the floor from when Ben had made love to her earlier. She became acutely aware of the fact she was completely naked, and heat suffused her cheeks. She glanced over and saw Ben watching her, his gaze sweeping unabashedly over every inch of her flesh, the heat in his gaze like a searing fire against her very soul. Instinctively, she started to cover herself, then froze at his whispered command.

CHAPTER 15

His voice was soft, so soft she almost couldn't make out the words, but there was emotion behind them, the same emotion that had driven his expectation that she would reject him after his revelation about his past.

She bit her lip against the instinct to dive into the bathroom and shield herself from this man who lived and breathed everything that gave her nightmares. She wasn't afraid he would hurt her, but she was terrified of what getting involved with him would bring into her life. Her hands trembling, she grabbed her bra and pulled it on, not turning her back, but not giving him a full show either. A compromise. It was the most she could offer him.

He said nothing while she got dressed, but he was still leaning forward, his elbows propped on his thighs, watching her intensely, his face inscrutable and dark. Her breasts burned under his attention, and part of her wanted to throw herself into his arms and beg him to make love to her again until she forgot everything else. But she couldn't do it. She couldn't make herself vulnerable to him again. "So, what do we do? What's the plan?" She kept her voice brisk and professional, trying to build the distance between them to protect herself.

"I don't know yet."

His candor was unsettling, like the ominous ticking of a clock. "Well, we have three days until the wedding."

"It's two and a half now."

Two and a half days didn't feel like much time to devise

a plan to defeat a man who had been murdering women for years, who had no doubt been plotting her death since the day she'd met him.

She sat down on the edge of the bed nearest to Ben, digging her toes into the carpet. "Getting dressed didn't help."

He raised his brows. "Help what?"

"It didn't help me come up with a great plan, or make me feel particularly brave and unstoppable."

He laughed softly, his gazed fixed on hers. "We'll get there. We have time, but you're going to need to be okay with me carrying a gun."

She looked past him at his jacket on his desk and let out her breath. There was a gun under there. She let the knowledge settle in her, then glanced at Ben. Which was stronger? Her fear of the gun, or her belief in Ben's ability to keep them safe? Trust or fear? She didn't have to ask herself. She knew the answer. Ben was the first respite she'd felt since the day her family had been murdered. She believed in him. That was just the way it was. She took a deep breath, and let out a shaky exhale. "Just don't point it at me, okay?"

He didn't smile. "I would never, ever put you at risk." His response was so vehement, so absolute, that a ripple of relief rushed over her. She believed him, and that felt good.

She smiled, and after a brief moment, he smiled back. It was a real smile, a smile of bonding, a smile that said they were in this together, no matter what baggage each of them had. Suddenly, the thought of him seeing her naked didn't scare her. She wanted to feel him against her. She wanted his strength wrapping around her. They had so little time, but right now, for just a few minutes, she wanted what he could give her. "Ben—" She cut herself off, unsure what to say or how to say it. She didn't even know what she wanted, not exactly.

Then he held out one hand to her. No words, and no entreaty. Just one hand, silently asking her for more than she was giving him.

For a moment she hesitated, and still he sat there holding out his hand to her. Suddenly, tears tightened her throat, and she knew what she wanted. Without a word, she stood up and walked across the room toward him. As she took his hand and felt his fingers tighten around hers, she felt like everything was going to be all right. He pulled her gently toward him, and she slid onto his lap, her legs wrapping around his hips as he enfolded her in his arms. His body was warm and muscled against hers, and it felt so good as she buried her face in his neck and held him. In his embrace, with their bodies melted together, she knew this was the man she could trust, the one who could take away the darkness.

His arms tightened around her, as if he was feeling the same thing. She felt him press his lips to her temple, a kiss so intimate and gentle that she felt the shields around her heart begin to crack. She pulled back slightly, her heart tightening as his mouth found hers. The connection was instant and electric, so much more than it had been last night. The gun had forced her to make a choice to truly trust him, and now that she had, his kiss seemed to lodge in her heart and breathe light into the tightness of her chest.

With a low groan, he deepened the kiss, his tongue ruthlessly demanding her response. Excitement and anticipation leapt through her, and desire pooled in her belly. White heat seemed to lick down her thighs, and suddenly she felt his cock harden beneath her, pressing against the junction of her jeans.

"I need you," he whispered, his voice so vulnerable that her heart leapt in response. She knew what he meant. He'd exposed his dark past to her, and he needed her to accept him as he was. Likewise, she needed to connect with the man she'd just opened her heart to.

"Yes," she whispered. "*Yes.*"

Desire darkened his eyes as his hands went to the waistband of her jeans. Moments later, her jeans were on the floor and his pants were unzipped. They had no time to make it to the bed. Their need was too great.

The kiss was frantic and intense, a fire trying to incinerate them both before they could control it. Their hands were desperate as they tried to touch, hold, and caress. He pulled her back onto his lap, and this time there was no denim between them. He was hard and ready, and he slid right into her as she settled on him. Her body was slick and wet, and she shuddered at the feeling of him filling her so completely. He caught her hips, moving her in a seductive, tantalizing motion that sent spirals of heat, fire, and chills shivering through her body.

Tension built inside her. It twisted and tightened, coiling through her until she felt like she was going to explode. He was relentless, moving inside her so fiercely, as he assaulted her mouth with kisses beyond anything she had ever experienced, until she couldn't think of anything but the enormity of his presence and his being.

The orgasm exploded through her so forcefully she screamed, and her heart seemed to burst when Ben shouted her name, his voice almost cracking with the intensity of what they were both feeling. They clung to each other as the orgasm shook them, an intimacy so much more than what had been between them the night before. This time was about them. It was about who they were, what they wanted, and what they needed from each other. It was beautiful.

When the orgasm finally released them, she collapsed against him. They were both breathing heavily, and their thighs were slippery with sweat where she was draped over him. She didn't move, and she knew she would never want to move again. This was where she belonged. This is where she wanted to be. And when he pulled her closer and whispered her name, she knew he was feeling the same thing. Yes, the world around them was hell and there was no way to predict what was coming for them, but in this moment, it was right.

Peace at last, her first respite since the day her family was killed.

Her phone rang suddenly, and she jumped, startled by the sudden intrusion into the moment.

Ben's head jerked off her shoulder, and he spun the chair around to face her purse. They both stared at her bag. "Expecting a call?" he asked.

She shook her head wordlessly, sudden fear clamping her chest.

Swearing, Ben lifted her off his lap as he leapt to his feet. He grabbed her phone, and checked the display even as he yanked his jeans back up. "Blocked number," he muttered as he answered it. "Yeah?" He had it on speakerphone, and she could hear the static.

There was no reply. Just static. She looked at Ben, and saw his grim face.

Then, a man spoke "Ben Forsett?"

Dear God Almighty. She knew that voice. A chill shot through her, a deep-seated terror that seemed to plunge right through every bone in her body. She jumped to her feet, her fists clenched. "That's him," she whispered to Ben. "That's Joseph." Dear God, she hadn't thought she'd ever hear that voice again. She'd been praying it was all a mistake, but it wasn't. It was him on the phone, calling her.

"Turn yourself in," Ben said, as he sprinted across the room and dialed his own phone. He threw it at Mari as he muted her phone. "When Mack answers, tell him to track your phone right now."

"Why should I turn myself in?" Joseph ranted on. "I've done nothing. You're the one who murdered your sister."

Mari fumbled with Ben's phone as an unfamiliar voice answered it. "You hung up on me for a girl?" a man said. The voice was rough and deep. "What's up with that? Your track record with women is shit. Don't get involved—"

"This is Mari," she interrupted, as she lunged for her jeans and underwear. "Ben's on my phone talking to Joseph. He wants you to track the number right now."

The man on the other end was all business. "What's your number?" She could hear clicking as if he were typing in the computer, and she quickly gave him her phone number, watching Ben as he talked with Joseph, trying to stall him. Ben's jeans were already back in place, and he was pacing restlessly, his body tense and ready for combat.

"Hang on," Mack said.

She yanked her jeans on, her heart pounding as Joseph's voice filled the room. "You think it's fun to steal my woman?" Joseph said. "You know you'll pay for that. Mari belongs to me."

Nausea roiled in her belly at his words. She remembered so clearly the night he'd said those exact words to her. The strange gleam in his eyes as he'd said it, as if he had the right to do anything he wanted to her. That had been the first night he'd scared her, the night that all the uncomfortable feelings she'd been having around him had started to clarify. That had been the night she'd realized she had to get away from him, that he wasn't the man he'd presented when he'd appeared to help her pick herself up after her family's deaths. *You belong to me,* he said. *I own you.* Her hands shaking now, she tucked the phone against her shoulder as she fastened her jeans.

"He's at 6100 East Maine Drive," Mack said. "The Eastern Lake Retreat."

"The Eastern Lake retreat?" she repeated, the phone sliding to the floor as she whirled toward Ben. "He's at the hotel," she whispered. *"He's here."*

✖✖✖✖

Adrenaline exploded through Ben at Mari's words. Son of a bitch. The bastard was here!

Ben lunged for his gun, whipping it out from under his jacket as he held the phone to his ear. "Turn yourself in," he said again, as he threw his back up against the outside wall and flicked the shade slightly so he could see out the glass. There was faint sunlight outdoors, enough for him to see out across the field, but there was no one there. Shit! Where was he? "You're a danger to innocent people." He kept the conversation going, trying to occupy Joseph while he figured out where he was.

"They're not innocent!" Joseph bit out, his voice dripping with venom. "Those bitches betrayed me."

Ben clenched his jaw, and anger coursed through him as he sprinted across the room toward the door, gesturing Mari to stay back. "My sister was not a bitch," he snarled. He slammed his back against the wall beside the door to the corridor, listening intently for sounds from the hall. Was Joseph only feet away from them? Was he within striking range of Mari? Ben tightened his grip on the gun, and his focus narrowed to two things: survival, and protection of Mari.

"Holly betrayed me, and deserved to die," Joseph shouted. "I tried to help her! I tried to save her! I gave her everything I had, and she betrayed me." He hung up, leaving nothing but stark silence behind.

The hallway was quiet. Ben hesitated. As long as they were in the room, they were safe, but the threat would not go away. Joseph could sit in the hallway and outwait them, setting a trap until the moment they were finally forced to walk out the door. He had to deal with this, and he had to deal with this now.

Ben looked back at Mari, who was standing in the middle of the room, her eyes wide and her fists clenched. No matter how much danger lay outside their room, he couldn't leave her behind for Joseph to attack in his absence. Ben jerked his head at her, indicating for her to follow him. They had to go to the cocky bastard and find him now.

Mari paled, and for a second, he thought she was going to refuse. Then she grabbed a small frying pan from the kitchenette and hurried to the door, clenching it in both hands. She gave him a fierce nod, and he couldn't help but grin. Yeah, screw Joseph. Mari was not going to be a victim. Not today.

His gun ready and up, Ben eased open the door to the hallway. It was empty, nothing but a row of closed doors. Shit. Joseph could be in any of the rooms. Was there any chance of finding him?

They had to try. They had one of the best advantages possible right now, because Joseph didn't know that they knew he was there. Joseph liked to catch people when they weren't ready. Maybe he wasn't good face-to-face with opponents who were on the offensive. Maybe he wasn't good on someone else's timeline.

Gesturing Mari to stay close beside him, on his left side away from his gun, Ben raced down the hall, moving silently, checking every door to see if it was locked. With each passing second, the tension rose. Where the hell was Joseph?

Together, they moved fast, down the hall, down the back stairs, into the lobby. It was crowded. Shit. Ben shoved his gun behind his back, skidding to a stop while Mari lowered her frying pan. He couldn't go in there with a gun.

Swearing, he faded back into the hall, grabbing Mari's arm to keep her close. There were eight people in the lobby. An aging front desk clerk. A young couple who looked hormonal enough to be on their honeymoon. A pregnant woman who looked like she might deliver at any moment was dragging a heavy bag toward the front door, no partner to help her. Two old guys were sitting in chairs by the fire playing checkers.

Ben's gaze narrowed on the old men. "Do either of them

look familiar?"

Mari peered past him, her grip tight on the waistband of his jeans. "I don't know. Maybe. Are they in Haas's group?"

"Maybe." Swearing, Ben scanned the room again. No one looked familiar. Everyone appeared to be legit. "You don't see him?"

"No, but you said he changes his appearance." Mari was tucked up against him, using his body as a shield, which was exactly where he wanted her. "I don't know if he could change it enough that I wouldn't recognize him.

"You'd know if it was him." Ben was sure of it. But he really didn't like the fact he'd never seen so much as a picture of the bastard—

He suddenly noticed a phone sitting unattended on the reception desk, right on the front corner. "That's it," he whispered, pointing at it. "That's where he was. That was the phone he was using, I would wager anything on it." It had to have been only seconds since Joseph had been there. He had to be on the run, still within range. "I'm going outside." Ben looked at Mari. "Go stand next to the concierge desk. Don't move until I get back, no matter what."

She gripped his arm. "What if you don't come back?"

"Call the troopers and don't move until they get here." He shoved her toward the desk even as he broke for the front door. His instincts were screaming at him not to leave her behind, but he knew he had to. He had to catch this guy while they could. He threw open the front door and bolted out into the parking lot. The wind was still raging, a biting cold that ripped through his flesh.

The parking lot was quiet. It was packed with parked cars, but Ben saw no sign of Joseph, or anyone at all. He glanced back into the lobby and saw that Mari was on her knees, helping the pregnant woman pick up what appeared to be the contents of a broken suitcase. Behind her, watching intently, was the old man in the red hat, who was sitting up straighter than he had been. Walking into the lobby was a heavyset man with huge jowls and rough, blond hair.

Hell. Any of them could be Joseph. Ben glanced back at the parking lot, and then back in the lobby. Son of a bitch.

Where was he? Where was Ben supposed to be? Inside with Mari, or outside? Headlights illuminated at the far end of the parking lot and a truck engine roared to life. The pickup was the same model as the one Ben had seen outside O'Dell's, though it had been too dark that night to see the color. This one was red.

Adrenaline blazing, he took a step toward the truck, then looked over his shoulder again. Someone else had just entered the lobby. A tall woman with broad shoulders and breasts that strained at the front of her jacket. Dark brown hair cascaded down her shoulders, and heavy makeup adorned her face. She definitely had wide enough shoulders to be a man in drag.

Shit!

The truck pulled out of the parking spot and drove ever so slowly toward him. Ben's hand went to his gun, and he stiffened, watching the truck approach. He checked the lobby again and saw a man approaching Mari from behind. He was moving slowly, his gaze fixated on her.

Ben swore and looked at the oncoming truck, and then back at Mari. The man was getting closer, and she hadn't noticed him approaching. "Turn around, Mari," he muttered. "See if you recognize him."

But she didn't turn, still helping the pregnant woman repack her bag.

The hum of the engine grew louder, jerking his attention back to the parking lot. The truck had reached the end of the lane and had its left blinker on to pull out onto the main road. Shit! He had only seconds to act before the truck would be out of reach!

Already moving toward the truck, Ben stole one last glance into the lobby. The man was reaching for Mari, his hand extended toward her hair. "No!"

Instantly forgetting about the truck, Ben bolted back into the lobby, charging across the floor just as the man's hand went down on her shoulder. "Get back, Mari!" Ben launched himself at the man, tackling him as Mari scrambled back. They skidded across the floor and crashed into the reception desk. Around them, chaos erupted as Ben rolled off the guy and hauled him to his feet.

"Hey!" The pregnant woman shouted. "Let go of my

husband!"

Ben blinked, jerking his gaze back at her as she waddled toward him. "Your husband?"

"Yes!" she screamed, her face a splotchy red. "Get off him!"

People were shouting now, and he heard someone yell orders to call the police. But he didn't relinquish his grip on the man. He simply turned toward Mari, who was sheet white, her hands fisted in front of her. "Is this him?"

"No." She shook her head. "I don't think so."

Swearing, Ben let go of the man's shirt just as the pregnant woman reached him. "What's wrong with you?" she shouted at him as she shoved at his chest. "Are you insane?"

"Sorry." Ben dropped his hands and stepped back, as the room converged in rising outrage that he'd attacked an innocent man. "My mistake. My wife...has a stalker. I thought your husband was that guy."

"A stalker?" One of the old men from the fire looked over. "You're Mari Walsh, aren't you? Who's stalking you?"

"An old boyfriend," he muttered, moving toward Mari to get her out of there before more rumors could start. Shit.

"You're that new guy, John Sullivan, who Haas was talking about," the other old man said. "I heard you're no slouch, eh?"

Ben grimaced. "Just trying to protect my woman. Have a nice day." He apologized again as he herded Mari back down the hall. Murmured outrage chased them down the hall, and he grimaced.

Mari looked over at him as they hauled ass back toward the room. "Did you find Joseph outside?"

"I don't know." Swearing, he kept vigilant as they walked along, watching every doorknob to make sure it wasn't going to open. Had he made the right choice by coming back inside instead of following the guy in the truck? Had it not been for Mari's safety, he would have gone after him, but there was no way he could have left her unattended. Shit.

He reached their room and made her wait in the doorway as he checked it out. Once he was sure it was secure, he let her in. He stepped back to guard the door as Mari hurried into the room. As she passed him, he noticed something metal gleaming in the hood of her sweatshirt. "Wait a second." He caught her arm.

"What is it?" She tried to turn, and he held her secure.

"You have something in your hood." He reached in, and his fingers closed around cold metal. He drew it out slowly, horror welling around him like some great black beast. It was a knife identical to the one that had killed his sister. The blade was caked with fresh blood that had stained the fleece of Mari's hoodie with dark, maroon blotches. A scrap of white paper was jammed on the end of the blade, spattered in blood.

Mari whirled around, and her face turned ashen when she saw what was in his hand. "That was in my hood?"

Numbly, his fingers actually shaking, Ben tore the paper off the end of the knife. Scrawled in blood across the soiled parchment was one short sentence.

Say good-bye.

CHAPTER 16

Mari went cold, staring in shock at the knife in Ben's hand. "He killed something with that knife. Something recently." Images started flashing through her mind, horrible images that she quickly shut out.

Swearing, Ben dropped the knife on the kitchen counter. It clattered against the tile, and the blood spattered in tiny droplets on the beige backsplash. "Maybe it's his own blood. Maybe he did the world a favor and jammed the thing in his own neck." But from the look on Ben's face, she could tell he didn't believe it.

"We have to get that to the police," she said, grabbing for her phone, her hands shaking so much she dropped it twice before she could hang onto it. "They can run prints on it."

"Prints?" Ben swore again and lunged for the knife. He swept it off the counter and shoved it in the sink, where he turned on the faucet and blasted it.

"What? What are you doing?" She grabbed for his arm as he snatched a sponge and began to scrub it down.

"You think he's stupid enough to leave his own prints on it? There's never been a single print at any of the murder scenes. The only prints ever are those of the bastard he set up." His face was grim. "I grabbed the knife with my bare hand when I took it out of your sweatshirt. It's my prints that are on it. It's my hands that the blood is on."

"Oh, God." She stared at him. "He's setting you up for something, isn't he?"

"Pack your things," he said sharply. "We need to get out of here." He looked at her with sudden urgency. "And get that sweatshirt off, because the blood's on that too."

Her stomach dropped, and she yanked the fleece over her head. "What do I do with it?" There was no washing machine in the place.

"We'll have to take it and ditch it. Wrap it up in a plastic bag." He was still scrubbing the knife, trying to get every last bit of evidence off it. "And fast. We need to get out of here."

His urgency had a sharp edge to it. Mari sprinted across the room and shoved her things into her bag. She raced into the bathroom and swept her toiletries into the duffel as Ben bolted for the desk and began packing up his electronics with well-practiced efficiency.

"You think he's going to come back here?" Mari's hands were shaking as she pulled a plastic laundry bag out of the closet and shoved her sweatshirt in it. "And how did he find us?"

"No, I don't think he's coming back." He zipped his computer case and then started loading his clothes into his duffel. The last thing he grabbed was the knife, wrapping it in a pair of his jeans and burying it deep.

She flinched at the sight of it. "Why are you bringing that?"

"Because I think he has called the troopers, and they're on their way here to bust me for whoever's blood is on that knife."

Mari's stomach dropped. "You think he killed someone?"

"Yeah, I do. And I think he wants me to hang for it. My guess is that he called in a tip and they're on their way here now." His bags packed, he slung them over his shoulders, and then grabbed Mari's, hoisting it up as well. His hand was in his jacket pocket, and she knew his fingers were wrapped around the gun.

She jerked her gaze away, and she strained to listen for sirens. To her relief, she didn't hear any. "What about me?" She hurried up behind him as he strode for the door. "I'm not dead yet. How can he get you arrested? Then who will kill me?"

"I think it's a game." Ben cracked the door and peered into the hall. "He gave us a chance to get away. If we make it," he said as he nodded at her and opened the door, stepping briskly out into the hallway, "then it just makes the game go on longer. If we don't make it, then I get to go to prison, and he activates option two as to who to pin your death on."

"Oh, God." Joseph was crazy. *Crazy*. She kept close behind Ben as he sprinted for the back stairs. Just as they reached the door, she heard the unmistakable wail of a siren. Her stomach dropped. "They're here!"

"Then let's go." Ben threw open the door, and they bolted down the stairs. Ben was hunched under the weight of all their bags, but he was fast, taking the stairs four at a time while she sprinted after him.

Booking a room on the third floor had seemed like such a good idea when they'd arrived, but now, as their feet hammered on the metal steps, each moment to freedom seemed an eternity. As they hurtled past the doorway to the second floor, Mari couldn't take her eyes off it, waiting for the state troopers to surge through, their guns aimed right at her heart.

They made it past, and there was only one more level. "Where does this come out?" she gasped, breathing hard.

"Next to the lobby."

"The lobby?" she said faintly.

"The lobby." He skidded to a stop at the door to the lobby. They could hear a loud commotion, and her heart started to hammer frantically.

"Oh, God, they're already out there."

Ben swore and dropped his bag. He unzipped it, and rifled through it. Within a split second, he pulled out a faded Red Sox cap with what looked like a short blond wig glued to the inside of it. He shoved his dark hair up under it, tucking it out of sight, until all she could see was the edges of a short, blond haircut, making him look like a preppy tourist...except, of course, for the dark whiskers on his jaw and the heavy jacket he was wearing. It changed his look significantly, but would it be enough? It didn't feel like much. Then he handed her a pale gray stocking cap, with long blond hair cascading from it.

"This hat is yours, too? You dress like a girl sometimes?" She tucked her hair up and jammed the wool hat on her head.

"Some guys have long hair," he said as he hauled the bags over his shoulder again.

She fluffed the hair, pulling it over her shoulders. "Good?"

"You look like a California girl." He swung his arm over her shoulder, pulling her close. "As of this moment, we are a honeymooning couple. We're going to cut right and go out the back door, but if anyone sees us, all they'll notice is that we're unable to keep our hands off each other. Got it?"

She nodded, her mouth dry. Was a little kissing and blond hair really going to make a difference? She knew it had to be enough. They didn't have time for anything else.

Footsteps thudded down the hall. With a grim look, Ben hauled her against him. He planted a heavy kiss on her as he swung the door open and tumbled them out of the stairwell and into the hallway. "Laugh," he whispered.

She managed to shriek with laughter as they stumbled, even though she was so aware of two uniformed men walking toward them from the lobby. *Oh, God. Oh, God. Oh, God.* She thought of the knife in Ben's duffel, the bloody sweatshirt in her bag, and the gun in his pocket.

Ben grinned at her, his green eyes intense as he pulled her close. "I think we should go back upstairs before we hit the road," he said, loudly enough for the entire world to hear. "I don't think I'm through with you yet, pusskins."

Pusskins? What the hell was that? "What? Is your gleaming rod of passion ready to play again?"

He blinked, then a real grin swept his face as he slammed her against the wall. "Oh, yeah." He kissed her again, hard, but she could tell his focus was elsewhere, as was hers. It felt good to have his body around her, protecting her, but at the same time, she was terrified that at any second, someone was going to rip him off her and throw him down onto the ground.

Still kissing her, he dragged her down the corridor. She managed a peek over his shoulder, and saw two troopers in the lobby. The elevator door was just closing behind another, and the ones who had been so close to them were already headed upstairs, their feet pounding on the steps. Had she and Ben pulled it off?

"Almost there," Ben muttered against her ear as he swung his arm around her and hauled her against his side, shepherding her rapidly toward the rear door of the building. "Our truck is parked around to the right, so we're going to have to walk over that direction…unless he called in our vehicle."

Oh, God. What if he'd reported which car was theirs? "If we don't have a car, what do we do?"

"Steal one."

She looked sharply at him as he shoved open the door, but he wasn't smiling. "You're serious?"

He gave her a droll look. "Mari, I grew up in a gang and saw my first murder before I was a teenager. You really think I don't know how to steal a car?"

She didn't even bother to protest that he could be arrested. It was a little beyond that now. As they rounded the corner, they saw half a dozen police cars in the lot, their lights flashing. A few officers were standing around, but most were apparently inside. Ben's truck was ten feet from the nearest car.

"We can't get to it," she whispered.

"I think we can. I don't think they've identified it. They aren't paying any attention to it."

"What?" She grabbed his arm. "We can't. Let's go in back and steal another one." Dear Lord, had she really just suggested they steal a car?

He gave her a grim look. "I know how to be a fugitive, babe. You don't take the wrong chances, but you don't make life more difficult than it has to be. They aren't watching our ride. I can tell." He flashed her a smile. "Trust me. We're taking our own wheels back."

And then, with a boldness that made her want to scream in terror and run the other way, he slung his arm over her shoulder and strode right toward the chaos.

※※※

Ben's senses were so attuned that he could see and hear things as clearly as the night he was almost murdered when he was a kid.

Keeping Mari close, Ben strode toward his truck, aware of every movement of the remaining officers, the angle of their bodies, where they were looking, the tone of their voices, and the placement of their guns. He knew exactly how far it was to his truck. He could smell the faint cigarette smoke of the nearest trooper, who was leaning against one of the cop vehicles. Ben knew exactly what direction the wind was coming from, and how much sound it was muffling. His state of hypervigilance was exactly the same as it had been when he was fifteen and being hunted by three kids from a rival gang, through the back alleys of the part of town where no decent human being would want to live.

He hadn't felt like this since that day...because survival had never been critical for him...until now.

His grip tightened on Mari as they neared his truck. He was every bit as aware of her as he was of their surroundings. The shallowness of her breath. The tension of her body. The way she kept her face averted from the troopers, even though her attention was on them. Adrenaline pulsed through him as he kept his body between her and the troopers. This was different from when he was fifteen. This time, he had someone else's life in his hands.

Failure before had meant his own funeral.

Failure this time meant Mari's.

As they approached, the smoker turned his head toward them. Ben immediately pulled Mari into his arms for a kiss, a decadent, obnoxious kiss in which he shoved one hand halfway down the back of her pants. Her body was stiff and cold, but she kissed him back, leaning into him.

Ben heard the low guffaws of the troopers, and he broke the kiss. Mari's eyes were wide as she stared at him, but she said nothing.

He managed a grin as he continued to head them toward the truck. He was aware of the troopers watching them, and his adrenaline pulsed. Shit. Had he been too cocky, walking right up to that truck? Acting as if he had nothing to hide was one of the best covers, but as he watched the bastards who were only thirty feet away, his nerves were strung tight as hell.

Keeping his attention fixed on their surroundings, he hustled Mari to the passenger side, which was the same side as where the troopers were standing. He unlocked the door, grateful that the old beater he'd scavenged didn't have the loud beep of keyless entry. The less attention, the better. Mari quickly climbed in, but before she could scoot away from him, he grabbed her by the hips and kissed her again. "Make it count," he whispered against her mouth. He had to convince the troopers so no one tried to stop them when they drove out.

There was only one exit from the lot, and if he'd stolen a car from the back, he would still have had to drive past them to get out. This was their chance. They wouldn't get far enough on foot, so they had to drive. He dropped the bags on the ground, then grabbed her thighs and yanked her against him so her legs were on either side of his hips. Then he kissed her, kissing her the way he wanted to, unleashing all his tension into her.

She stiffened, and then kissed him back. The kiss quickly went from hot to deadly. It was all Ben could do to keep his attention on the troopers as he kissed Mari, the kiss igniting all the same need that had almost eclipsed his self-control earlier when they'd made love. She still tasted incredible, her mouth that same decadent temptation as it had been before, but this time, there was an edge to the kiss. A danger. A knowledge that at any second he could feel a gun in his back.

But he had to do it. He had to make those state troopers notice only the sex, see only a couple in love, and never focus on the man driving the truck.

Again, he heard the low guffaws from their audience, and knew they were being scrutinized. Swearing, he dragged Mari closer, deepening the kiss as he slid his hand up the front of her jacket, cupping her breasts through the outside of the material.

She stiffened, and for a split second, he thought she was going to pull back. "Stay with me," he urged against her lips, breaking the kiss just enough to talk to her. "Come on, babe. You can do this." He took over the kiss again, knowing that the angle of the troopers made his hand on Mari's breast visible.

Then she palmed his crotch, her hand cupping his balls. Ben jumped, almost breaking the kiss. "Jesus, woman," he muttered. "You gotta warn me before you do that."

In answer, the infernal woman actually started to unbutton his jeans, the backs of her hands brushing against his bare stomach as she got the button undone. Then his fly was down, and then she slipped her hand inside his pants, through the gap in his boxers...

"Oh, you're in trouble now," he growled, as he grabbed her thighs and flipped her backwards into the front of the truck. She tumbled across the seat, and he heard the loud catcalls from the troopers as he flung their bags into the back of the cab. Then he slammed her door shut, sprinted around the front of his truck, and swung himself into the driver's seat. Mari was leaning back against the passenger door, her feet still up on the seat.

"God, Mari. If those guys weren't out there, I'd take you right now." He grabbed her by the waistband of her jeans and hauled her across the seat toward him. She fell into his arms and he kissed her again, rough, carnal, and possessive. He was well aware that the smoker had moved so he could see into the cab, and Ben gave him a show, but as he fondled the woman in his arms, his cock was as hard as a rock, and the lust burning through him was not for show.

After another two minutes of kissing that was more intense than anything he'd ever experienced, Ben knew it was time to go. The glow of voyeurism lasted only so long when actual flesh wasn't going to make an appearance. "We gotta go," he said as he broke the kiss.

Mari's eyes were wide, and she nodded. They spoke no words as he started the engine, but he carefully watched the men in his mirrors. They were grinning and watching the truck. "You better stay all over me," Ben said.

"Okay." Mari scooted up next to him, perched on her knees, and began to nibble at the side of his neck. Gritting his jaw against his body's response to her seduction, he shifted into reverse and backed out of the parking spot. As he swung the truck toward the entrance, two of the other cops came out the front door. "Shit," he muttered. "They're reporting that they couldn't find me."

Mari's fingers dug into his shoulder, but still she played her role as he drove past the smoker and his friend. He rolled to a stop at the exit, tension hammering at him as he put on his blinker. He waited a fraction of a second longer than he wanted, as if he had all the time in the world, then he eased the truck out onto the road, turning left so he didn't have to drive by the troopers amassing in the parking lot.

Mari stopped kissing him and spun around in her seat, watching the flashing lights as they eased down the road. "The others are coming outside," she said.

"I know. We need to get out of sight fast. It's not going to take them long to figure this out." They rounded the corner out of sight, and he gunned the gas. The old truck leapt forward, as he'd known it would when he'd carefully selected it. It looked like shit, but worked like a breeze.

They hurtled down the road. A few winding roads passed by on the sides, but he had no idea where they led. Dead ends would not be a good place to wind up. He hadn't had time to complete his reconnaissance of the area they were in before Joseph had made his move. "Mari," he said, suddenly slamming on the brakes. "You drive."

"What? Me? What are you going to do? Shoot everyone?" But she was already scrambling over him into the driver's seat. The exchange took less than three seconds, and then they were off again, traveling even faster than when he'd been driving.

He lunged into the backseat and dug his computer out of his bag. It booted up in a tenth of a second, and he immediately called up maps of the region, including satellite images. There were still no sounds of sirens behind them, but he knew it wouldn't be long. Quickly, carefully, he scanned their options, looking for a place to hide. They had to get off the main road and out of sight. Now.

He'd already done some checking when Mari had been sleeping, and he quickly zeroed in on their best option. "In six miles, there will be a dirt road on the right."

"Six miles?" She gripped the steering wheel. "They'll be on us in six miles."

"Hopefully not." He continued to plan their route, his fingers flying over the keys as he listened for the sound of sirens.

He heard the wail of pursuit when he and Mari were still two minutes away from their turnoff. "Shit!"

Mari gripped the steering wheel and glanced in her mirror. "I don't see them."

"Turn off the headlights."

"But it's dark. I won't be able to see where I'm driving—"

"Turn them off." He twisted around in his seat,

watching, waiting. And then he saw it. Faint blue lights in the distance, sparkling through the trees.

He spun around, checking his computer. "Fifty feet," he said, "slow down."

She slowed as the sound of sirens grew stronger, her face pale.

"Twenty feet."

She slowed further.

"Here."

She turned the truck, and then stopped. In front of them were heavy foliage and a thick forest. "There's no road here."

"Yes there is. Drive."

"We'll crash."

"Drive!"

She gave him a look of trepidation, but to her credit, she hit the gas and the truck flew forward. They crashed through the foliage, and the branches hammered at the vehicle, swallowing them up.

For three endless minutes, she drove, and neither of them could see a damned thing.

Then suddenly, finally, the woods parted, and they were on an ancient dirt road. "Stop."

Mari hit the brakes, and the engine idled as sirens roared past them. Together they waited, tension rampant in the truck until there was silence. "You think they're coming back?" she whispered.

"I doubt it. This road isn't on any maps more recent than fifty years. I doubt anyone knows it's here." He grinned at her. "But we do, so let's get out of here."

Mari nodded, but she didn't start driving again. He noticed that her hands were trembling. "Hey," he said, touching her shoulder. "You okay?"

She looked over at him, her eyes wide. "Whose blood was on that knife, Ben? Who did he kill? And how can we ever stop him? He was close enough to me to kill me if he wanted to, but we never saw him. How can this ever end?"

CHAPTER 17

Mari's hands were trembling even more now, shaking so violently she could barely hold the steering wheel. The aftershock of all that had just happened was finally hitting her now that the immediate danger was past. They had come so close to dying. To being caught by the police. Joseph had been so close that he'd touched her sweatshirt. *Dear God.*

"Hey." Ben leaned forward, his hand on her shoulder. "You did great, Mari."

She bent her head, resting her forehead on the steering wheel, as she tried to pull herself together. The steering wheel was hard and cold, and it felt good against her skin. "That sucked."

He laughed softly as he tugged the modified stocking cap off her head. "Don't worry. After a few more times, you'll start to have some fun running from the cops. It's really quite an adrenaline boost."

"What?" She gaped at him in disbelief, and then saw a twinkle in his eyes. Her heart flipped at his amusement, even as a part of her wanted to break into hysterical sobs. "You're making a joke? How can you joke about this?"

"Because we have no other choice." He leaned forward, his gaze intense. "Listen to me, Mari, okay?"

She nodded, staring into those green eyes, hoping desperately that he could say something that would make all of it better and offer her some miracle. "Okay."

"So, we're going to focus on the fact that we got out of there. He didn't get us. He's good, but we beat him, right? We're safe, the cops are chasing their tails, and Joseph doesn't know if we got away or not. So, victory to us right now."

"Victory?" she echoed blankly. "There's no victory. Someone is dead, Ben. Dead!"

He flinched. "We don't know that for sure, Mari, and if he did kill someone, then it's even more important that we keep our shit together and be smarter than he is, or there will be more deaths."

Was Ben delusional? Seriously? "We aren't smarter than he is! He found us and almost got us caught!"

"But we *didn't* get caught." He lightly clasped her shoulders, his grip warm and firm. "Listen to me, Mari. I saw people die when I was a kid. I learned to be tougher than it—"

"I'm not you! I'm not that cold! If someone I know is going to be killed because of me, I'm going to be upset about it!"

"I wasn't finished." Ben touched her mouth with his finger, asking her to listen. "I got tough as a kid, but when I walked into the door of my sister's house, it all changed. When I saw her lying there with a knife in her chest and her blood all over everything, I thought I was going to shatter. It was beyond what I could cope with or what anyone should ever have to face. So, when I sit here next to you, and I think of the fact that Haas or Charlotte might be dead or dying because of this bastard who I stirred up, I know exactly how bad it is. I feel the weight of it crushing me. But I also know that if I let it break me, then I can't stop Joseph and more people will be killed. He'll keep doing it again, and again, and again. So, I have to keep my shit together, and so do you." His hand slid to the side of her neck, cupping her gently. "Mari, a lot of people have tried to kill me over the years, and I'm still here. That lunatic at your family's store tried to kill you not so long ago, but you're still here. We're survivors, and neither of us is giving up, right?"

She closed her eyes, fighting back tears. His words made sense, and in a way, they gave her the freedom to pull herself together and not let fear for Haas and Charlotte overwhelm her. Falling apart didn't help them, and it hadn't saved her family. She took a deep breath that was too shuddery and shaky to be convincing, but still, it felt better. "I'm not giving up. I'm just... freaking out a little bit, okay?"

He laughed softly and pulled her into his arms, pressing his lips to her forehead. "It's totally cool to freak out," he said.

God, it felt good to feel his arms around her, to be swallowed up by his strength. His body was warm and hard, reminding her that they were both alive, and that she had a partner who was smart, brave, and desperate. "Whose blood was on the knife, Ben?" she whispered against his jacket, unwilling to pull herself away from him. She could catch the faint scent of his aftershave from the night before, a hint that somewhere beyond them was normalcy, things like a man who smelled good and a woman who could appreciate it. But even as she tried to focus on his scent, she couldn't get that knife out of her mind, the bright red of the blood.

Ben was grim. "I can think of only two people."

She didn't need to ask as two faces came to mind. She already knew, as did he, which is why they'd both already mentioned them. "Charlotte and Haas," she whispered. "If he wants to target someone we know well, it has to be one of them. They're the only ones we're close enough to. Do you really think he killed one of them?"

"I don't know." He squeezed her gently, then pulled back. "Do you have Charlotte's cell?"

She nodded, already reaching for her bag in the back. "I'll call now."

"I'll call Haas's number, and then O'Dell's if we can't reach them."

Mari found her phone in the pocket of the duffel Ben had brought for her, and she grabbed it. To her surprise, her hand was steady. She realized Ben had calmed her. Somehow, he'd taken a situation that had terrified her and used it to make her stronger. She'd been terrified of being killed by a madman ever since her family's massacre, and finding out Joseph was after her had made it even worse. But now....she felt different. Yes, she was still scared, but at the same time, she didn't want to crawl under the seat and whimper.

She wanted to fight the bastard and take her life back. Of course, she couldn't do it by herself, but she didn't have to anymore. She had Ben. Hope raced through her, hope that maybe, just maybe, she wasn't as broken as she'd thought she was. Still broken, yes, but maybe not irrevocably.

She managed a small smile at Ben as she flipped through her contacts to find Charlotte's number. Once she found it, she raised her gaze to Ben's as she put the phone to her ear, watching Ben as he did the same.

They sat side by side in his dark, beat-up truck, hidden in the deep woods of Alaska, staring at each other as their phones rang and rang. Ben reached out and took her hand, wrapping his fingers around hers and squeezing.

Charlotte didn't answer, and the call went into voicemail. Mari's heart began to pound. "Charlotte," Mari said quickly. "Call me as soon as you get this. It's an emergency." As she hung up, she realized Ben was talking to Haas.

She put her phone away and scooted across the seat. She pressed her ear to Ben's head so she could listen.

"I'm at O'Dell's," Haas was saying. His voice was even more rough and raspy than usual, as if he'd spent too much time shouting over the noise at the bar with his buddies. "Charlotte's not here. Let me ask where she is." The phone was loud, rumbling with the background noise of the crowded bar.

Ben put the phone on speaker and turned toward Mari. "Haas said he hasn't noticed anyone shadowing him. He said everything's fine. I told him to get in his truck and take off for a few days." He grimaced. "He said he's going back to his house to get his guns ready—"

"Sully." Haas came back on the phone, using Ben's fake name. "Charlotte's fine. Apparently, she asked for a few days off to go out of town with some new boyfriend. So, she's not even around."

Some new boyfriend. The words hit Mari like a sledgehammer in the chest as she recalled Charlotte mentioning that she had a new man. Oh, God. Not Joseph again. Suddenly terrified, she grabbed the phone from Ben. "What's her boyfriend's name? Do you know him? Is it a local guy?"

Haas didn't even hesitate at her interruption. "No, I don't. It's some guy from out of state. I've never heard anyone mention meeting him."

A cold chill seemed to burrow into her bones as she stared at Ben. "It's him," she whispered. "Something terrible happened to Charlotte in the past. She has a huge dog because she's so scared. She fits the profile of the type of woman he targets."

Swearing, Ben took the phone back. "Go to Charlotte's house. Call the state troopers and have them meet you there."

"What's going on?" Haas's voice was tight and clipped. "Is Charlotte in danger?"

Ben didn't reply. "Don't go in there alone," he repeated. "Whatever you do, *don't go alone—*"

"Wait a sec." There was a murmured conversation in which Mari could hear Haas talking to another woman, but she couldn't make out their words. She looked at Ben, who shook his head. "She left a note for me," Haas said, coming back on the line.

"Who did?" Ben's face darkened. "Charlotte?"

"Yeah." Haas laughed softly. "I can tell it's been read about six times. Did she really think that no one in this place would open it if she left it unsealed?" His voice faded into silence as he read the note.

"Haas? Haas!" Ben shouted into the phone. "What does it say?"

"It doesn't make sense," Haas said slowly. "It says that she can't deal with me harassing her anymore, and if I don't stop stalking her, she's going to call the state troopers. What the hell is that?"

Mari sucked in her breath. "Haas would never stalk her," she whispered. "It's a lie."

Ben's fingers were white-knuckled on the phone. "Joseph is setting you up, Haas! He's going to kill Charlotte, and he's setting you up for it!"

"Who's going to kill Charlotte? That bastard who did your sister?" Haas swore. "He has her now? Where? At her house? Is that where?"

"No! Don't go after her! Stay at the bar! Stay in public!"

"She's not going to die," Haas snapped. "I'm going after her!"

"No!" The phone line went silent as Haas cut them off.

Swearing, Ben dialed 9-1-1. "What's her last name?" He asked Mari.

"Charlotte Murphy." Mari quickly scanned her phone. "I have her address in here because I picked her up for work one night when her car battery was dead." She handed her phone to Ben.

The operator picked up.

Ben rattled off the address and Charlotte's name. "She's just been attacked," he told the operator. "I think she's dead! Hurry!" He then cut off the call as the operator started asking him for details.

"Shit!" Ben gestured at the wheel. "Drive!"

The engine roared to life, and Mari hit the gas. The truck leapt forward, spinning out across the old road. "We're an hour away. We'll never beat the cops there."

"We have to try." Ben grabbed his phone, and called Haas again, but he didn't answer. Frustrated, Ben slammed the phone shut. "I don't want Haas there. This isn't right. We're all playing into his hands."

"So, what do we do? Not go? Leave Haas?" They couldn't do that. They couldn't risk it. She drove faster, barely able to see the trees in the darkness. Was it too soon to turn on her headlights? Were the police still nearby? Frustrated by her inability to drive faster, she slammed her palm on the steering wheel. "What if she is there? What if he's waiting for Haas?" Oh, God. The thought made her stomach turn. What if Charlotte was already—

"Stop the truck!"

Mari slammed on the brakes, and the truck skidded to a stop. "What?"

"If Charlotte's at her house, the cops are going to get there faster than we are. We can't help her by rushing over there."

"But—"

"I rushed over to my sister's house, and that's exactly what he wanted me to do. We need to think for a second." He leaned forward, resting his forehead in his palms, as if he were fighting for control. "This doesn't feel right. He never makes a mistake like this, like allowing us time to call the police. That's such a rookie mistake."

Mari gripped the wheel, her heart pounding. She wanted to drive to Charlotte's, to do something. They couldn't just sit there. "Maybe he's gotten sloppy. He's trying to kill two women at the same time..." She swallowed, the horror of her words weighing down the night. "People make mistakes."

"Not this mistake. It's too big, too obvious." He shook his head. "He knew everyone would read that note if he left it unsealed at the bar. He did that on purpose."

"He wanted people to read it," she said slowly, trying to think. "He wanted to set up the connection between Haas and Charlotte. But who would believe Haas would be stalking her? No one would buy that. Haas is too well-known for the quality guy he is."

Ben ground his jaw. "Haas has a shadowed background. No one knows what he did for the fifteen years he was gone, but no one in this town thinks he's harmless. You know that."

She bit her lip, well aware of the sharp intelligence in Haas's wrinkled face. Would people really believe the worst of him? Maybe they would, if they were given enough proof. She thought back to the man she'd almost married, to the equally vivid intensity in his gaze. "Joseph timed it on purpose," she said slowly. "It wasn't a fluke that Haas was handed that note when he was on the phone with you, was it? It wasn't given to him until after he asked about Charlotte, while he was still on the phone."

Ben swore. "Joseph wanted me to know about the note, and he wanted to give me time to react and call the cops. Son of a bitch, he set that up."

Cold realization dawned on her. "There's something at her house he wants the police to find, isn't there? When they get there, there's going to be evidence against you, isn't there? He's laughing that we sent the cops over there to find whatever it is he put there." She leaned her forehead against the steering wheel, her head starting to pound. "We're just playing into his hands, aren't we? We can't even see him coming."

Ben was bent over, his head still in his palms. "We know how he works now. But this time is different, because for the first time, someone knows what he's planning. All criminals have patterns. We just have to figure out what his is. We're missing something."

Mari stared at him, her heart thundering in fear for

Charlotte and Haas. She wanted to barrel right into Charlotte's driveway and run to the house to find her, to save Haas, to do *something* to protect the people who had become her only friends. "What do you mean?"

"He always wins because he knows how people respond to certain stimuli. He plays us, and we walk right into it." He looked at Mari. "He knows we'll go after Charlotte and Haas to save them. He knows we'll call the cops. He knows we'll tell Haas and that Haas will go to her house. And then he knows we'll head there too, to protect them."

She stared at him. "Unless he knows that we would figure that out before we got there, and not show up."

"That, too." Ben swore again, and a siren sounded in the distance.

They both looked over their shoulder, but she couldn't see any blue flashing lights through the thick trees.

"We need to get out of here."

Silently, Mari started driving the truck again, slower this time. "So, where do we go? What do we do? We have no idea, do we?"

"No, we have no idea where he is." Ben ground his jaw, lacing his fingers behind his head.

Tense silence reigned in the cab of the truck. All Mari could think about was the knife wrapped in their duffel in the back, and the blood on her sweatshirt, both of which were evidence of some terrible thing that Joseph had done, evidence that had their fingerprints on it. "He's a ghost," she said. "No one sees him unless he wants to be seen. There's no way to find him."

Ben still said nothing, and she looked over at him. His face was taut and grim, his hands fisted as he leaned forward and braced his forearms on his thighs. "No, there's not." He looked over at her. "Did you ever go to his house? Did you ever see where he lived?"

Mari shook her head. "Never."

"It was always at your house?"

"Yes. Or we went out of town for the weekend sometimes. We never went out locally. I have no idea what kind of places he goes to or where he might live. Even when I was dating him, I had no idea where to find him." Mari swallowed. They didn't have time to wait for him to make his move. Not with Charlotte and Haas targeted. "We need to take control back."

Ben looked over at her. "Yeah, we do. We need to make him act before he's ready. He always sets it up with methodical precision, setting his players exactly where he wants them. We need to put him on our timelines. We need to play his game, only better."

Understanding dawned. "We set the trap for him."

"Yeah."

"How?"

He met her gaze. "We make him come after me now."

"Not you. Us." She stopped the truck again, staring at him, guessing the words he hadn't said, but she knew were true. "We bring him after *us*, don't we? I'm the key player. I'm the one he needs to kill." For a long moment, Ben didn't answer, and she saw the tension on his face. "It has to be us," she said, amazed that she could actually say the words without wanting to run away screaming. Well, she sort of did, but not as much as she wanted to stop looking over her shoulder, waiting for him to jump out of the shadows with a knife. "If we're separated, he could come after me." She shivered at the idea of facing Joseph alone. She needed to be with Ben. Going solo, they had both already failed to defeat Joseph. Together, they might have a chance. "We have to be together, Ben. There's no other way."

He still didn't answer, but after a long moment, he turned his head toward her. His face was haunted and stark, almost gaunt. He reached over and took her hand, and his fingers were like ice. "I swear on my life I won't let him hurt you," he said, his voice hoarse. "*I swear it.*"

Mari nodded. She knew he would give his life to protect her, but she also knew that it might not be enough. But it was the only choice. If they ran away, if she ran away, Joseph would find them eventually. He would never stop until she was dead. The battle had to happen. "Okay," she whispered.

Ben cursed under his breath, then he reached out and dragged her into his arms. She didn't resist, and closed her eyes as he held her against him. His embrace was so tight, as if he was pouring into his hug all the words and emotions he couldn't articulate. It was a moment of connection, far deeper than even when they'd been making love. It was the interlacing of two lives, two souls that could very well be torn apart and destroyed within hours. Tears filled her eyes, and she hugged him back, burying her face into his shoulder. They held each other for what felt like an hour, both of them holding tightly.

It was the flash of blue light across the dashboard that ripped them apart.

Ben swore and looked over his shoulder as she yelped and lunged for the steering wheel. "They're right at the end of the road. I think they're looking for the entrance."

"Oh, my God." She shifted into drive and eased the truck through the woods, not daring to hit the gas hard enough to make the engine roar. Every crack of broken branches beneath the tires made her jump, and the light of the dashboard seemed unbearably bright in the darkness.

Without a word, Ben reached across and turned the dimmer on the dash, plunging them into total darkness. The tires crept along the ground, the dark cover of forest making the woods almost impenetrable. "I can't see," she whispered. "I can't drive."

Ben opened his computer again, and she saw him pull up a satellite map, setting it up right beside the old map from years ago, the one that showed the road they were on. On the satellite map was a blinking red light in the middle of the woods. With a quick movement of his fingers, he merged the maps, so that the blinking cursor was now on a thin, winding line that was their road. "In ten feet, veer to the right."

She swallowed and did as he said. Miraculously, the trees opened up in front of them, giving them just enough space to pass through. "They're going to catch up to us," she whispered. "And then Haas and Charlotte won't have anyone to save them—"

"He won't kill them until he has you and me where he wants us."

She bit her lip. "What about the blood? What if it was Charlotte's?"

He reached over and took her hand. His grip was warm and strong, making her throat tighten. "We'll find her, okay? It's

going to end tonight."

She glanced over at him. "Tonight?" His eyes were dark and his jaw was clenched, and she knew he'd figured out a plan.

They were going to face Joseph *tonight*.

CHAPTER 18

Mari shifted restlessly as they sat in the truck outside O'Dell's. The parking lot was full, packed with trucks and cars. A brisk snow was blowing across the ground, stirring up dusty, white swirls. "You think he's here?"

"I think he knows we won't go to the house. I think he's waiting for us, yeah. I think he thinks we'll come here to try to find him." Ben was leaning forward, scanning the parking lot. "The logical plan for us, the only one that makes sense, is for us to go in there, to have you stand up on one of the tables, and to announce that some guy is stalking you and you think you're going to end up dead. You should announce to the community that Charlotte and Haas are innocent and in danger, and that everyone needs to know that Joseph is the culprit and to hunt him down until they find him, no matter how long it takes. Since the cops won't listen to you, you need to put the entire community on a mission to defend Haas. Make it public. Tell them you know what's going on. They'll hunt down Joseph for you after you're put in prison for whoever's blood is on that knife and I'm hauled back to Boston. That would be our best defense against him."

Personally, she thought it seemed like a logical defense. The town was tight-knit and would protect their own. And if she did die, she wanted someone to know the truth and go find him. "But we're not going to do that?"

"No, because he'll be prepared for us to do something like that. He knows that he has us in a tight spot, and he'll be ready for us to call in the community to rally. I really expect that he thinks we'll do that, even at risk to ourselves and our own future. He knows we're both honorable and will try to protect our friends."

She looked over at him. "So, we're going to do the unpredictable?"

"Yeah." He winked at her. "No man can almost marry you and not know how brave, strong, and loyal you are. He will be absolutely certain you won't abandon the people you love to save yourself, and that's what he's planning to capitalize on."

The genuine respect and warmth in his voice made her throat tighten. "You really think I'm that brave?"

"Shit, yeah." He leaned closer to her and slipped his fingers through her hair. "Your heart is so amazing, Mari. I had nothing left in my soul after my sister died. All I wanted was revenge, and then, when I met you, it changed. It became about you, and keeping you alive." He brushed his mouth over hers. "Despite all you've been through, you still have the most beautiful soul." He grinned. "And somehow, you believed in me. No one else has done that for me."

She heard the depth of emotion in his voice, and she smiled, resting her fingers on his whiskered cheek. "Some things that are covered in dirt are actually the most beautiful gifts the world can offer."

He grinned. "See? You notice my dirt, and somehow think I'm still a good guy." His smile faded. "I'll never forget that, Mari. Ever."

The front door opened and they both turned to look. A young couple stepped out. The woman was tucked under the man's arm to shield her against the wind as they hurried across the parking lot. "It's time," he said quietly.

She nodded, her stomach roiling at what she had to pretend to do. "You really think he would believe that I'm going to run away and abandon Haas and Charlotte? If he's so convinced of my selfless bravery, why would he buy this story?"

"He doesn't know you that well," Ben interrupted. "If he knew the real you the way I do, he would have married you for real and never let you out of his sight. He would have fallen in love with you and given his life to keep you safe. No man who truly knows you could do anything else. There are gaps in his knowledge of you, and we're going to insert this into one of those gaps. He won't be able to afford not to believe you."

Mari stared at him in shock at his words, barely even registering the last of his short speech. His voice was so intense and urgent that it seemed to plunge right through her and settle in her heart. No man who knew her the way he did could do anything but fall in love with her? Did that mean that Ben loved her?

Ben didn't seem to have noticed what he'd said, or her reaction. He just leaned forward, watching the building. "So, that's what we're banking on. He's not going to expect you to slink away and abandon your friends, and he's going to panic when he realizes he's losing you. We're going to jerk him off his carefully planned path, and that's going to trip him up." He glanced at her. "I hope."

"And you?" She managed to find her voice, refocusing on their situation. "He'll really believe you'll give up on him?"

"It'll take a bit of convincing, but yeah, in the end, I imagine he'll be willing to believe I'm a piece of shit." He rubbed his hand over his jeans, as if ridding himself of Joseph's taint. "Right now, he's sitting in there all smug, knowing that after hunting him all this time, the last thing I'm going to do is walk away and let him go. He's counting on that." He finally turned to look at Mari. "He's not going to be expecting the two of us to fall so much in love that we're willing to run to save ourselves instead of saving others."

She swallowed. "He won't believe it," she whispered. She didn't believe it. How could they fall in love in this short of time? No one could. But even as she thought it, she couldn't take her gaze off Ben's face. His eyes were so burdened by guilt and sadness, the pain of losing his sister. But he was so kind, with so much love. So brave. He'd held her when she was scared. He made her brave. He protected her. There was so much about him she didn't know, but at the same time, she'd seen into his soul, and she knew exactly who he was. Her heart tightened with emotions she was afraid to feel, with love that she was too scared to risk.

"He can't afford not to believe us. If we really disappear,

he's lost." Ben entangled his fingers with hers and squeezed. "You ready?"

Her instinct was to say she wasn't and to run and hide, but she thought of the blood on her sweatshirt, of Charlotte and Haas, and of Ben, and she knew she wouldn't run away. She'd just barely begun to rebuild her life, and she wasn't going to let it go. "Yeah." She surprised herself with the confidence in her voice and managed to smile at him. "Yes, I think I am."

He grinned. "Then let's do this." He opened the door of the truck and held out his hand to her. She met his gaze, took a deep breath, then put her hand in his. He squeezed tightly as he pulled her close, tucking her against his side as he swung his arm over her shoulder. He locked the truck carefully, and then they headed in.

In about two minutes, they were going to poke the sleeping dragon.

She could only pray that they were doing it in time, and that it would not wind up killing them.

▨▨▨▨

Ben's adrenaline was thudding through him so fiercely he could hear his own pulse roaring as he grabbed the handle of the front door and pulled it open. Mari's body was trembling against his side, but her chin was held high with courage he knew she'd had to summon over the fear that had stalked her for so long.

A fierce swell of admiration raced through him, along with a raw need to protect her. His instincts were screaming not to bring her into the bar and expose her to a madman, but he would never leave her behind unprotected. *Never.*

Pulling her even closer, he looked carefully around the joint as they stepped inside. It was somewhat quieter than it had been recently, but still crowded enough that he couldn't begin to target every person. Haas's crew was at a table in the corner. A girls' night out of forty-something women had taken over the far end, and there were more than a few tables of random people, most of whom looked unfamiliar. He didn't recognize anyone, and no one appeared to be watching him with particular interest. There was no indication that Joseph was there.

No indication at all, except for the sudden prickling of the skin on the back of his neck. Ben looked around carefully again. "He's here," he whispered into Mari's ear. "I can feel him."

She looked sharply at him. "Where?"

He shook his head. "I don't know."

She took a long look around the room, too, her gaze moving from table to table, but after a moment, she grimaced. "I can't believe I don't recognize him."

"He's good." Ben's instincts were screaming at him. "Let's get this done and get out of here. Where's your boss?"

Mari pointed to the bar. "Over there. The guy with the blond hair."

Keeping her close against him and making sure his body was shielding hers, Ben guided her toward the bar. He was scanning the room with rigid scrutiny, fighting to see past the obvious hair and facial features. Which one was Joseph? There were too many men of all different types. A few women who were tall. Several couples. No one he recognized from the hotel lobby. Shit.

"David?" Mari reached the bar, and Ben turned his attention to the rugged male working the bar. He hadn't noticed him before. How had he missed him? The man was built like a house, and his blue eyes were piercing and intelligent. A man who should be sprinting across a flaming battlefield with a rifle, not pouring beer in a small town in Alaska. He knew instantly that David was more than he seemed. Where had he been all the other nights?

David jerked his head around, then grinned when he saw Mari. "Can you work? Charlotte didn't show up tonight, and we're understaffed. She was supposed to be back, and I don't know where the hell she is."

Charlotte didn't show up tonight. Ben swore and looked around again. Several tables were watching with interest. Haas's group was watching, along with the table of women, but they were looking at him, not Mari. He was used to that look, and it had nothing to do with wanting to hurt them.

"No," Mari said. She raised her voice, as if to be heard over the bar, and Ben carefully looked around to see who was paying attention. "I need my final check. I'm leaving town tonight."

David began to protest, but Ben didn't listen. He turned toward the mirror over the bar and began to watch closely. There were six people sitting at the bar. Four men and two women. The one sitting closest to them was lean with hunched shoulders, and he turned his head to look at Mari. Ben stared intently at him, memorizing his cheekbones, his ears, and the shape of his eyes, things that were more difficult to conceal. He worked his way down the line, studying each person, as he kept his arm tightly around Mari, his body pressed against hers.

"I can't stay," Mari said. "I'm being stalked, and he found me." She glanced at Ben, and he took his cue, speaking loudly to David across the noise of the bar.

"I can keep her safe," he announced. "We're leaving town tonight." He looked down at her, and smiled, not needing to fabricate the softening in his chest when she met his gaze. "She's mine now," he said loudly. "Mine to protect."

She smiled. "Yours to love, right?"

Something thudded in his heart. Something sudden and unexpected that seemed to tie up his tongue. His to love? The words that he was supposed to say were frozen in his throat.

Her smile faded, and her forehead furrowed in question. Vulnerability flashed across her face, and he swore under his breath. "Mine to love," he echoed.

Her answering smile was uncertain and tentative, and sudden tension seemed to crash over him. He yanked her tightly against him, and suddenly the whole damn bar disappeared, and all that remained was the woman in his arms. "I swear on my life, I will keep you safe, Mari. I swear it."

All the uncertainty vanished, and her eyes seemed to shimmer for a split second, as if tears had suddenly filled them. "I know you will."

David interrupted them with a grunt of irritation. "Can't you work tonight and then bail? He's not going to hit you here. We're swamped, Mari. I need your help."

She glanced at Ben, and he shook his head. "We're going back to her house to pack, and then leaving within the hour. We need to disappear, David. This guy is bad shit."

David met his gaze, and sudden understanding appeared

in them. The hardened wisdom of a man who'd seen the kind of shit they were facing. "What's he look like?"

"We don't know."

David nodded once, understanding. Then he looked past Ben, scanning the room with the same vigilance that Ben had used. "Leave me your phone number," he said.

Ben knew then that he had an ally. He jotted his private line down on a paper and handed it to him. "For no other eyes."

David looked down at the paper, read it carefully twice, then picked up a lighter and burned it. "Got it."

Ben raised his brows. "You're good."

David nodded. "Yeah, I am." Again, he looked around the place. "If he's here, I'll find him."

Shit. He could have used this man earlier. "Where have you been all week?"

David met his gaze, and said nothing.

It was Ben's turn to understand the silence, and he nodded. "Come on, Mari. Back to your place, and then we're on the road."

"Where you going?" David asked.

Ben looked at him. "We're ghosts, David. No one will find us, not even that bastard." He said it loud enough that anyone who wanted to hear it would, then turned with Mari and headed toward the door. He watched the room carefully as they left, searching for the person who would respond.

No one got up, but Ben knew that Joseph would know what had just happened. He would know, and he would come after them.

They had less than an hour until the whole damned thing was going to be over.

▨▧▨▧

Using the rearview mirror, Mari watched the exit of O'Dell's carefully as they drove out of the parking lot. The door didn't open. No one followed them, and no car started up to pursue them. Disappointment raged through her, a sense of frustration so great it seemed to eat away at her. "It didn't work. He's not following us." What now? What other card did they have to play?

But Ben didn't seem concerned. "He knows. He'll be at your house shortly." Ben reached over the seat into the back and grabbed one of his bags. He pulled it over into the front and began to rifle through it. "Watch the road," he ordered.

The edge to his voice caught her attention, and she glanced into the bag in time to see a flash of metal. Another gun. That meant he had at least two, including the one in his pocket.

Sudden panic seemed to hit her, and she jerked her gaze from it, staring at the road in front of them. "What if he gets it away from you?"

"I won't let him." Ben kept the gun pointed toward the passenger door as he fiddled with it, but she couldn't stop the rising bile in her throat. "Watch the road, Mari. You need to get us there safely."

She realized she was staring at the gun again, and she dragged her attention off it...for a split second until she looked at it again. She had to know where it was to make sure it wasn't pointing at her, or at Ben. She swallowed, her mouth suddenly dry, and her hands shaking. Sounds began to hammer in her ears, the loud cracks of the gun going off. She gripped the steering wheel tighter, fighting to keep her attention on the street and not the gun.

Her phone rang, making her jump. Ben picked it up and looked at the screen. "Charlotte."

She gasped in surprise. "It is? She's okay?"

Ben shook his head as she reached for it. "Joseph knows we're leaving town. He's making his move. If this is Charlotte on the phone, remember that he's probably telling her everything that she says." He hit speakerphone and held it near enough for her to answer, but so they both could hear. As she answered, he sent a text message on his own phone to Mack, his friend who had helped track the phone before.

"Charlotte?" She couldn't keep the desperation out of her voice. "Are you okay?"

"Mari?" Her voice was pinched and weak. "I need your help."

Dear God. *Charlotte was alive.* Relief rushed through her, and tears filled her eyes. "I'll do whatever you need. Where are you?"

"I'm at a cabin in the woods. It's an hour out of town. I need your help. Please come, now!"

Mari's throat tightened. "Is he there, Charlotte? Is your boyfriend there?"

"Something's so wrong." Charlotte started to cry, and answering tears slid down Mari's cheeks. "Please hurry. I don't know what to do. It's at the end of East Mountain Lane. I don't have a car. Don't tell anyone you're coming. It's so embarrassing for me. I just want you." Then she hung up.

Mari stared at Ben as the car went silent, struggling to keep focused and not whip the truck around and race to her friend's aid. "It's like when you got the text from your sister to go to your mom's house in Maine. What do we do? Is she really there? Or does he just want us there?"

Ben's phone beeped and he looked down at his phone to read his message from Mack. "He didn't get an exact location, but the call bounced off the tower near your house. She's not an hour away."

Despair ratcheted away the momentary relief she'd felt at hearing Charlotte's voice. "Then where do we go?"

"Same plan. Your house." His hand tightened around the gun. "And then we wait for him to come get us."

<hr />

Fifteen minutes after arriving at Mari's house, Ben realized his plan was fatally flawed.

The site he had chosen to face down Joseph was too vulnerable. It was in the middle of the woods in a house that was physically compromised. Joseph could come from any direction. Through a window. Through the plywood on the back door. They were baiting him, but as the minutes wore on, Ben began to feel like they were the ones being played. He should've gone to a hotel, a place where there were only two ways, or even only one way, into the room. He'd tried to get the advantage by forcing Joseph to act before he was ready, but in the process, he'd had to rush his own planning, and he'd made a strategic mistake in judgment. *Shit.*

There was no way for him to protect all possible approaches in Mari's house. The woods gave Joseph unlimited access from every direction. All Ben could do was wait for him to access the building itself, and he didn't like that at all. *At all*. He had positioned himself in the center of the small cabin. From this angle, he could see into the kitchen, the living room, and the bathroom. Mari was standing several feet over, still in the hallway, but facing her bedroom.

Their strategic placement allowed them to see all the entrances, but he didn't like the fact that Mari was closest to some of them. He needed to be her shield, but he couldn't do it the way he wanted to as long as they were in this indefensible house. All they could do was wait for Joseph to make his move.

A loud thump slammed against the front door. Mari jumped and Ben raised his gun, aiming at the wood.

"Mari!" Haas's voice rang out. "Sully! You in there?"

Mari started to move toward the door, but Ben held up his hand. She froze, her eyes wide.

Haas banged on the door again. "Son of a bitch, man! Open up! Your truck is outside. He set you up, man! The shit at Charlotte's house makes it look like you were having an affair with her. Your clothes are there. Letters you wrote to her. And blood, man, there's blood all over the place. Where's Charlotte? What the hell is going on? The cops want me to go in tomorrow for questioning. I showed them the damned note to explain why I was there, and now they want me. Ben! Open the door!"

Ben swallowed as the images of his sister's living room flashed through his mind. So much blood everywhere. It had been so bright, sprayed across the white couch and splattered across the pale yellow walls. He could still see that bloody handle sticking out of her chest. Dizziness assaulted him and he staggered, losing his balance under the onslaught of the hell savaging his mind.

"Ben," Mari whispered. "Are you okay?"

He jerked his gaze back to Mari, and he nodded, fighting against the memories.

"Sully!" Haas shouted again, pounding on the door. "Are you okay?" His voice was worried now. "Talk to me!" There was another crash, and then the door burst open.

Ben dropped to his knee and aimed at the door. Mari screamed as Haas stumbled through it, landing on his knees. He froze when he saw Ben's gun aimed at him. "Sully," he said. "It's me." His baseball hat was askew, his old, lined face shadowed, and his gnarled hands gripped the wooden floor. He was wearing the same coat he always did, the same battered jeans, and he looked even more frail and older than usual.

Ben didn't avert the gun. "Where is he, Haas?"

"Where is who?"

"Joseph." Ben searched the dark night behind Haas, but he could see nothing but darkness. He knew that Haas had been set up. Why else had Haas chosen to come here? "Where the hell is he?"

"Ben," Mari whispered. "Can we get the door shut?"

Swearing, Ben realized she was right. They were all vulnerable with the door open to the dark night. "Get inside," he ordered Haas as he sprinted to the front door. Haas scrambled to his feet and leapt up as Ben slammed the door shut. The wooden frame was shattered where Haas had busted out the lock. Shit. How had the old man done that kind of damage to the solid doorframe? Not that it mattered. The noose was tightening around their necks, and they still had no idea what direction the final assault would be coming from.

Ben spun around, frantically trying to think. Haas was standing in the middle of the living room, splotches of blood on his jacket from Charlotte's house. Ben swore, and again, flashed back to that moment when he'd found his sister. He fought against the memories, but they swirled around him. It was happening again. Someone's blood was all over Charlotte's house? Her blood? Someone else's? "How much blood, Haas? How much?"

The old man's eyes glittered at him. "A lot. Enough."

Enough. That meant that there had been enough that someone had died, or was almost dead.

Mari's voice split through his agony. "It's not Charlotte. She's still alive. I talked to her." She was still in her spot, her gaze flickering between the bedroom window and the men, not abandoning her vigilance.

But even as she spoke, a grim realization began to settle upon Ben. "No," he said quietly. "You talked to someone using her phone who was screaming and sobbing. You expected to hear her voice, so that's what you heard."

She paled. "It was Charlotte—"

"Not if that blood was hers." Ben edged up beside the front door, pressing his back against the wall. He couldn't lock it, but he could be prepared if Joseph burst through. "People see what they expect to see," he said softly. "He preys on that, with the cops, with the friends of the victim, with the victim herself. We see what we expect to see, and that's how he gets us." Swearing, he searched the room again, looking at the ceiling, the walls, and the furniture. He studied everything. "What aren't we seeing? What the hell are we looking at that we're not noticing?"

Mari was staring at him, and slowly, she began to look around, too.

Haas was still standing in the middle of the living room, looking ragged and strung out. "It's about the guy who killed your sister, isn't it?" he asked. "That's what this is."

"Yeah." Ben still didn't move from his spot. "He's setting you up for Charlotte's death." Guilt tore through him as he looked at the old man. "I feel like shit that you got dragged into this."

"Screw that. You need my help. If this bastard touched Charlotte, he has to die." Pure venom coursed through Haas's voice, and Ben looked at him sharply. The old man's hands were curled into tight fists, and his jaw was tight. But it was his eyes that Ben noticed now. They were cold. Ice cold. Not the warm and intelligent eyes of the old man who had become his friend. These were the eyes of a ruthless killer. Was this the man Haas had been when he'd been on his military duty? They were intense and lethal. Ben had seen eyes like that before, when he was in a gang. The eyes of the gang leader who had stared him down as he'd raised the gun to shoot him in cold blood. He'd never seen Haas look like that. Warning rippled through him, a cold chill easing down into his bones. "Who the hell are you, Haas?"

"I'm the sleeping tiger," Haas growled. "No one brings this shit into my world. Come on." He jammed his hat down over his head. "We're going to my place. I have a fortress over there. He'll never win."

Ben hesitated and looked at Mari. She was so vulnerable, standing in that open hallway. There was no way to defend against all threats. But was Haas's house any better? He tried to recall the layout of the building and property. "What do you have there?"

Haas was already moving toward the door. "You've never been in my barn, have you?" He grinned as he reached for the doorknob. "That's where I have all my shit from my days in the military. This bastard won't know what hit him."

His shoulder brushed against Ben's as he reached for the door, and Ben shifted to cover him as he pulled the door open—

"Watch out!" Haas suddenly bellowed a warning and lunged at him. Ben caught him and stumbled back just as a searing pain exploded in his right chest, just under his arm. He gasped and tripped, clutching his chest as the agony tore through him. His gun clattered to the floor, his fingers too numb to hold it.

"Ben!" Mari screamed in horror as he recoiled.

He realized instantly that he'd been shot. Son of a bitch. Joseph had been outside, waiting for him to walk out. "Shut the door," he gasped at Haas. "Mari," he croaked as he hit the ground, weakness flooding him. His gun was several feet away. He had to get to it. "Call 9-1-1!" It was over, way beyond his control. He didn't give a shit if he was arrested anymore. The time for revenge or redemption was over. All that mattered was getting Mari to safety.

Haas slammed the door shut, accidentally knocking the gun away just as Ben reached for it. Swearing, Ben gripped his chest, fighting the nausea as Mari ran across the living room and fell to her knees beside him, her face ashen. "What happened?"

"Bullet." Shit, it hurt. It *really* hurt. "Get my gun. I need my gun."

Ignoring his request, Mari shoved his jacket back, and then let out a small cry of distress. "You're bleeding. Oh, my God, you're bleeding! What happened? Did Joseph shoot you?"

"Yeah," Haas said, "he did."

"But when? I didn't hear a gunshot." Tears were streaming down Mari's cheeks as she pressed her hand to his bleeding wound, trying to stop the blood. Ben ground his jaw, fighting against the pain. He had to pull it together. He had to protect Mari. He had to get up.

"He used a silencer." Haas's voice was quiet. Too quiet.

Too late, much too late, a warning rang in Ben's head. He jerked his gaze off Mari and looked up. Haas was standing in the doorway, pointing a handgun at Mari's head.

Chapter 19

Mari froze, horror seizing her when she saw Haas pointing the gun at them. It was a small, gleaming handgun exactly like the one that had killed her family...and it was aimed right at her.

"What are you doing, Haas?" Ben gasped, his hand closing around Mari's arm, tugging her back.

"Don't move," Haas said...only this time, it wasn't Haas's voice. It was a voice she knew and recognized, a voice that sent chills of sheer terror shooting down her spine.

"Joseph?" she whispered, her voice trembling. But she didn't need to ask. She could never forget that voice. But how was it Haas who was staring at her, while she heard Joseph's voice?

"Joseph?" Ben echoed. "What the hell?"

Haas grinned, triumph gleaming in his eyes. "Joseph, it is." His eyes were cold, glittering with that same lethal hostility that had haunted her the nights before she'd finally left him. "Or Abraham. Or whatever name you choose for me." He looked at Ben. "I'm impressed you figured out as much as you have," he said. "No one else has gotten this far."

Mari's heart was hammering, and she frantically tried to think of what to do, but all she could focus on was the gun. His finger was on the trigger. One tiny twitch and they would both be dead.

"Stand up, Mari," Joseph ordered.

Ben's fingers closed around her arm. "No," he growled. "Don't move." Blood was pooling on the floor beneath him, and

Mari sucked in her breath, gasping in horror. "Ben—"

"Get up!" Joseph grabbed her arm and yanked her up. She stumbled, falling against him as Ben lunged for her. Joseph kicked Ben in the chest, his foot slamming brutally into Ben's wound. Ben sucked in his breath and collapsed back to the floor, gripping his chest. His breath was rasping, and his face was ashen.

"Ben!" she screamed, reaching for him, but Joseph grabbed her hair and yanked her back.

Ben roared in protest and tried to get up, but Joseph kicked him again sending him crashing into the wall. Ben stumbled and fell, but tried to recover almost immediately, using his shoulder to brace himself against the dented plaster as he fought to get upright.

"No!" Joseph shouted. "Get down!" He aimed the gun again, and Ben went still, his eyes fastened on Joseph, barely contained rage simmering in those green depths.

Mari fought against Joseph's hold, twisting desperately to try to free herself from his iron grip, but he was so much stronger than she was, barely even moving in an effort to contain her struggles. "Let me go!" she screamed, but he only laughed as he jerked her backward. She saw a glint of something shiny in his jacket pocket. Another gun? Then she saw a black hilt. A knife. A dagger. The same thing he'd used to kill Ben's sister.

Dear God, it was going to end now. He was going to kill them both! She jerked her eyes to Ben, and then almost cried out when she saw him half-propped against the wall, having made it only to his knees. His jaw was clenched with pain, and a thick bloodstain was spreading across his shirt, just like in her dream. But his eyes were sharp and wary, and she met his gaze, a silent determination spreading between them. They weren't dead yet. They still had a chance.

"You both ruined my plans," Joseph snarled. "It wasn't supposed to be this way! What the hell are you doing running away? You are supposed to save your friends." He swore again, and then threw Mari face-first into the wall. She crashed into it, and then gasped as he pinned her against the plaster.

"No! Let me go!" She ducked, trying to get free, but he merely shoved her harder against the wall, knocking the breath out of her lungs.

Her head spun as she fought to stay conscious. Dear God, no, this couldn't be happening. "One more move and you die," Joseph growled in a low voice. "And so does he."

Mari slid down the wall, her head throbbing from where she'd hit it against the plaster. Joseph was walking toward Ben, his gun out. What was he going to do to him? Panic hit her, and she lurched to her feet. "No!" She lunged toward Ben, but Joseph spun toward her just as she reached him. He smacked her across the head with his gun. Pain exploded through her, then darkness closed in, and she knew nothing.

※※※

"No!" Raw terror and violent outrage exploded through Ben when he saw Mari fall. He lunged to his feet just as Joseph whipped toward him. For a split second, time seemed to freeze, and then the gun exploded and pain slammed into Ben's knee. He bellowed and fell to the ground, writhing in agony as he gripped his knee.

"This ends my way," Joseph said as he walked over, standing above him. His eyes were so sinister and evil, Ben had no idea how he hadn't seen it when he'd first walked in. When had Joseph made the switch? Had Haas actually been Joseph since the first moment they'd met? Or had there been a switch out at some point?

Swearing, Ben thought back to his phone call with Haas at the bar, and grim realization dawned on him as he recalled the roughness of Haas's voice that he'd attributed to agitation. It hadn't been the real Haas. That had been Joseph, playing them. Of course it had been Joseph. How the hell else would he have arranged the delivery of the note at the exact moment he was on the phone with Ben. Shit! Ben had done exactly what Joseph had planned, and now Mari was going to die—

No! This wasn't over! He wasn't going to let her die. *Never.*

"Under normal circumstances, you'd already know the drill," Joseph said, his voice suddenly reverting to a charming, friendly tone, the one Ben knew he used to woo the women he was going to kill. "I'd stab Mari and let her die. I'd put my gun in her hands, and then help her dead, lifeless body shoot you one more time just to show the police how hard she was working to protect herself from you, the obsessed killer. Permanently maimed, you go to jail, she's dead, and it's all good." His voice grew hard again. "But that's not how I planned this all out. It is supposed to go down at Haas's house, not here, not in this way. I have other players involved this time, and it has to go the way I planned." He pressed the muzzle of the gun into Ben's temple. "So, get up. We're relocating."

The cold metal was like a sudden surge of focus for Ben. He dragged his gaze off the inert Mari, staring into the cold eyes of the man who had killed his sister. As long as he and Mari were both alive, it wasn't over. They still had time. He would bide his time and act when Joseph wasn't ready. "Where are we going?"

"You don't have time to ask." Joseph walked over to Mari, scooped her up with an ease that belied the old man he was pretending to be. He tossed her over his shoulder, and then pulled a knife out of his pocket, the same type of knife that he'd lodged in Holly's chest.

Ben went still, his gaze riveted to the knife as memories came screaming back at him as Joseph angled the blade at Mari's throat. "Get up, or it ends here."

"Don't! I'm up." Ben grabbed the edge of the couch and lunged to his feet, putting all his weight on his good leg. He could barely feel the pain in his knee or chest. All he could see was the knife aimed at her jugular. Swearing, he fought to remain still and look harmless. He had to do everything to keep from spooking Joseph.

"Get into the back of my truck. Now."

Slowly, searching for that opportunity, that split second of a chance, Ben dragged himself out the door and across the frozen earth to the truck that was sitting in the front driveway. The truck bed was covered with a hard canopy, and the tailgate was open. "In."

The interior was pitch black, but Ben suspected there was nothing inside that he could use as a weapon. Desperate, he hesitated, knowing he could not get in there alone. There would be no way out, no way to protect Mari. "I'm not getting in."

"Yes, you are."

"No—"

Joseph suddenly plunged the knife into Mari's upper arm. Ben shouted and lunged for her. His knee collapsed, and he hit the ground a yard away from her as Joseph yanked it out. Mari was still unconscious, and Joseph hurled her into the bed of the truck, where she landed with an agonizing thud. "Get in."

Ben forced his way back onto his feet and then hauled himself into the back of the truck with Mari, wrapping his good arm around her as he slid in beside her. Joseph slammed the tailgate shut, locked them in with a click, and darkness consumed them.

"Mari," Ben whispered, pressing his lips to her ear as he pulled her against him, trying to warm her cold body. "Wake up, sweetheart. I need you to wake up."

She didn't respond, and the engine of the truck roared to life. The tires spun out on the gravel, and then Joseph hit the gas. Ben and Mari slid across the metal truck bed, their bodies grinding over debris. Ben swore and used his good arm to keep Mari's head from hitting the side of the truck. He'd barely managed to stop their slide when the truck lurched over a deep hole and slammed them down on the hard metal bed. Pain shot through Ben's chest and knee, and he sucked in his breath, fighting for consciousness as the pain blasted violently through him.

"Mari," he whispered again as the truck tires began to hum, and he knew they were on the highway now. The ride would be smoother now. How long did they have? Minutes? He forced himself to release Mari. He inched over to the back and tried to get the canopy open, but it was immovable. Frustrated, he leaned on his hip, protected his bad knee, and slammed his foot into the plastic. The jolt sent shards of pain through his body, and the plastic didn't flinch. Swearing, he went still, sweat pouring off him as he fought the wave of unconsciousness trying to take him. He kicked it twice again, and then gave up, realizing that he had to find another way. Tension rising within him, he began to feel his way across the bed of the truck, searching for anything he could use.

Leaves.

An old sweatshirt.

Nothing he could use as a weapon.

"Shit!"

"Ben?" Mari's muffled voice jerked his attention. Relief hit him hard, tightening in his chest as he spun toward her. "Mari!" He crawled back toward her, his hands reaching blindly for her. He needed to touch her, to hold her, to reassure himself that she was really all right.

He touched her shoulder, and she immediately grabbed his hand. "What's going on?"

"Haas is Joseph." He pulled her against him and buried his face in her hair, his entire body shaking with the enormity of what it felt like to hold her, to know she was okay. "He's taking us somewhere."

"Did he shoot you? Is that what happened?" She reached for his chest with her free hand, but he blocked her.

"I'm fine." Shit. He had to pull himself together. Now was not about crushing Mari in his arms. The worst was still coming. They had only minutes to find a way to save themselves. Forcing himself to relax his grip on her, he pulled back. "Help me look for something we can use. There has to be something he overlooked in here." He didn't allow himself to ask if she was all right. She had to be. "Are you all right?" The question shot out of his mouth before he even had time to think it, and he knew it was because he would never be able to concentrate until he knew she was okay.

Shit. He was so deluding himself that he could focus on the job and not her. When had she become so much more than simply the next woman on Joseph's list? He couldn't afford this kind of distraction or emotional entanglement right now. But at the same time, he knew that it was Mari who was giving him the strength to continue, despite the two bullets he'd taken already.

"My arm hurts," she whispered, as she rolled to her side. "What did he do to me?"

"He stabbed you." The words were like a knife in his own gut.

"When I was unconscious?" To his surprise, there was no fear in Mari's voice. Just anger. "That's just being a bully. I hate bullies." She moved away, crawling across the bed of the truck as she searched.

He realized that it would have been different if Joseph had shot her. Mari didn't do guns, but apparently a knife was okay. Respect rushed through him, along with intense and incredible admiration for her. He smiled into the darkness as he began to sweep his good arm across the truck bed, feeling for something that would work. "You kick ass, you know that, don't you?"

She was silent for a moment. "Do you think we're going to die?"

Ben closed his eyes against the horrific images trying to take over his mind. "Eventually, yes. Not tonight."

"Okay."

She didn't ask any more questions, and he knew that was the answer she'd wanted. There was no room for doubt right now. Fear would paralyze them and strip them of whatever sliver of opportunity they had.

The truck suddenly slowed, and they both slid across the bed and crashed into the front of the truck. Pain shot through his chest and knee, and Mari yelped. The truck began to bounce again, and he knew they were going off-road. Wherever they were headed, they had almost arrived. "Shit," he muttered, grabbing Mari and helping her right herself. "We don't have much time."

He swept his hand more desperately across the truck bed, and pain sliced through his hand as he hit something sharp. Quickly, frantically, he retraced his movement, and he found a gouge in the metal. It hadn't been an implement he could use to save them. All it had been was a crack in the truck bed. "Shit!"

The truck stopped suddenly, and they both flew forward again. Swearing, they scrambled up. A light from outdoors shone through the seams in the truck bed cover, illuminating Mari's face. Her skin looked pale and wan in the shadowy light, and his heart tightened. Suddenly, all he wanted to do was sweep her into his arms and run for the hills, protecting her for the rest of his life.

Footsteps crunched around the truck, jerking him back to the present and the reality they were facing. "Pretend you're still unconscious," he whispered, unable to think of anything else. That was his plan? To make Joseph not notice her because he thought she was still out? Shit! He had nothing better than that.

The handle to the tailgate clicked, and Mari dropped to the truck bed, her eyes still fastened on his. Then, her gaze flicked to just above his shoulder, and her eyes widened.

He whipped around. In the dim light, he could see a screwdriver stuck in a crevice in the corner. He lunged for it as the tailgate opened. He jerked it free and slid it up his sleeve just as Haas's face appeared in the doorway. No, not Haas. Joseph. But son of a bitch, it looked like Haas.

A bright light shone in, temporarily blinding Ben. He shielded his eyes, fighting against the sudden onslaught.

"Get out," Joseph ordered. "Now."

Fisting his hand to keep the screwdriver hidden, Ben inched his way toward the tailgate. Mari was lying motionless, and every part of him screamed to grab her and protect her, to fight the bastard, but he couldn't risk her. He had to deal with Haas...Joseph...whatever the hell his name was.

Joseph turned the light onto Mari, freeing Ben from the blindness, and he quickly inspected Joseph as he slithered across the truck bed. The gun was in his right hand, aimed at Ben, but he was watching Mari.

Could he make a move? Could he get him?

Ben edged closer, barely noticing the numbness of his injured chest or the shattered knee. He just watched Joseph, waiting for an opportunity—

Joseph suddenly swung toward him, the gun in both hands. "Drop it."

Ben kept moving slowly, knowing he had to get out of the truck. He couldn't afford to be locked in there. "Drop what?"

"Whatever's in your hand." Joseph aimed the gun at Ben's hand where he'd hidden the screwdriver. "Drop it, or you lose your hand."

Swearing, Ben let the screwdriver slide out of his sleeve. It landed with a clatter on the truck bed, rolled off the edge, and then thumped into the dirt, out of reach. Despair wrenched through him as he watched his last chance roll away from him. Sweat poured down his temples as he edged off the tailgate, not giving Joseph the chance to keep him inside.

"Stay." Joseph grabbed Mari by the ankle and dragged

her across the bed of the truck toward him. Adhering to Ben's order to feign unconsciousness, she allowed her head to thud over the bumpy surface. Ben had to fist his hands to keep from bellowing his outrage and lunging for her. He had to keep his shit together. He had to stay focused. He couldn't move too soon.

Joseph hoisted Mari over his shoulder again, his body tall and strong. He was no longer bothering to project the hunched shoulders of Haas anymore. He couldn't have been Haas this whole time, could he? Ben would have noticed, right? He was certain he would've sensed it. But what was going on? Even now, Joseph looked exactly like Haas, except the visible strength in his lean body. Was he simply that good at disguise?

History said he was.

Joseph flicked the gun at Ben. "Walk." He jerked his head to the right. "Go."

Ben turned and saw a small shed. To his left was the same house that he and Mari had spent time in that first day when they'd all gone shopping, when the tile had nearly crushed Mari while she'd been talking to Charlotte and the abrasive woman who had run into Mari with her shopping cart. Haas had been there. Had it been Haas/Joseph who had made the tile fall? Not an accident?

Not that it mattered. The past was irrelevant. The moment was *now*.

They reached the shed, which Ben saw had a padlock on it. Joseph tossed Ben a key. "Open it."

Ben fumbled with the lock, as he scanned the ground around him, looking for a weapon, but there was nothing. Their only chance lay in the dirt behind the truck. Shit. What was he going to do?

"Open it *now*, or I'll shoot your other knee."

Ben jammed the key into the lock and it sprang open. He jerked the padlock off, jammed it locked again, and then fisted it, the hard metal base lodged between his fingers. His adrenaline was screaming through him, his entire body shaking with the need to act.

"Open the door."

Ben twisted the handle and kicked it open, still gripping the padlock as he stepped back, refusing to get close enough for Joseph to push him in. Something moved inside, and he instinctively glanced at the interior. Tied up like a pig was an old man, an old man he knew, an old man with blood caked on his head and crusted down the side of his neck. "Haas," he whispered, unable to stop the stab of grief that gripped his chest. That was his *friend*.

Haas didn't look up and didn't even move. He remained on his side, his eyes closed, and his thin body so small and frail.

Ben swung around, studying Joseph more intently now. "When did you make the switch?" The man pointing the gun at him looked like Haas, even now when he knew for certain it wasn't him.

Joseph grinned, flashing the same crooked teeth that Haas had. "I'm not one of those stupid bad guys that starts spilling all his secrets at the end," he said. "No bedtime story for you. Just hand me the lock and get in there."

Ben looked down at the padlock in his hand, and his grip tightened around it. Get himself locked in the shed while the bastard kept Mari? No way. *No way.*

Joseph raised his gun, pointing at Ben's heart. "You know I won't hesitate to kill you. I never do. If you go in the shed now, you get to live a little longer. If you're alive, you have a chance to save Mari, right? If you're dead...not so much."

Son of a bitch. The man knew exactly what to say. He knew how to twist the situation. He knew what choice every one of his victims would make. Shit. Ben had tried to be unpredictable and act against his nature, and Joseph had known he was going to do that. "What are you, a psychologist?"

True to his claim, Joseph did not answer, or appear to feel the need to gloat over his victories. He simply flicked the muzzle of the gun toward the shed, leaving it trained on Ben's heart.

"Why do you kill them?" Ben persisted. Out of the corner of his eyes, he saw Haas's eyelids flutter. Was he still alive? Conscious? "Why do you kill the women?"

"Get in the shed!" Joseph shouted suddenly. "Just get in!"

And that's when Ben knew. Joseph *wasn't* ready to kill him. He had set up his plan the way he wanted it, and shooting

Ben out in the dirt wasn't how he wanted to do it. But could Ben afford to have his other knee blown out? He was already on one foot, his body shaking with the effort of staving off the pain. His hand fisted around the padlock still clenched in his hand. Did he risk it? Did he move? Or did he wait for a better chance? *Shit!*

He began to inch toward the shed, intentionally dragging his injured leg and trying to look as defenseless as possible. As he did, he quickly scanned the shed, trying to figure out how secure it was. If he went in, could he get out fast and come after Joseph when he wasn't prepared? Or would he be rendered helpless while the bastard stabbed Mari?

Bile rolled in his stomach at the image of Mari sprawled on the ground like his sister, and he knew there was no way he could take the chance that he'd get a better opportunity later. He had to act, and he had to act, *now.* He stepped up into the doorway of the cabin and intentionally tripped. He let out a yowl of pain as he pretended to fall. "Get down," he shouted as he whipped his arm back to throw the padlock.

Moving with sudden quickness, Mari wrenched herself free of Joseph, and Ben hurled the padlock. It slammed into Joseph's head, and he staggered for a split second. Ben lunged for him, but then Joseph raised his gun and pulled the trigger.

CHAPTER 20

"Ben!" Mari screamed in terror as Ben fell to the ground. He didn't move.

"Ben!"

"Shut up!" Joseph grabbed her by the hair and flung her to the side. She landed on the dirt, her face smashing into the ground.

She gasped in pain, fighting for breath. "Ben! Wake up!"

But he didn't react as Joseph dragged him across the dirt with an ease that suggested a terrifying amount of strength. He shoved Ben into the shed, kicking his booted feet out of the doorway. He slammed the door shut, jammed the padlock closed, and then paused to lean against the door.

Dear God. Ben was trapped. He couldn't help her now. She had to fight Joseph *alone?*

Blood was pouring down the side of his face. The gash from the padlock Ben had thrown had hurt Joseph more than she'd realized. He closed his eyes, as if trying to summon the energy to continue. She immediately rolled onto her side, fighting to stand up, but his eyes jerked open.

He pointed the gun at her, and she froze. "Don't."

She went still, her heart pounding. "Is Ben dead?" she whispered. She hadn't seen where the bullet had hit. She'd only seen him fall, but there'd already been so much blood on him from before that she wasn't sure that she'd even notice new blood. Her body was shaking now, and she couldn't get the image of Ben out of her mind. Her family's slaughtered bodies floated in and out of her mind, her father's face merging with Ben's, all of them gazing sightlessly in that blank stare of death.

Tears seemed to overwhelm her, and sudden weakness flooded her. The loss. The grief. The terror. How could this be happening again? She didn't want to die. She didn't want Ben to die. She couldn't go through this again.

"Ben will die in prison," he said as he levered himself off the doorframe. "He has to go to prison. That's how it works."

"Prison?" Sudden hope leapt through her. Joseph never made a mistake. He always put someone in prison. If Ben had to go to prison for Joseph to be happy, then that meant he'd made sure he didn't kill him. Maybe it wasn't over. Maybe Ben was still alive.

Fierce determination seemed to flood her, and her mind suddenly calmed as she studied Joseph. Violence had stolen her family from her. Guns had killed those she loved. Terror had hunted her for over a year. But if she let it win this time, then she would lose the one man who had made her believe again, in love, in hope, in herself.

She would not let it end badly. Not this time. *Not again.*

"Get up." Joseph flicked the gun at her, and this time, as she looked into his eyes, she didn't see Haas anymore. She saw those same, cold ruthless eyes that she knew. She saw the man who had tried to destroy her. She saw evil. And she also saw a man that she had been smart enough to get away from once. Why not again? He didn't always win. If he had, she wouldn't still be alive now.

Slowly, she climbed to her feet, not taking her gaze off him. Her arm was throbbing where he'd cut her, but she didn't bother to grab it. A little cut didn't matter. All that mattered was making this hell end.

"To the house." Joseph nodded toward Haas's cabin.

Her mind spinning over all the options she had, trying to figure out what to do, she turned to walk toward it. As she spun around, she noticed the handle of the knife sticking out of his jacket pocket. Her arm suddenly started hurting again, and fear rippled through her, real fear, for herself. Terror that in minutes, he would stab her to death like he'd done with Ben's sister—

No. She couldn't think like that. She had to stay focused. For herself. For Ben. Her heart tightened as she thought of him trapped in that cabin. He would never forgive himself if she died. It would break him, and dammit, he was too good of a man to suffer like that. For him, she would stay alive. She would stay alive for the man she loved.

The moment she thought it, a comforting warmth seemed to spread through her, and she realized it was true. She did love him, and for him, she could survive anything.

New energy seemed to surge through her as she reached the front door of Haas's cabin. Yes, she could do this! Then she opened the door, and all her confidence fled.

Charlotte was on the couch, tied up, her eyes wide with terror so stark that it seemed to plunge like an icy dagger into her heart. One sleeve was torn off, and a bloody bandage was wrapped carelessly around her arm.

It had been Charlotte's blood on the knife, but he hadn't killed her.

He was keeping her alive, so he could kill them all in whatever horrific order he had planned out. As hard as she and Ben had tried to derail him from his perfectly orchestrated plan, he was right on track to make it all unfold exactly as he wanted. Again.

※※※

"Sully."

The hoarse whisper grated through his mind, and Ben struggled to surface from the fog crushing his mind.

"Ben."

The familiar voice of Haas finally penetrated, and Ben jerked awake, instinctively lurching to his feet, his hands fisted in a defensive position. It took a moment for his eyes to adjust, then he saw the old man he knew so well, huddled in a tiny, frail ball on the cold floor. Swearing, he lowered himself beside Haas, his shattered knee now screaming with pain. His head was throbbing, and his chest was on fire. "How do I get out of here?" He pressed a hand to his head, and it came away covered in blood. He realized that the bullet had grazed his head. Too close.

He didn't question his luck, though. He had no time for

that. All he could think of was Mari at the hands of the madman who had killed his sister.

But Haas shook his head. "No way out," he whispered. "I made it secure against animals when I built it. Nothing's getting in or out." His eyes were glazed with pain and weakness, a man too old to be trussed up and left in a cold shed in Alaska.

"There has to be." Ben shrugged off his jacket and wrapped it around Haas, even as he scanned the inside of the small shed. Moonlight was slipping through the cracks, casting a faint light around the small building. The walls were bare, and even the floor was void of clutter. There was a crack of light coming from beneath the door, but it was only an inch high, not enough to make any difference. He peered beneath the door, but all he could see was the abandoned yard. Mari? Where was Mari? Fear hammered at him as he whirled toward Haas. "Where is everything that was in here?"

"He tossed it." Haas's eyes were closed again, his voice weak. "Guess he didn't trust an old man not to kick his ass. He was right, you know. I would've. If he'd left me even a cotton ball, he'd be dead, but he didn't even grant me that. Stupid fool."

Ben stumbled as dizziness assaulted him, but he nevertheless began a careful but fast assessment of the shed, his hands touching every inch of the floor and walls. His fingers hit dirt, splinters, and dislodged nails, but that was it. "When did he take you?"

"Two days ago," Haas muttered. "Remember the pushy lady from the home supply store? The one who was talking to Mari when the tile fell?"

Ben looked sharply over at Haas. "Yeah."

"Well, that was our man. He showed up at the bar a couple nights ago dressed as her, all upset because she'd seen a truck in the ditch a little ways down." He opened his eyes and gave Ben a weary look. "She described your truck, Sully. I thought it was you. I hauled ass out the door, and he clocked me over the head just as I opened the door to my truck. I woke up here." He swore again. "How did I not notice how big her hands were? No woman has hands that size. I should have known." His face was bleak, and he looked old, so damn old. "I lost my edge, Sully. I lost it. I got beat, and now everyone's gonna die."

"No." Ben balled his hands into fists. "No one dies—"

A woman's scream split the night, ripping apart his very soul. "No!" He lunged at the door. He slammed his shoulder into it, hitting it so hard he bounced back and crashed into the other wall, almost stepping on Haas. Stunned by the impact, he staggered to his feet, sweat pouring down his temples. "He'll let us out," he said. "As soon as Charlotte and Mari are dead, he'll let us out, so that we run there, and try to save them, and we're covered in their blood." He howled with agony and charged the door again. Again, it shook under the impact, but held against his assault. He rebounded and fell on his ass, his body screaming with pain so intense that black spots swam before his eyes. And still, he lunged to his feet, lurching sideways into the wall as he fought for balance.

"Stop it!" Haas bellowed. "Just stop it! You can't get through there! We have to think!"

"I can get through!" Ben charged again, but Haas moved his foot and tripped him. Ben slammed headfirst into the wall, landing on his injured knee. Groaning, he rolled onto his side, fighting to stay conscious. "Whose side are you on?"

"The good guys, of course." Haas had worked himself into an upright position, his face deathly pale. "What's your talent, boy? What's that past you're hiding? What the hell can you do?"

Ben stared at him. "I can get people off for a crime they did."

"Before that," Haas scoffed. "You've got a past uglier than mine." Haas leaned over and grabbed Ben by the shirt. "What the hell do you know, Sully?"

Ben stared at him, his mind flashing back to his childhood and his teen years. "I can hotwire a car."

"What else?" Haas shook him.

"I can shoot a gun. I can pick a lock with a pipe cleaner. I can smell death from a hundred yards away. I can outrun cops for three miles. I can walk into a room and know where all the exits are within three seconds. I can look a man in the eye and kill him without remorse, but how the hell does that help us?" There was another scream and Ben lurched to his feet, his body slick with sweat. "Sweet Jesus," he whispered, saying a prayer for the first time since the day his best friend lay dying in his arms as a teenager. "Help me save her," he whispered. "Don't let this happen again."

"What else?" Haas barked at him.

"What else?" Ben swung to face him. "We're locked in a shed without a single implement to help us get out, while the woman I love is about to be *murdered!* What the hell does it matter what I can do?"

"It has to matter," Haas yelled at him, his voice raspy and harsh. "Because there has to be something! Just *think!*"

But Ben couldn't think of anything but what was going on in that house. What was Joseph doing? Who had screamed? What in God's name was happening fifty yards from him that he couldn't stop? He was numb with terror over the thought of what was happening to Mari.

There was another scream, and Ben felt the life drain from him. "Mari!" He screamed her name and shook the door handle, helplessness flooding him.

"If you love her," Haas shouted at him, "you have to save her."

Ben turned toward him, feeling more lost than he'd ever felt in his life. "How?" he whispered. He'd failed his sister. And now he was going to fail Mari. He never got there in time. He dropped to his knees, welcoming the stab of pain that almost knocked him out. He looked at Haas, begging the old man for answers. "How? How do I save her? I don't know what to do."

Disappointment flashed through Haas's eyes. "Then she's going to die."

※※※

Mari tried to scramble backwards, but there was nowhere to go. She was up against the wall, her hands trapped behind her back. Charlotte was slumped on the couch, no longer conscious, which was a blessing for her, because the moment she'd passed out, Joseph had left her alone.

Instead, he'd turned toward Mari. On his hands were rubber gloves that went all the way up to his elbows, and he was still wearing the Haas outfit. No one would ever know that anyone besides Haas has been there. Ever.

"Mari." The eyes she knew so well were bearing down on her, those pitiless black eyes that were no longer hidden by the colored contacts he'd had on when they first arrived. The rest of his Haas disguise had stayed intact, but it was as if he'd wanted her to see who he really was. "You ran from me."

Tears were staining her cheeks, but she lifted her chin, her voice steady. "It's over, Joseph. You need to let me go. It's time for this to stop."

"I tried to help you." He walked closer to her, and she shrank back against the wall, the rough wood unyielding against her back. "You were broken, and I saved you."

She swallowed as he lifted his hand, trailing his bloody rubber glove across her cheek. "It's time to break the cycle," she said. "It's time for you to stop killing."

"I have no choice. You leave me no other options." He met her gaze. "I saved you, but then you showed me that you're not worthy. None of you are worthy." He looked over at Charlotte, an expression of such regret on his face that it almost seemed real, as if he truly felt great regret about his obligation to kill them. "So many good women who are too tainted to deserve life. I try to save you all, and I fail. I have been sent here to save you, to heal your soul, and all of you fail." He turned his attention back toward Mari "I fail, because you aren't worthy." Sudden anger flooded his face, and he gripped her chin, trapping her. "You ran too soon," he said. "You ended it too soon! One more day, and then we would have been married!" His hand slid around her neck and he grabbed her hair, jerking her head back. Out of the corner of her eye, she saw him slide that knife out of his pocket.

Terror slammed into her. It was going to be the exact same as Ben's sister. He'd leave her with a knife in the chest, and then release Ben too late. How could it happen again? How could it be happening the same way again?

The same... *the same*! A sudden idea popped into Mari's mind, Ben's conviction that Joseph had a pattern that he had to keep, that it had to be the same each time. "I wish I hadn't left," she blurted out, her voice shaking more than she'd hoped. "You helped me. I wish I'd married you. Can we..." She swallowed, praying that it would work, that it would buy her time. "Can we...still get married?" She thought of Ben and pictured him, and then whispered three words, pretending she was saying them to Ben. "I love you." She raised her gaze to the madman standing before her. "Joseph."

His eyes went wide with shock, and for a split second, she saw that same soft expression that had won her over that first day she'd met him, when she'd been stumbling home from her family's funeral.

She knew she had him. She was the only woman that he hadn't managed to marry before murdering. And Charlotte... She looked over at her friend, and her gut went cold. Had he married Charlotte? She didn't even know. "I want to marry you," she said again. "Can we? Please?"

Yearning was etched on his face, an almost maniacal need for what she was offering him. "Do you still have my ring?" he asked.

"At O'Dell's," she answered quickly, hope surging through her. "I keep it in my locker at work." A total lie, but if she could get him out of there—

"No." Darkness flooded his face. "It must be now. Here." He ripped his gloves off, and then yanked a ring from his own hand and held it up. "We marry with this. Now."

Now? Now didn't give her enough time! "I need a wedding dress," she protested, trying to think of a reason to stall. "I've always dreamed of marrying you in a beautiful white gown—"

"Shut up!" He spun her around and slammed her face into the wall. She gasped at the pain, turning her head to the side for air as he twisted her arms behind her back in agonizing contortions. "I am not a fool," he whispered, his breath hot against her ear. "I never lose, so don't think you can get away from me. We get married, and then you die."

She nodded. "I understand." Dear God, he was beyond insane, if he believed that telling her that he would kill her after they got married would make her compliant. But she could use that, right? Somehow, she could take advantage of the fact that he was delusional, right?

He jerked her around, and he placed the cold muzzle of the gun against her forehead.

A cold sweat broke out, and she started to shake. "Put that away," she whispered. "Please. I'm afraid of guns."

"I know that, my darling. I know that all too well." He pressed the gun harder into her forehead. "We are gathered here today to witness and celebrate the marriage of Joseph and Mari, brought together by love and a common understanding of the beauty of life, to join them in holy matrimony."

She stared at him, horrified by the realization that he was going to marry them right there, right then, and then kill her, the gun to her head the whole time. There was no chance for her to escape. "You can't marry us. We need a pastor—"

He pressed the gun harder into her head, making pain burn through her flesh. "This marriage will be blessed by God, and torn asunder by Satan, if Mari proves unworthy," he continued, his gaze piercing and cold.

"Don't you love me? I thought you loved me. Put the gun away and let this be real and beautiful. It's our wedding, Joseph—"

"Do you, Joseph, take this woman to be your wife, to live together in matrimony, to love her, to honor her, to comfort her, and to keep her in sickness and in health, forsaking all others, for as long as you both shall live?" He nodded. "I do."

Oh, God. This wasn't going to work. She needed time, not an instant wedding—

"Do you, Mari, take this man to be your husband, to live together in matrimony, to love him, to honor him, to comfort him, and to keep him in sickness and in health, forsaking all others, for as long as you both shall live?"

"Joseph—"

"Say I do."

God, this was happening too fast. "Joseph—"

He pretended to pull the trigger, and she jumped. "I do," she gasped. "I do—"

He nodded in satisfaction "I, Joseph, take thee, Mari, as my lawfully wedded wife—"

"What's your name?" she interjected desperately. "I want to know your real name. I don't want to get married to a lie!"

The gun didn't budge from her forehead. "From this

day forward, I promise to honor and love you, to protect and preserve, through richer and poorer, through sickness and health, until death do us part."

Oh, God, he was halfway done with the ceremony! "Joseph—"

"Say it." His upper lip sneered. "Say your vows, Mari. Say them. I, Mari, take you, Joseph—"

"I want a white dress! I can't marry the man I love with a gun to my head—"

"Say it! I, Mari, take you, Joseph—"

"I can't—"

His hand went to her throat, cutting off her air. "Say it," he snarled. "I, Mari, take you, Joseph—"

She couldn't breathe. She couldn't save herself if she were unconscious. Dammit, she had to change her tactic. She had to stop fighting. She had to make him trust her. Her heart pounding, she nodded, and licked her lips. His gaze dropped to her mouth instantly, and nausea churned through her stomach. "I, Mari," she whispered, "take you, Joseph."

A smile curved at the corner of his mouth. "As my lawfully wedded husband."

She lifted her hand to his chest, barely able to stop herself from recoiling when she felt the heat of his body through his shirt. "As my lawfully wedded husband," she said, meeting his gaze.

His eyes darkened, and he leaned closer. "To love and obey."

"To love and obey," she repeated. She slid her hand up his shirt, so her fingertips brushed the bare flesh of his neck.

He flinched and then moved closer. "Through richer and poorer." His voice was husky now.

"Through richer and poorer." Bile churned through her, and yet she still managed to move her hand higher, caressing his jaw.

"Through sickness and health," he whispered, his mouth less than an inch from hers.

"Through sickness and health," she whispered, her heart pounding through her.

"Until death do us part." His fingers laced through her

hair, trapping her with an unyielding grip.

Death. *Death.* The death that would be coming for her in minutes, or even seconds. Oh, God, she couldn't do this. She couldn't say it. But she had to. She couldn't put him on alert again. "Until...death...do us part." She stared at him, searching his eyes for some intent, for some warning of what he was about to do.

Joseph held up his bloodied ring and took her hand. His hands were rough and raw, and she had to force herself not to pull away as he slid it over her ring finger on her left hand. "I now pronounce you man and wife," he said.

"You may kiss the bride," she whispered, her voice so faint she could barely even hear her own words.

But Joseph heard them. "You may kiss the bride," he repeated. His grip on her hair tightened, and for a moment, he simply stared at her.

What was he going to do? Was he going to kill her now? Was he going to kiss her? Did she have a chance? Did she—

He slammed his mouth down onto hers.

CHAPTER 21

The moment Joseph kissed her, Mari grabbed the front of his shirt and pulled him close. She kept the image of Ben in her mind, desperately trying to pretend she was kissing the man she loved, but even that didn't keep the revulsion from roiling through her. But still she held on, and forced herself to respond to Joseph's assault.

One of his hands went to her hip...and then he clamped onto her other hip. He was gripping her with both hands, the gun no longer pointing at her head, his knife safely in his pocket. Slowly, as seductively as she could, she trailed her hands down his chest to his waist, nearly gagging when he thrust his tongue into her mouth. Easing her left hand to the side of his jacket, she slammed her right hand over the front of his jeans, over his erection. He sucked in his breath and then groaned as she cupped him, gripping hard, so hard she knew it had to be almost hurting him, and he groaned again, gasping her name.

"Yeah, that's right," she whispered. "Let me have you one last time."

"God, yes—" He moved closer, using his body to pin her against the wall. She heard the clunk of his gun against the plaster.

She kept her hand between them, grinding her knuckles into his erection to distract him as she found the opening of his jacket pocket with her left hand. He stiffened, and she immediately went for the button of his jeans and started to undo it.

"Yes, Mari, Yes—"

She plunged her hand into his jacket pocket, grabbed the knife, and slammed it into his side, right through his clothes. She felt the resistance of the blade as it plunged through his flesh, and she gagged as he screamed in agony. He stumbled back, and she sprinted past him, running for the front door. "Ben!" she screamed as she yanked the door open. "Ben!"

She vaulted down the steps, knowing that Ben was her only chance. She couldn't outrun Joseph, and they were isolated in the middle of the woods. Her only chance was Ben. He had to be okay. She had to get the door to the shed open. "Ben!" She shouted again as her feet pounded across the hardened earth. Behind her, she heard the thud of Joseph's feet as he raced after her.

"Mari!" Ben's roar was like a great burst of energy through her, and she heard him crash into the wall of the shed, as if he were trying to break through.

Still running as hard as she could, she bolted toward the truck, drawing Joseph away from the shed. She ran past the passenger side, skidded around the rear, and scooped the screwdriver off the ground just as Joseph lunged around the tailgate at her. She screamed and ducked, just barely dodging his grab. Her lungs were burning as she ran toward the shed, and Ben's desperate shouts echoed out against the night.

"Ben!" She was only ten feet away when Joseph tackled her. She hit the ground with a thud, and the screwdriver spilled out of her hand, coming to a rest inches from the base of the shed door. Dammit! "Ben! Look under the door!"

Joseph grabbed her ankles and hauled her back toward him, dragging her over the rough, cold ground. He flipped her over, and raw terror ripped through her. His eyes were glazed with the fury of the insane, and a bright red bloodstain was spreading over his shirt. "You betrayed me for the last time, bitch."

Then he ripped the knife out of his side, and she knew it was too late. "I love you, Ben," she shouted. "I will always love you!"

Then Joseph struck with the knife.

"Mari!" Ben dropped to his knees as he heard the clatter of a metal implement on the ground outside the door. He pressed his face to the wooden floor to look beneath the crack. Mari was on the ground, being dragged away from him by Joseph. Her hand was stretched toward him, as if in a final, desperate supplication for his help. Her face was pale, etched in agony, and he felt his heart stop. "Mari," he whispered, her name tearing at his throat.

Then, a flash of metal caught his eyes, and he shifted his focus. The screwdriver was only a few inches away. *They had a chance.* The intense focus of his youth ripped through him, and he instantly spun to Haas. A tarnished metal buckle gleamed at the waist of the old man. He lunged for it, even as Haas seemed to read his mind and reach for his own belt. They had it off him within a split second, and then Ben was back on his stomach. "I'm coming, Mari," he shouted. "Don't give up!"

As he watched, Mari suddenly rolled sideways, and Joseph's knife blade crashed into the earth where her torso had just been. "That's it," he yelled as he shoved the leather belt beneath the door. Working with a deftness of a teenage miscreant, he hooked the screwdriver with the belt buckle and dragged it swiftly beneath the door.

Joseph lunged for Mari again, and she kicked his side. He gasped with pain, and then grabbed her again—

"Fight him," Ben ordered as he grabbed the screwdriver and leapt to his feet. His hands were steady and focused, but sweat was pouring down his face as he jammed the screwdriver into the hinges, frantically working to pry the pin out. Outside, he heard Mari scream again, and his fingers slipped. How long could she avoid him? "I'm coming," he yelled.

He finally got some movement, and the pin popped up. He yanked the pin out, then went down on his knees, and jammed the screwdriver under the lip of the second pin, desperately tracking the sounds of the scuffle outside while he worked it free. *Please let me be in time. Please let me be in time.* He got the second pin out, then grabbed the handle of the door and pulled—

The door didn't move.

"Shit!" He jammed the screwdriver into the crack

between the wall and the frame, and shoved against it while he yanked on the doorknob, trying to leverage the door out of the frame.

"Ben!"

Her scream ignited his fury. Strength surged through him, desperation so strong that his world seemed to burn with his need to get to her. "Argh!" He roared with rage, slammed the tool so hard into the crevice that a loud crack exploded through the shed as the doorframe shattered. "I'm coming!" He tore the door free, hurled it aside, and lunged across the barren earth just as Joseph reared back, the knife glinting in his hand. Mari was on her back, trapped between his knees.

"No!" Ben bellowed, and Joseph looked up at Ben.

"Too late," Joseph screamed as he thrust the knife toward Mari's heart. "Too late—"

"Never!" Ben slammed into him, knocking him all the way across the driveway. Both men skidded, the rough ground tearing at flesh, but Ben was on his feet before Joseph had even begun to rise. He slammed Joseph's face into the dirt, lodged his knee into his back, and pinned him to the earth. "Don't even breathe."

But Joseph twisted beneath him, nearly dislodging him as he rolled onto his back, fists flailing. Ben swore as Joseph punched Ben's injured knee, knocking him off balance. Shit—

"Ben!" Mari's voice broke through his concentration, and he glanced toward her just in time to see her grab Joseph's gun off the ground and throw it to him.

Swearing at the sight of a loaded gun sailing through the air, Ben concentrated on catching it without firing the damn thing. He caught it, and aimed it at Joseph's forehead. "I've killed two men," he snarled. "Give me one reason to make it three." His entire body was shaking with the need to pull the trigger, but his hand was steady, ready to do it.

Joseph went still, staring at him, clearly trying to decide whether Ben had the goods to actually shoot him.

"Just blink," Ben said, his voice low. "That's all the reason I need. Just one blink."

For a long moment, they just looked at each other, Ben staring into the face of the man he'd been hunting for so long, the man who had stolen so much from him. Those pitiless eyes burned into his brain, and he knew he would never forget them as long as he lived.

Joseph suddenly closed his eyes, and let his head fall back to the earth in defeat.

But Ben didn't move, not trusting him, not for a minute. He was afraid to even take his eyes off him. "Mari?" he could barely croak out her name. His body was beginning to shut down, a coldness creeping up his limbs. But still, he kept the gun steady on Joseph. "Tell me you're okay."

"I'm okay."

He jumped at how near her voice was, jerking his gaze off Joseph for a split second, just long enough to see Mari walking toward him. Her clothes were streaked with blood, her face filthy and bruised, but she was alive.

His throat suddenly tightened up, and all he wanted to do was hold her. "Mari," he whispered. "Mari."

"I got it," Haas said, limping up to them, his eyes flashing with that old intelligence Ben recognized. "Give me the gun. You look like you're about to pass out."

"I'm fine." But even as he spoke, his strength seemed to give out, and he slithered off Joseph, no longer able to hold himself up. Haas grabbed the gun from his hand, pointing it at Joseph before the bastard could move.

Ben held up his arms for Mari, and she fell into them, going down on her knees to hug him. He buried his face in her hair as pain and weakness seemed to close in on him. Now that it was over, and now that she was safe, suddenly all his injuries were beating at him, his adrenaline no longer able to carry him for even one more minute. He focused on the warmth of her body against his, on the softness of her hair against his face, on the strength in her body as she held him. "I love you, Mari," he whispered.

"I love you, too, Ben," she said back. Her voice was beautiful and warm, filling him with the most amazing peace.

He'd done it.

It was over.... Over? Suddenly he became viscerally aware of the intense weakness engulfing his body and the coldness creeping through his limbs. Sudden terror hit him. He wasn't ready to die. Not yet. Not when he had finally found a reason to live. "Help," he whispered, before collapsing into her arms.

⧓

Mari gasped as Ben fell against her, his body a dead weight in her arms. "Ben?" She touched his cheek, but his skin was ice cold. His eyes were closed, his dark lashes flush against his cheek. She looked at her hand, and saw it was caked in blood. His blood. "Oh, my God. He's dying." She carefully eased Ben off her lap, then lunged to her feet to run to the house to call 9-1-1, but before she could take a step, she saw Joseph move ever so slightly.

Terrified, she spun toward him, her heart pounding. Haas was standing over Joseph, the gun aimed at Joseph's head. Haas looked pale and weak, and she saw Joseph eyeing him, as if trying to decide if he could move before Haas could react.

"I'm fine," Haas said, answering the question she hadn't even asked. "I can shoot the eyelashes off a turtle when I haven't slept in a month and have lost ninety percent of my blood. If this piece of shit so much as blinks, I'm going to get my first kill in three years, and I'm going to love every second of it." He raised the gun. "Move, you piece of shit. Just move."

Joseph put his head back down and stared at the sky.

"Go, Mari," Haas said. "Go!"

Mari dropped to her knees beside Ben, and pulled him onto her lap. "You stay alive, dammit," she ordered. "You just took down my ex-fiancé, and you owe me a new one!"

A faint smile curved the corner of Ben's mouth. "Is that a proposal?" he rasped, not even opening his eyes.

Relief rushed through her at the sound of his voice, and tears burned in her eyes. "No, it's a threat!" She kissed him quickly, and his hand inched across the ground to her calf, brushing against her in a tender gesture that made her throat tighten. "Don't die on me," she whispered. "Don't you dare."

"Trying my best," he mumbled back.

"Go!" Haas shouted. "The phone is on the kitchen wall!"

Mari set Ben aside, then scrambled to her feet, racing desperately along the same path that she'd run only moments before, trying to save her own life. Now it was Ben whose life was in critical danger. And Charlotte. Dear God, Charlotte! Mari leapt up the front steps and raced into the house. She didn't even take time to check on her friend, knowing that all that mattered right now was getting help for them both.

She skidded around the corner into the kitchen, lunged for the black cordless phone stuck to the wall and frantically dialed for help. As she rattled off the address and told the operator what had happened, she raced back into the living room to Charlotte. Her friend's eyes were closed, her face ashen, her body utterly still, bright red blood still oozing through her shirt. "Oh, my God," she whispered into the phone. "I think she's dead."

She threw the phone on the coffee table, not even bothering to listen to the operator's questions. She knelt beside the couch and pressed her fingers to Charlotte's neck. For an agonizingly long moment, she felt nothing, and then, a faint heartbeat. Tears filled her eyes, and she pulled back Charlotte's shirt to see her stomach and check the damage. "Oh, God," she whispered, horrified by what she saw. He hadn't stabbed her. He'd carved letters into her belly. *Mine*. A claim of ownership she would carry for the rest of her life.

Charlotte's eyes fluttered open, and she looked dully at Mari.

"It's over," Mari whispered. "It's done. Haas has him at gunpoint, and we're waiting for the police."

"I want to see. Show me."

Mari's gaze flickered to the wounds on Charlotte's belly. "I don't want to move you."

"Please," Charlotte whispered, her voice barely rasping from her cracked lips. "I have to see."

Mari knew what she meant. She'd relived the murder of her parents a thousand times since it had happened, and she'd been unable to get those horrible images out of her head. Charlotte's last sight of Joseph had to be the right one, one that she could recreate when the memories of what he'd done tried to overtake her. "Come on." Her arms trembling with fatigue she refused to acknowledge, Mari scooped up Charlotte. Her friend's arm snaked around her neck as she gasped in pain, resting her head against Mari's shoulder. Willing herself the strength to carry the other woman, Mari staggered toward the door and down the steps.

In the pale light of the moon, Haas was still standing over Joseph, and Ben was lying on his side, facing the other two men, as if he were standing guard even in his prone position. Her heart tightened at the sight of the two men who had saved her, who had stood by her through so much. She had come to Alaska to find herself, and she had found her new home, her new family. Violence had shattered her old life, but violence had also brought her a new one.

She tripped over a rock, and lost her balance. She fell to her knees, and Charlotte spilled out of her arms. Her friend cried out in agony, and Haas looked sharply over.

The instant he did, Joseph leapt to his feet, lunging toward the gun.

Mari screamed a warning, but it was too late. His hands were already closing around Haas's fist, turning the gun toward Ben—

Ben erupted off the ground with sudden ferocity, lunging for Haas's hand as the old man fell backward, knocked off balance. The gun went off in a deafening explosion, and Mari screamed as time seemed to stand still for an eternity.

Then, to her shock and disbelief, she saw Joseph flying backwards, his hands outstretched as he fell onto his back, a broad stain spreading across his chest. He landed with a thump, his eyes open and glazed as he gasped for breath.

Ben collapsed on his side, somehow still pointing the gun at Joseph. Behind him, Haas struggled to a sitting position, his elderly body shaking.

For a long moment, no one moved, everyone frozen in time, watching Joseph as he fought for breath, as he struggled to hold onto life. And then, in the distance, she heard the wail of sirens, the same sirens that she and Ben had run from such a short time ago.

Then, through the darkness and the tension, came Charlotte's voice. "Die," she whispered. "Just die."

Sudden realization swept over Mari, and with it, sudden horror of what would happen if Joseph died. "No," she shouted.

"If he dies, then there's no way to prove that Ben is innocent." She leapt to her feet, ignoring the shouted warnings of the others, and raced over to Joseph. She tore her jacket off and pressed it to the wound in his chest, trying to stop the flow of blood.

"Mari," he gasped, trying to grab her hand.

"No." Ben's voice was a low warning, and she turned to see that he had dragged himself beside her. He was pressing the gun into the side of Joseph's head, somehow summoning strength he shouldn't have anymore. "One move, and you die."

Joseph looked at her, and in those eyes she saw regret and sadness. Regret not for what he had done, but rather, for what he had left undone. There was no more bitterness or hate. Just a man who had failed. In his eyes, an angel who had failed. A man so crazy he thought all he had done was offer the mercy of God to souls in need.

"Tell them," she said, as she pressed harder on his chest. "Tell the police everything. Cleanse your soul of the filth. Free your soul." He met her gaze just as the night filled with flashing blue lights, his face cold and ruthless. Doors slammed and troopers shouted, and she knew Joseph would never tell. He had no soul to be cleansed. He was the clean one. The women he'd murdered had been the tainted ones.

Frantic, she pressed harder on his chest, realizing what she had to say to him, realizing the words that would matter to him. "Tell them," she whispered, "so they understand what needs to be done, and they can continue your work. More women need to be saved, and..." She almost choked on the words, but Ben leaned his head against her leg, giving her strength. "Someone needs to punish the women who deserve it," she whispered. "Someone needs to finish what you started, but no one will know if you don't tell them everything you've done."

Joseph's eyes met hers, and there was a sudden desperation in them, but she couldn't tell what he was thinking. "Please," she whispered. "I'm still alive. Someone needs to finish me off—"

"Enough," Ben snarled. "Don't say that again, even if you don't mean it."

Suddenly, they were surrounded by officers with their guns pointing at Ben, shouting at him to put his weapon down.

"No," she shouted. "He saved our lives! He needs an ambulance! Don't arrest him!" She pointed at Joseph. "This man is the one who hurt us!"

The shouts of the cops changed, and suddenly the guns were all aimed at Joseph. With a low groan, Ben finally lowered the gun, and his whole body shuddered in relief. His face was bloody and dirty, pain etched in his eyes. Then he smiled, a private smile just for her. "We did it," he whispered to her even as the paramedics rushed over to him. Someone told him to drop the gun, and he did. Booted feet kicked it aside, out of his reach and Joseph's, and then they were rolling him over, quickly checking his injuries.

But Ben didn't take his gaze off her. "Nothing else matters. It's all okay now."

Her heart swelled with love for the man who had given so much for her and for his sister, but she knew it wasn't over. Once the police found out Ben's true identity, hell would begin again. He couldn't go to prison. She couldn't allow it. "It's not okay. Not yet." She turned back to Joseph. "Tell them the truth," she ordered bitterly. "You have a duty to make sure I die."

Joseph met her gaze, his lips whispered something she couldn't understand, and then strong hands pulled her off him. She stumbled to her feet as the paramedics and police swarmed them. Charlotte was already in an ambulance, Haas was standing and talking, and Ben was being lifted onto a stretcher. She fought past the officials trying to talk to her and ran across the battered earth toward Ben as they strapped him onto a gurney.

His eyes were closed now, his breathing shallow. "Ben?" She grabbed his hand as they began to wheel him across the dirt. "Ben!" There was no response. She looked at the paramedics. "What's wrong?"

"He's in shock. Please stand back." Someone grabbed her and pulled her away as they thrust Ben into the ambulance. The doors slammed shut, the sirens flashed and then he was gone, leaving her behind as he fought for his life.

CHAPTER 22

The light was too bright.

Swearing, Ben closed his eyes against the glare. His body hurt like hell, and his mind felt thick and foggy. Where the hell was he? He struggled to remember, and then recalled the scene with Joseph. "Mari!" He croaked out the words, terror ripping through him. "Mari —"

"Ben, it's me. It's okay." The most beautiful voice in the world whispered his name, and gentle, familiar hands touched his shoulder.

"Mari?" He couldn't stop the warmth that seemed to expand from the depths of his soul, and he cracked his eyes open. Leaning over him, her dark hair cascading past her cheeks, was the woman he'd been hunting for so long. Alive. Smiling at him. Safe. Relief seemed to crush him. "Mari," he croaked, his voice rusty with emotion and disuse.

She smiled, moisture glimmering in her beautiful eyes. "How do you feel? They operated on your knee and chest. They said the bullet hit so close to your heart. They have no idea how you managed to do all you did after you were shot. Your knee was a mess. How on earth did you stand on it?"

He grinned, ignoring how much it hurt to move, to even breathe. "I had to save my woman. There was no time to be hurt." He wasn't lying. He hadn't felt any pain until this moment, when he'd woken up and finally realized she was safe. He tried to move his hand toward her, but his arm seemed stuck. "Mari—"

She entwined her fingers with his, as if she knew what he wanted. "I'm here, Ben."

He squeezed her hand, his grip pathetically weak, but it just felt so incredibly good to feel her hand in his. Fatigue swam over him, and he closed his eyes again. "Joseph?"

"He told them everything," she said gently. "His real name is Walter Wainwright, and he killed a total of eleven women. You're exonerated, Ben. He confessed that he killed your sister. Her death is avenged."

At her words, his chest and throat tightened, and he suddenly couldn't breathe. A tear slid out of the corner of his eye. Grief washed over him, and guilt, but this time, there was also the faintest hint of redemption. Holly's death had stopped the cycle and prevented countless other women from suffering the same fate, including Mari. Her death had not been in vain.

Suddenly, all he wanted to do was hold onto his anchor, his life, his breath. "Mari," he whispered.

One word was all he'd said, but she understood, sliding into his embrace and wrapping her arms around him. He pressed his face against hers, inhaling her warmth and her scent. Together, they held each other, two people who had been through hell and had somehow, someway, survived. This woman, this amazing woman, had saved him, and he knew, without a doubt, that he never wanted to take even one step without her by his side. "I need you."

She pulled back slightly to look at him. With her shoulders blocking the light, he could see her better. There was a dark bruise by her eye, scratches on her face, and her short-sleeved shirt showed a heavy bandage on her arm. "Shit, you're so beautiful."

She smiled, her eyes softening. "You see things in me that no one else sees."

"As you do with me." Using his uninjured arm this time, he managed to lift his hand enough to trace his index finger down the curve of her nose. "I can't go back, you know."

She raised her eyebrows, snuggling more comfortably against him, but careful not to bump any of his injuries. Not that he'd care if she slammed her elbow into a wound. Having her tucked against him was worth any cost. "Back where?"

"To Boston. To the law firm. To that life." He shook his head, thinking of the empty existence he'd lived for so long. "I have to be here, with you. With Haas. In this wild land where all that crap doesn't matter."

She stared at him, her face paling. "But your career—"

"—made me choose work instead of my sister. I'm not that guy anymore, sweetheart." He took her hand, tightening his grip on her fingers. "I lost everything, and now that I've found it again, I'm not going to let go. I need to be here, with you, living and breathing with all of my soul." He kissed her lightly, not the deep kiss he wanted to do, but a kiss that simply promised the truth of his words. "I want to be the guy who holds you when the nightmares take away your peace. I want to be the guy who rebuilds your living room wall. I want to be the guy who gets to call you his wife and holds you every single night for the rest of his life." His voice thickened with emotion he'd denied for so long. "I love you, more than I ever knew was possible. Marry me, love me, and let me be a part of your life. I swear I won't let you down."

Tears filled her eyes. "There is no way on this earth that you could *ever* let me down. I love you, Ben. You've given me life, too. I'll hold onto you and what we have more tightly than I've ever held onto anything before."

He couldn't keep the grin off his face. "So, that's a yes, you'll marry me?"

Her face erupted into a broad smile that lit up her eyes. "Yes, of course it is."

"Say it," he whispered, lifting his uninjured hand to slide it behind her neck, urging her closer. "Say the words." He needed to hear it. He needed to know that this incredible woman, who knew all his darkest secrets, who had lived the hell that would always be a part of him, saw in him the things he had never thought were there. He needed to know it was real.

"Ben Forsett," she whispered against his mouth, "I will love you for all eternity with all of my soul, and I will absolutely marry you at the first possible chance we have. I don't want the big wedding. I don't want the fancy dress. I just want you."

And with that, she gave him everything he had needed for so long. She gave him her heart, and he gave her his, broken as it was, but he could already feel it starting to heal. "I love you," he whispered again, just as he kissed her, a kiss that promised the future that neither of them had ever thought would be theirs.

⬩⬧⬥⬧⬩

Ben wedged the crutch more securely under his arm, pretending to scowl as Mari gripped his arm more tightly. "I can walk, you know."

Yeah, it was vastly uncool to have to be practically carried down the hallway by a woman, but Ben had to admit that he'd almost be willing to have his other knee shot out just for the chance to have Mari wrapped around him so damned tightly. Yeah, in the week since he'd been home from the hospital he'd had Mari wrapped around him plenty, but it wasn't enough. He had a feeling it would never be enough.

"Don't be a manly man and deprive me of my joy at helping you," she teased, her eyes cheerful. There were still shadows haunting her, but there was also lightness and love radiating from her.

"I have to be a manly man. It's what I'm good at," he grunted as a sharp wave of pain knifed through his knee. Okay, never mind. Maybe he'd just tackle her in bed and skip the second knee-shattering thing.

She raised her brows. "Was that a groan of pain? Because that sounded like a groan of pain."

"Never." He managed a cocky grin, his pain fading in response to her gentle ribbing. "Damn, woman, you do realize that you're exactly what I need, don't you?"

Her smile widened. "Yes, I do. You can't live a moment without me."

"Not even one second." He slid his hand around her neck to pull her close for a kiss, until movement behind her drew his attention to the room they were approaching. A petite figure was curled up in the bed, and Haas was sitting next to her. Haas. Damn, it was good to see him. He still couldn't believe that Joseph had been able to fool him into thinking he was Haas, but Mari had told him that Joseph had grown up with a mother who worked in Hollywood as a makeup expert. He'd learned his trade well, apparently. Too well.

Haas and Charlotte appeared to be playing cards, but the feminine laughter drifting out into the hallway was forced and weak.

Charlotte. He hadn't seen her since the attack. She hadn't been taking visitors until today. Shit. She looked thin, too thin, and her shoulders were hunched. There was nothing left of the bold, sassy woman he'd met at O'Dell's.

"Charlotte?" Mari tapped lightly on the doorframe. "You want more company? Ben's here."

"Hey," he said quietly as he let Mari help him into the room. Mari had warned him, but Charlotte was so much worse than he'd expected. No wonder Mari had come up with the plan she had. He wasn't sure it would help Charlotte, but damn, she needed something.

"Hi, guys." Charlotte rolled toward them, her arm over her belly as if trying to contain the pain. She smiled faintly, and Mari touched her shoulder, giving her a light squeeze.

Noticing how bony Charlotte's shoulder felt beneath her touch, Mari felt her heart tighten. She was still so pale. But worst of all, was the fear in her eyes. Haas was sitting close to her, hunched over her protectively, giving her as much reassurance as his battered old frame could provide.

"So, great news," Charlotte said, with forced cheerfulness. "The doctor said I can go home." There was no joy in her eyes, though. Just the raw, stark fear of going back to the home that Joseph had snatched her from. Too many memories. Too many nightmares. "No lasting damage to my body, so yay, right?"

That was such a lie. The damage was not only lasting, but entirely permanent, etched on her body and soul forever. "What about the plastic surgery?"

Charlotte shook her head. "Not right now. I still have to heal, and they'll never make the skin flat again anyway. Just more scars, you know?"

Yes, maybe there'd be more scars, but at least the marks wouldn't have the claim of a madman etched across her flesh. Not that it would really matter. Even if the doctors were able to get "mine" off Charlotte's stomach, every time she saw her scarred skin, she would see the word that Joseph had carved there. Mari knew exactly how it would be for her: a nightmare that would never let her go.

"It will be good to be out of here," she said encouragingly. "Home is better than the hospital." Mari grabbed a chair for Ben, and he eased down beside the bed, leaning on her for support more than she knew he wanted to acknowledge. Mari perched on the mattress next to Charlotte. "Joseph—I mean Walter can't get you anymore," she said. "You'll be safe at home now."

"I wish he was dead," Charlotte said, her voice cracking. "Why can't he be dead? I don't want to know he's alive somewhere, even if he's in prison forever."

With a heavy sigh, Mari took her friend's hand. "Even if he's dead, it won't take away the nightmares, Charlotte. Only you can do that." There were so many shadows in her friend's eyes, shadows that had been there even before Joseph.

Charlotte's jaw tightened and she nodded. "I know. I can do it." But Mari knew it wasn't that easy.

"We'll all help you," Mari said. "Everyone in the area is on your side."

"Everyone in the area?" But instead of looking reassured, Charlotte stared at her. "How do they know?"

Mari blinked. How would anyone not know? "Well, it's been in the newspapers, and in the news. Everyone knows. But you don't need to worry, the whole community is on your side. Whatever you need, just ask.

"On the news? In the newspapers?" Charlotte's already pale face seemed to drain of all residual color. "Oh, my God. He'll see the reports. He'll know. He'll come back."

"He?" Mari stiffened, and she thought of the dog that Charlotte kept with her all the time to keep her safe. Safe from what? Safe from who? Beside her, Ben's body went rigid, and Haas sat up straighter as both men went on alert.

"*Who* will come back?" Ben's voice was low and tense, and chills pricked down Mari's spine.

But Charlotte just bit her lip and shook her head. "Nothing. It's fine. I just…" She fell silent, but she didn't need to say anymore. It wasn't only Joseph who gave her nightmares. It wasn't only Joseph who had taught Charlotte that some nightmares were real.

Maybe Mari had remembered Charlotte's hints about her past when she'd made her suggestion to Ben a couple days ago. Or maybe she was just all too aware of the nightmares that she'd had after her parents' murder, and the ones she still had about Joseph, night demons that went away only when Ben wrapped his arms around her in the middle of the night. Charlotte needed her own protector to give her peace so she could find her strength again.

Mari nudged Ben. "Ben has a suggestion for you."

Charlotte looked at him, and somehow she managed to sit taller and shut away the fear that Mari knew was lurking beneath the surface, still gripping her so tightly. "I still can't get used to your name being Ben," Charlotte said, tilting her head to study him. "You're much more of a John Sullivan. 'Ben' is too civilized for a guy who runs around shooting people with a shattered knee and a bullet in his chest."

Mari smiled at Charlotte's comment, a tiny indication that her friend's spunky spirit still lay buried in her somewhere. Charlotte was prepared to fight, and all she needed was someone to stand behind her to back her up.

Ben smiled gently as he took Mari's hand and held it between his. "My best friend is even less civilized than I am," he said. "And he's not happy that I got shot repeatedly."

Charlotte's brow knit. "So, what's he going to do? Come beat you up?"

"Nah, but he's going to come stay for a while." He leaned forward, his finger still tracing circles on Mari's palm even as he focused intently on Charlotte. "Mack Connor has been my best friend since I was a kid. He handles a gun as well as I do, and he can kill with his bare hands." His voice became rough. "I would trust him with my life," he said softly. "He's the most honorable man I know, and he's a completely untamed, pain-in-the-ass, badass."

Mari snorted. "Oh, come on, you're making him sound like a stereotype."

But Charlotte was staring at Ben, listening intently, just as Mari had suspected she would. "So?"

"So, he needs a place to stay while he's here. Haas said you've got extra space at your house." Ben grinned. "He's too cheap to stay at a hotel, and he's too damn surly for me to put up with him, but he sleeps with a gun under his pillow and likes to pace the house at night to make sure nothing is sneaking up on him."

Charlotte's gaze swiveled to Mari, disbelief gleaming in her eyes. "You guys are setting me up with a bodyguard?"

Mari grimaced. "You weren't supposed to figure that out."

Charlotte rolled her eyes. "It's not like I got hit in the head *that* many times. It's kind of obvious." She met Mari's gaze steadily. "I don't need charity."

Mari shrugged. "No, but Mack is in dire need of some, apparently. According to Ben, he's a messed-up train-wreck of a man who has some problems he's dealing with, and he's got nowhere else to go."

"What's wrong with him?" Charlotte looked at Ben suspiciously.

Ben just shrugged. "Not my place to tell. But as long as he's camped out at your place, you might as well be living in a fortress. He needs a place to crash, and he enjoys shooting anyone he doesn't like, which might come in handy for you."

A small smile flickered across Charlotte's face. "Doesn't that kind of thing get him put in jail sometimes?"

Another shrug. "Prison doesn't bother some people."

Charlotte's eyes widened, and Mari had a bad feeling that Ben was in the process of talking her out of taking Mack on as a boarder. She surreptitiously elbowed Ben in the side and interrupted him. "Ben said that Mack is so loyal that he'll give his life to save anyone he cares about. He's pretty sure that would extend to landlords who open their house to him." She held her breath, hoping that Charlotte would say yes. If nothing else, Mack would give Charlotte the security she needed to be able to relax enough to heal, at least physically.

She knew what it was like to hide in fear. Joseph might be behind bars, but Mari suspected that the threat that had made Charlotte get a guard dog meant that the other threat in her life wasn't entirely over. Charlotte needed help, even if it was simply feeling safe enough to sleep at night...but she had a feeling it was more than that, and if it was, then she definitely wanted Mack in

Charlotte's house. No way could her friend take another round like she'd just been through.

Charlotte looked at Ben. Her jaw was tensed in defiance, but there was a desperate hope in her eyes that belied her toughness. "Does he like dogs?"

"He was bitten when he was a kid, so he's scared shitless of them."

Charlotte raised her brows, the corner of her mouth curving up ever so slightly, and Mari could see her friend relax, knowing that she had a weapon against this man who wanted to invade her home. "Seriously?"

"We all have our flaws," Ben said with a grin. "So, you'll need to be gentle with him at first. Is it a deal? Can I tell him he can camp out at your place?"

Charlotte glanced at Mari, and she quickly nodded to show her support for the idea. "He helped us out with Joseph," she said. "And Ben trusts him."

Haas leaned forward, his intelligent eyes gleaming with the same intensity they had once had. "If he messes with you, just let me know, and I'll shoot his ass."

Charlotte burst out laughing at Haas's wink, and so did the others. It was good to have the real Haas back with them. With a grateful smile, Charlotte finally nodded. "Okay, he can stay with me while he's here. How long will he be in town?"

"I don't know," Ben said while Mari grinned with giddy relief. They'd done it! Charlotte would feel secure, and be safe if any more threats came her way. "He's not the kind of guy to share long-term travel plans with anyone. A couple days? Ten years? You never know with him."

"Ten years?" Wariness flickered over Charlotte's face, and Mari knew that she was already beginning to second-guess her decision to let Mack stay.

But it was too late for her to back out. They'd timed it this way on purpose. Charlotte was stuck, exactly as they planned. As if sensing their underhandedness, Charlotte looked around at the three of them, her eyes narrowing in suspicion. "When does he arrive?"

Ben looked at his watch. "His plane lands in about two hours."

"What?" Charlotte almost shrieked.

He grinned at Charlotte's shocked face. "Don't worry, he's the kind of anti-social miscreant that everyone hates, and you'll love him the minute you meet him." He looked over at Mari. "Just like me, right?"

A beautiful warmth seemed to spread over Mari, and she smiled. "Utterly loveable, in every way," she agreed.

Ben grinned, a wicked gleam in his eyes as he bent over to kiss her, his hand sliding along her thigh in a secret, intimate promise of what was to come. Oh, yes, utterly loveable, and all hers.

SNEAK PEEK: ICE

ALASKA HEAT
AVAILABLE NOW

Kaylie's hands were shaking as she rifled through her bag, searching for her yoga pants. She needed the low-slung black ones with a light pink stripe down the side. The cuffs were frayed from too many wearings to the grocery store late at night for comfort food, and they were her go-to clothes when she couldn't cope. Like now.

She couldn't find them.

"Come on!" Kaylie grabbed her other suitcase and dug through it, but they weren't there. "Stupid pants! I can't—" A sob caught at her throat and she pressed her palms to her eyes, trying to stifle the swell of grief. "Sara—"

Her voice was a raw moan of pain, and she sank to the thick shag carpet. She bent over as waves of pain, of loneliness, of utter grief shackled her. For her parents, her brother, her family and now Sara—

Dear God, she was all alone.

"Dammit, Kaylie! Get up!" she chided herself. She wrenched herself to her feet. "I can do this." She grabbed a pair of jeans and a silk blouse off the top of her bag and turned toward the bathroom. One step at a time. A shower would make her feel better.

She walked into the tiny bathroom, barely noticing the heavy wood door as she stepped inside and flicked the light switch. Two bare light bulbs flared over her head, showing a rustic bathroom with an ancient footed tub and a raw wood vanity with a battered porcelain sink. A tiny round window was on her right. It was small enough to keep out the worst of the cold, but big enough to let in some light and breeze in the summer.

She was in Alaska, for sure. God, what was she doing here?

Kaylie tossed the clean clothes on the sink and unzipped

her jacket, dropping it on the floor. She tugged all her layers off, including the light blue sweater that had felt so safe this morning when she'd put it on. She stared grimly at her black lace bra, so utterly feminine, exactly the kind of bra that her mother had always considered frivolous and completely impractical. Which it was. Which was why that was the only style Kaylie ever wore.

She should never have come to Alaska. She didn't belong here. She couldn't handle this. Kaylie gripped the edge of the sink. Her hands dug into the wood as she fought against the urge to curl into a ball and cry.

After a minute, Kaylie lifted her head and looked at herself in the mirror. Her eyes were wide and scared, with dark circles beneath. Her hair was tangled and flattened from her wool hat. There was dirt caked on her cheeks.

Kaylie rubbed her hand over her chin, and the streaks of mud didn't come off.

She tried again, then realized she had smudges all over her neck. She turned on the water, and wet her hands...and saw her hands were covered as well.

Stunned, Kaylie stared as the water ran over her hands, turning pink as it swirled in the basin.

Not dirt.

Sara's blood.

"Oh, God." Kaylie grabbed a bar of soap and began to scrub her hands. But the blood was dried, stuck to her skin. "Get off!" She rubbed frantically, but the blackened crust wouldn't come off. Her lungs constricted and she couldn't breathe. "I can't—"

The door slammed open, and Cort stood behind her, wearing a T-shirt and jeans.

The tears burst free at the sight of Cort, and Kaylie held up her hands to him. "I can't get it off—"

"I got it." Cort took her hands and held them under the water, his grip warm and strong. "Take a deep breath, Kaylie. It's okay."

"It's not. It won't be." She leaned her head against his shoulder, closing her eyes as he washed her hands roughly and efficiently. His muscles flexed beneath her cheek, his skin hot through his shirt. Warm. Alive. "Sara's dead," she whispered.

"My parents. My brother. They're all gone. The blood—" Sobs broke free again, and she couldn't stop the trembling.

"I know. I know, babe." He pulled her hands out from under the water and grabbed a washcloth. He turned her toward him and began to wash her face and neck.

His eyes were troubled, his mouth grim. But his hands were gentle where he touched her, gently holding her face still while he scrubbed. His gaze flicked toward hers, and he held contact for a moment, making her want to fall into those brown depths and forget everything. To simply disappear into the energy that was him. "You have to let them go," he said. "There's nothing you can do to bring them back—"

"No." A deep ache pounded at Kaylie's chest and her legs felt like they were too weak to support her. "I can't. Did you see Sara? And Jackson? His throat—" She bent over, clutching her stomach. "I—"

Cort's arms were suddenly around her, warm and strong, pulling her against his solid body. Kaylie fell into him, the sobs coming hard, the memories—

"I know." Cort's whisper was soft, his hand in her hair, crushing her against him. "It sucks. Goddamn, it sucks."

Kaylie heard his grief in the raw tone of his voice and realized his body was shaking as well. She looked up and saw a rim of red around his eyes, shadows in the hollows of his whiskered cheeks. "You know," she whispered, knowing with absolute certainty that he did. He understood the grief consuming her.

"Yeah." He cupped her face, staring down at her, his grip so tight it was almost as desperate as she felt. She could feel his heart beating against her nearly bare breasts, the rise of his chest as he breathed, the heat of his body warming the deathly chill from hers.

For the first time in forever, she suddenly didn't feel quite as alone.

In her suffering, she had company. Someone who knew. Who understood. Who shared her pain. It had been so long since the dark cavern surrounding her heart had lessened, since she hadn't felt consumed by the loneliness, but with Cort holding her...there was a flicker of light in the darkness trying to take her. "Cort—"

He cleared his throat. "I gotta go check the chili." He dropped his hands from her face and stood up to go, pulling away from her.

Without his touch, the air felt cold and the anguish returned full force. Kaylie caught his arm. "Don't go—" She stopped, not sure what to say, what to ask for. All she knew was that she didn't want him to leave, and she didn't want him to stop holding her.

Cort turned back to her, and a muscle ticked in his cheek.

For a moment, they simply stared at each other. She raised her arms. "Hold me," she whispered. "Please."

He hesitated for a second, and then his hand snaked out and he shackled her wrist. He yanked once, and she tumbled into him. Their bodies smacked hard as he caught her around the waist, his hands hot on her bare back.

She threw her arms around his neck and sagged into him. He wrapped his arms around her, holding her tightly against him. With only her bra and his T-shirt between them, the heat of his body was like a furnace, numbing her pain. His name slipped out in a whisper, and she pressed her cheek against his chest. She focused on his masculine scent. She took solace in the feel of another human's touch, in the safety of being held in arms powerful enough to ward off the grief trying to overtake her.

His hand tunneled in her hair, and he buried his face in the curve of her neck, his body shaking against hers.

"Cort—" She started to lift her head to look at him, to see if he was crying, but he tightened his grip on her head, forcing her face back to his chest, refusing to allow her to look at him.

Keeping her out.

Isolating her.

She realized he wasn't a partner in her grief. She was alone, still alone, always alone.

All the anguish came cascading back. Raw loneliness surged again, and she shoved away from him as sobs tore at her throat. She couldn't deal with being held by him when the sense of intimacy was nothing but an illusion. "Leave me alone."

Kaylie whirled away from him, keeping her head ducked. She didn't want to look at him. She needed space to find her equilibrium again and rebuild her foundation.

"Damn it, Kaylie." Cort grabbed her arm and spun her back toward him.

She held up her hands to block him, her vision blurred by the tears streaming down her face. "Don't—"

His arms snapped around her and he hauled her against him even as she fought his grip. "No! Leave me alone—"

His mouth descended on hers.

Not a gentle kiss.

A kiss of desperation and grief and need. Of the need to control *something*. Of raw human passion for life, for death, for the touch of another human being.

And it broke her.

Sneak Peek: Chill

Alaska Heat
Available Now

"Yeah." Luke looked away from his friend. He didn't want to talk about his past. He didn't feel like opening doors with Cort that had stayed firmly closed during their long friendship. They'd been partners for eight years, but he'd hired Cort on several occasions prior when he'd come to Alaska to do research.

He shifted in his chair as he surveyed the bar. The juke box was blaring. A few pilots were hanging around. Some locals. Place was gloomy as hell.

It had never bothered him before. But right now, the moody atmosphere was grating on him big time.

"I'm going outside." He shoved his chair back to stand up, and then the front door opened. In walked a woman of the ilk he hadn't seen in eight years, since he left Boston. Her dark hair cascaded down her back. Even in the dim light of the bar it was glistening.

It looked as soft as the fur on a Husky pup.

It reminded him of the kind of hair women shelled out a thousand bucks a week to maintain. Women in Alaska didn't bother. Women in Alaska let their true beauty speak for themselves.

This woman was not from Alaska.

She strode up to the bartender and began hammering him with questions. She was gesturing furiously, her hands flying around like she was agitated beyond hell.

The bartender nodded in Luke's direction, and she turned and looked directly at Luke.

He immediately sat up, his body responding when he felt the heat of her inspection. Her eyes were black as the sky during a stormy night, but they were alive and dangerous. Sensuous and passionate. He knew instantly that this was a woman who ran hot, who didn't hold back from whatever was in her heart. She sort of reminded him of how he used to be, before he'd realized living that way made too many people die.

Her jaw was out, and she looked fiercely determined. Yet there was a weariness to her posture, and dark circles under her eyes, visible even in the dim light. She rubbed her shoulder and winced, her body jerking with pain.

Her vulnerability made him want to get up and haul ass over there and offer her help.

Her eyes widened at his expression, and a hint of red flushed her cheeks. The she plunked herself wearily down on a barstool and turned away from him.

Just as well. Luke still had issues when it came to woman in need. Big issues. The kind of issues that haunted his dreams and brought him screaming to consciousness, his body drenched in sweat.

His skin began to feel hot, and it wasn't just from the strip of smooth skin peeking out between the bottom of her sweater and the waistband of her very low-cut jeans... He peered closer and caught a glimpse of a bit of lacy black thong above her jeans.

He'd seen that action on plenty of women and it didn't do much for him, but on her...shit. All his blood was heading south at full speed. Despite her attire, there was a level of innocent sensuality that was drawing him like a grizzly to a picnic basket.

He inspected her more closely, needing to assimilate as much information about her as possible to explain his reaction to her. Her shoulder blades were strong, and her back narrowed into a trim waist and toned hips. The woman took care of herself. Yoga? Most of those wealthy women seemed to have so much time on their hands, they did nothing but spend hours in the gym to try to attract the powerful, rich men they had their sights set on.

Was that her? It didn't feel accurate. She was more than that. The fancy clothes were window dressing, meant to obscure a deeper truth she was trying to hide.

He narrowed his eyes, quickly tabulating all the data so he could make an accurate assessment. It was difficult to tell from this distance, but the sweater appeared to be cashmere. High quality, given its lines. He'd guess upwards of a thousand bucks for it. And her jeans...he recognized the designer brand on that fine ass of hers. His gaze dropped to her boots...heels were low and practical, but the leather was clearly soft and supple, and the seams had that extra bit of style he recognized from his own mother's closet. In fact, she seemed to be wearing exactly the kind of outfit all his dad's women used to wear, once he got finished dressing them up like the Barbie dolls they were willing to be for a chance at his money and his power.

From the brief glance Luke had at had her face, however, this woman was beautiful in a natural way. She didn't need all the glam to look good, but she apparently went in for it anyway. She was refined and beautiful, she was as far from Alaska and carnage as a woman got, and she was exactly what he wanted to bury himself in right now to forget the hell he'd been in for the last fifteen hours.

She turned toward him suddenly, as if sensing his continued perusal. When she saw him watching her, she sat up straighter, and he saw in her something he hadn't expected. Courage. Strength. The woman was a survivor. Not a weak female. She was strong, and that put him over the top.

After what had happened eight years ago, weak, scared, defenseless woman scared the shit out of him. But a woman who was a survivor? Hot as hell. The cashmere? It was escape from Alaskan hell he'd been crawling in the last two days.

Her gaze dropped to his mouth, but then she quickly averted her gaze, shutting him out.

"Too late, my dear," he whispered under his breath. "Too damn late."

He shoved back his chair and stood.

"You heading out?" Then Cort followed Luke's gaze, and he grinned. "She's a little too prettied-up for these parts, isn't she?"

"Damn straight she is." And then Luke headed right for her.

Sneak Peek: Fairytale Not Required

Ever After
Available Now

A car door slammed, and Jason tensed. Shit. He wasn't in the mood to be sociable right now. If the little old lady from his fantasies had finally shown up with a plate of cookies, she was too damn late. She was just going to have to leave them on the porch.

Jason sheathed the blade of the utility knife back into the casing, waiting for that inevitable ring of the doorbell. How many times had he answered his door to find another note of condolence or another casserole after Lucas's death, and then Kate's? Well-meaning acquaintances who thought that a smile and a slab of meatloaf would ease the gaping void in his soul. He'd stopped answering the door, because there was no way to pretend to be appreciative when all the darkness was consuming him.

And now, after fighting like hell to get past that, after scraping his way back into a place from which he could function, all those emotions had returned, brought on by the overwhelming silence of his house. That same silence that had flooded him when he'd come back home after watching his son die at the hospital and felt the gaping absence of Lucas.

Silence fucking sucked, but a doorbell was no better.

But the doorbell didn't ring, and the car didn't drive away.

Scowling, Jason walked across the landing to peer out the back window at the driveway.

Astrid Munroe's rusted junker was in his driveway. *Astrid.* He'd forgotten she was coming.

Adrenaline rushed through him, breaking him free from the tentacles of the past. His heart suddenly began to beat again, thudding back to life with a jolting ache. He tossed the knife aside, spun away from the window and vaulted down the stairs, taking them three at a time, almost desperate for the air he knew

Astrid would feed back into his lungs.

He jerked the back door open and stepped out onto the front porch, unable to keep the hum of anticipation from vibrating through him. "Astrid?"

Her car was empty, and she was nowhere in sight.

Trepidation rippled through him. Another woman dead? He immediately shook his head, shutting out the fear that had cropped up out of habit. Instead, he quickly scanned his property, knowing she had to be there somewhere.

But there was no Astrid. Frowning, Jason jogged down the pathway that led around the house toward the lake front, urgency coursing through him to find the one woman who had brought that brief respite into his life, that flash of sunshine, that gaping moment of relief from all that he carried. Where was she? He had to find her. *Now.*

Jason was almost sprinting by the time he rounded the rear corner of his house and saw her. The moment he saw her, he stopped dead, utterly awed by the sight before him.

"Son of a bitch," he whispered under his breath as he stared at the woman who'd rocked his world only a few hours before.

Astrid was standing on one of the rocks on the edge of the lake, silhouetted by an unbelievable sunset. The sky was vibrating with reds, oranges and a vibrant violet, casting the passionate array of colors across the lake's surface. Astrid's hands were on her hips, her face tilted up toward the sky, as if she were drinking the beauty of the sunset right through her skin. Her auburn hair was framed in vibrant orange and violet, a wild array of passion that seemed to mesh with the wild woods around her.

Her sandals were on the ground beside the rock, her bare toes gripping the boulder. She was wearing the same jeans and tank top as she had earlier, despite the slight evening coolness cropping up in the air. It was as if she hadn't bothered to notice, as if she couldn't deign herself to succumb to something so mundane as a cool breeze.

She was above it all, and Jason felt the tightness in his lungs easing simply from being in her presence. *Astrid.*

He knew then that he hadn't come to Birch Crossing for the town, or for the plate of cookies, or even for the damn pizza store he was planning to open. He had come for her. For Astrid. For the sheer, raw passion that she exuded with every breath.

She was the epitome of freedom, of passion, of life. Rightness roared through him at the sight of her on his land, basking in the sunset, breathing in the air that he suddenly noticed. The fresh, clean scent of woods and crystalline water filled him, as if Astrid's reverence of their surroundings had brought his own senses back to life.

She was beautiful. Not simply beautiful. She was beauty itself, the definition of all that it could be in a person's wildest, most desperate imagination.

Yearning crashed through Jason to lose himself in her, to use her vibrant energy to wipe away the smut covering his soul and give him the chance to breathe again, to find his path in this second chance that he'd tried to give his son. He was captivated by her, even the way she ignored protocol and had helped herself to his rock and the sunset, not even bothering to ring the doorbell. She was a free spirit, a woman who didn't fit into the town and didn't care.

He wanted that freedom. He needed to get caught up in her spell. He would never survive if he didn't find a way to forget, even for a minute, all the burdens crashing down on him. There was no choice, no other path, no other option, than to lose himself in the aura that was Astrid. To remember that there was something else in life beside the darkness that consumed him.

"It's beautiful, isn't it?" She didn't turn around, but her voice drifted to him, a melody that seemed to crawl under his skin and ignite flames within him.

"Yes, it is." He began to walk toward her, tentative, almost afraid of spooking her and losing the moment. But he couldn't keep from approaching her. He was drawn to her as if she were a magnet, calling to his soul, to the part of him that had once been alive. His need for her was pulsing through every cell of his body, so intense that it almost hurt, as if something inside of him was fighting its way to life after an eternity of being dead.

"This is the best place in town to watch the sunset. Is that why you bought it?" She spoke softly, almost as if she were afraid to disturb the beauty of the sunset.

"I haven't noticed a sunset in years," he admitted as he reached her. He stopped beside the rock, suddenly uncertain of how to approach. Of what to do next. Of how to get closer. "I bought the house because it has lake front, and I thought Noah would like it."

Astrid turned her head slightly to look at him, and he caught his breath at the sight of her face. The sun was casting a soft glow, illuminating her face so that her eyes seemed to vibrate with depth and passion... He realized suddenly that there was none of the levity in her expression that he'd seen before. Just pain and emotion, fighting to be free. His chest tightened for the agony he saw in her face, for the depth of trauma that seemed to echo what beat so mercilessly in his own soul. Outrage suddenly exploded through him, fury that someone had inflicted such damage on this angel that she could harbor such pain. Astrid was so free, so untamed, that she should be gallivanting across the surface of the lake, not looking at him as if her heart had been carved right out her chest.

"You don't notice sunsets?" she asked.

He barely heard her words or registered his response to her. All he could think about was the woman before him, the depth of her spirit, his need to somehow chase away the shadows and bring back the spirit that he knew was coursing through her veins. "No. I wouldn't have noticed this one if you weren't out here."

She shook her head, and that teasing glint sparkled in her eyes again, making his stomach leap. *Yes, Astrid. Come back to me.* He moved closer to the rock, ruthlessly drawn toward her.

She grinned at him. "Well, you've got some learnin' to do, Sarantos, if you're going to be living in this here town. Sunset appreciation is mandatory for all residents, and you'll be quizzed every morning at Wright's when you show up for your coffee." She held out her hand and beckoned with her fingers. "Up," she ordered.

Jason grinned at her bold command, and he immediately set his hand in hers. Electricity leapt through him as his skin touched hers, and she sucked in her breath at the contact. Wariness flashed in her eyes, and Jason sensed she was about to retreat.

No chance.

He wasn't missing this moment.

He immediately tightened his grip on hers and hauled himself up onto the rock beside her. The peak of the boulder was smaller than he'd expected, bringing them dangerously close to each other. For a moment, neither of them moved. He just stared down at her, and she gazed at him, her brown eyes wide and nervous. Her pulse was hammering in her throat, and he instinctively pressed his index finger on it, trying to ease it down. "Your heart is racing."

Those dark, expressive eyebrows of hers shot up, and she lifted her chin. "Beautiful sunsets get my adrenaline going."

"Do they?" They were so close to each other that he could feel the heat from her body. "Shouldn't they calm your soul and ease the stress from your body?" He moved closer, easing across the boulder. "Are you afraid of me, Astrid? I won't hurt you."

She blinked, and he saw doubt flicker across her face again. "Don't touch me," she whispered.

Instead of moving his fingers away from her throat, he traced her collarbone. Goosebumps popped up on her skin, and she sucked in her breath.

Awareness leapt through him at her transparent response, at the realization she was as affected by the touch as he was. Sudden desire blasted through him, raw, physical need that leapt straight to his loins. Jason froze, shocked by the pulse of physical need that shot through him. Son of a bitch. He hadn't responded to a woman in years. *Years.* "Jesus, Astrid," he whispered. "What is it about you?"

She shook her head once, her eyes so wide that he could read every nuance of her emotions. Unexpected, powerful desire, coupled with a fear so deep that it came from her soul. Excitement. Anticipation. Uncertainty. Vulnerability. "It's not me," she whispered. "It's you."

He spread his hand over the back of her neck, basking in the sensation of her skin beneath his palm. She felt so alive, vibrating with life, and yet at the same time, her skin was so delicate and soft that protectiveness surged through him. A need to be the strong male and take care of her, in the way that his former wife had never allowed him to do. His fingers tightened on her neck and he drew her closer. "No. It's both of us."

Astrid braced her palm on his chest, blocking him. "Don't," she said. "Please, don't."

"I can't help it." He couldn't tear her gaze off her eyes, off the myriad of expressions racing through them. He couldn't breathe. He felt like his soul was screaming with desperation, frantic for one chance, one moment, one kiss with this woman. As if the brush of her lips could save him from the free fall threatening to consume him. "I need to kiss you, Astrid. Now."

Sneak Peek: Inferno of Darkness

The Order of the Blade
Available Now

In the beginning, many centuries ago...

He wanted her.

There was no way for Dante to deny his response to the whispered warning she had sent dancing along the breeze to him. He had no idea who she was, or what she looked like, but her voice was like the harmony of early morning, the whisper of new leaves brushing against the dew, the delicateness of flower blossoms coming to life. The energy of her words spun through him with restless temptation, prying him from his dark thoughts about Louis and the bloodbath he'd left behind.

In his world, craving a woman this intensely was a very, *very* dangerous thing.

He wanted to race toward her.

He wanted to rip aside the canopy of leaves shielding her from his sight.

He wanted to find her, to claim her, to consume her.

So, instead, he stopped and went completely still. He reached out with his preternatural senses, searching the landscape ahead. The mountain was ominously tall. Turbulent dark clouds coated the sky above him, but it wasn't enough to block her. He caught the faint scent of woman, pure and delicate, and his gut clenched in response. But still, he didn't move. Instead, he carefully located the pulsing energy of the sword she was guarding. She was between him and the sword, an obstacle that he had to pass in order to retrieve the weapon.

Testing her, he turned left, circling around behind her. As he moved, she shifted, keeping herself between him and the sword. She could sense him? Was her awareness of him as intense as his awareness of him?

He looked down at the protective symbols on his arms and saw they were still blazing. As long as they were visible, the *sheva* bond could not affect him. No woman could be his soulmate. He was still safe from that fate...but if that was the case, why was he reacting to her so intensely? He had no time for women. He had no time for seduction. He was never distracted from what he had to do.

So, what the hell was going on with her?

He had no time to play games any longer. He needed that sword, and he needed it now, which meant he had to get past her. He was tempted to call out his spears, but he didn't. Never would there come a day when he approached a woman armed. Ever.

So, instead, he straightened up, fisted his hands, and strode right through the undulating shadows toward her.

His feet were silent on the forest floor, and the leaves moved out of his way as he walked, responding to his silent request for passage, as they always did. Ahead of him, he could see that the trees thinned, and he knew he was approaching a clearing.

His weapons still burning in his arms, responding to the risk she presented, Dante stepped forward through the last of the foliage and into the open, exposed area.

He didn't see her.

Disappointment surged through him as he quickly scanned the vicinity. Trees stood tall above him, their branches long and spindly, tangling into each other, weaving a canopy that protected this area from the rest of the world. Sparse grass clung to barren dirt. Ancient rocks lay battered, half-submerged in the weary ground. He could sense the suffering of this place, of the people who had once lived and died in this clearing. So much to tell him, and yet the one thing he wanted to know more about was hidden. He saw no sign of her, but her presence was strong, a vibrating energy of light and dark. "Show yourself," he commanded.

Again, no response. Not even another whispered reply on the wind.

Awareness still prickling on his neck, he walked further into the clearing, reaching out with his senses, searching for a ripple in the atmosphere that would reveal her location. Out into each direction he sent queries, and then he found her. A block in the transference of energy, a shield of sorts, in the northwest end of the clearing.

He turned toward it, his hands still flexing. Behind her, he could feel the sword's energy calling to him, more intensely than ever before. The urge to respond to its summons was thundering through him, almost impossible to resist, but he refused to acknowledge it. This woman, this mysterious woman who was guarding it, this sensual temptation of danger...she was what he needed to deal with first.

He kept his gaze riveted on the swirl of feminine energy that he'd located. He couldn't see her, but he knew she was there. "I am going to take the sword," he said.

"No." Her voice was clear, a shot to his gut with the raw intensity of it. It wasn't simply feminine, it was powerful and strong, rich with sensuality. "Walk away."

"It's been calling to me." He took a step closer, and felt a sudden burst of wind slam against his chest, as if she'd shoved the air at him as a warning. Could she manipulate air? He'd never heard of that. "The sword wants me to retrieve it."

"Do not touch it." As the words filled the air, a faint mist began to glisten in the location he was watching, like millions of dew droplets in the first rays of morning light.

Adrenaline and anticipation roared through him, and he was riveted by the rainbow-colored prisms as they glittered and sparkled, becoming less transparent. Then he saw her face beginning to take shape. An incredible, vibrant turquoise began to glow as it slid into the shape of her nose, a delicate slope of pure femininity. Smooth cheeks of perfection, the sensual curve of her jaw, parted lips. Her hair began to appear, tumbling down around her in violet and turquoise cascades of thick curls. And then her eyes. Dante stood, transfixed, as her eyes appeared, vibrant blue pools flanked with long, thick lashes, watching him intently.

Her body began to manifest. Long, delicate arms, a mystical dress clinging to her body, showing small breasts of surreal temptation, hips that bled into lean legs, bare feet that seemed to fade right into the grassy tufts by her toes.

"What are you?" he asked, his voice gruffer than he'd intended.

"I don't exist here." There was a sudden shimmer, as if a thousand prisms had shifted position, and then she was standing before him, fully corporeal, with flesh as human as his. Her cascade of colors shifted into a rich, decadent shower of brown curls, and an endless temptation of flesh so pale it looked as though it had never seen the sun. But her eyes were the same, a vibrant, iridescent symphony of violet, rich blue, and enchantment.

Stunned, he closed the distance between them, compelled by the need to touch her. To see if she was real. She lifted her chin regally as he neared. She did not retreat, but her muscles tensed, and a ripple of fear echoed through the air.

He stopped a mere foot from her and raised his hand. Gently, almost afraid that he would shatter the mirage, he brushed his fingers ever so lightly over the ends of her curls. Silken strands glided through his fingers, the softest sensation he'd ever experienced. She closed her eyes and went utterly still, as if drinking in his touch with every ounce of her being.

"You *do* exist here," he said softly, forcing himself to drop his hand, trying to shield himself against the depth of his urge to slide his hand down her arm, to feel the warmth of her skin against his. Again, he looked down at his protective markings and saw they were still blazing as black as they had the first time he'd finally succeeded in manifesting them. This wasn't a *sheva* compulsion. It couldn't be. So what was it?

She opened her eyes, and he saw that they had darkened into deep blue, though they still had the glittery sparkles in them. "You are worthy," she said softly. "I can feel your strength, your capability. The sword has chosen well. Too well," she added, the regret obvious in her voice.

Dante had no idea what the hell was going on, not with the sword that had been summoning him, not with this woman who had manifested from a glittery mist, and not with his own burning desire for her. Swords, he understood. All this? No, but he was going to figure it out, and fast. "My name is Dante Sinclair. I'm the leader of the Order of the Blade." He did not add that he was the only one left of a decimated Order. The last Calydon alive who had a chance to save the earth from the rogues. "Who are you?"

"Dante Sinclair," she repeated, sending warmth spiraling through him as she said his name. She made it sound poetic, like a great gift offered to the very earth upon which they stood. She gave a low curtsy. "My name is Elisha, daughter of the Queen of Darkness. Soon to be consort to the master Adrian."

Dante went cold at her words. "Consort?" That one word had chased every other bit of information she'd offered out of his mind. "What does that mean?"

She rose to her feet, and something flickered in her eyes, something he couldn't decipher, but she definitely had reacted to his fury about her becoming some guy's consort.

She raised her hand and brushed her fingers over his cheek. "Your anger at my words is beautiful." Her touch was like silk, like the whisper of a new dawn across his skin. Without speaking, he laid his hand over hers, pressing her palm to his face. Her hand was cool, drifting through his body like the cleansing rain of a raging summer storm.

Her gaze went to his. "You have freedom here, in the earth realm. I can sense it about you. Your heart—" She laid her other hand on his chest, moving even closer to him. "—it beats differently than mine. I can feel its freedom. It's like the purest magic, born of innocence and honor." A sense of awe appeared on her face, and Dante felt his world begin to close in on him as he tumbled into her spell.

Unbidden, his hand slid to the back of her neck. He needed to touch her. To kiss her. To claim her. To make her his.

Her eyes widened, and she froze, going utterly still. "No," she whispered. "This cannot be."

"Just like how you don't exist in the earth realm?" He bent his head, his lips hovering a breath from hers. "Because you *do* exist. And this *can* be, because it's happening right now."

"No!" A gust of wind suddenly slammed into his chest and thrust him backwards. He landed ten feet away, on his ass, a pawn in the grasp of her power.

Damn. That was impressive. With a groan that he didn't mean to let slip, he vaulted back to his feet, disgusted that he'd let his need for her dictate his actions. Had he really just considered seducing her when his last hope for the rebuilding of the Order lay dead, only half a day's run from here? Shit. He lowered his head, studying her more carefully. The power of a woman. A princess? What in the hell was going on? "Who is the Queen of Darkness? And what realm are you from, if you're not from the earth realm?"

Elisha was facing him, her hands dangling loosely by her sides, her gaze blazing. "You must leave," she said urgently. "You must."

There was no chance of that. "Where is the sword from, Elisha?" He began to walk toward her again, but this time, it wasn't about seduction. It was about his mission, his job, his calling. "How is it calling me?"

"No." Once again, she sent air at him, pushing him backwards, but this time he was ready.

He simply braced himself and shoved forward, cutting through the invisible wall.

Her face tightened with fear. "Halt!" she commanded, with the imperious force of the royalty she'd claimed to be.

He stopped. "Tell me why." She was soon going to be some man's consort? Really? *Shit.* Why was he thinking about *that* when he was facing down an enemy? He schooled his thoughts away from seduction, desire, and temptation, and faced the princess. "Tell me what's going on."

Select List of Other Books by Stephanie Rowe

(For a complete book list, please visit www.stephanierowe.com)

PARANORMAL ROMANCE

The NightHunter Series

Not Quite Dead

The Order of the Blade Series

Darkness Awakened
Darkness Seduced
Darkness Surrendered
Forever in Darkness (Novella)
Darkness Reborn
Darkness Arisen
Darkness Unleashed
Inferno of Darkness (Novella)
Darkness Possessed
Hunt the Darkness
Release Date TBD

The Soulfire Series

Kiss at Your Own Risk
Touch if You Dare
Hold Me if You Can

The Immortally Sexy Series

Date Me Baby, One More Time
Must Love Dragons
He Loves Me, He Loves Me Hot
Sex & the Immortal Bad Boy

ROMANTIC SUSPENSE

The Alaska Heat Series

Ice
Chill
Ghost

CONTEMPORARY ROMANCE

EVER AFTER SERIES

No Knight Needed
Fairytale Not Required
Prince Charming Can Wait

STAND ALONE NOVELS

Jingle This!

NONFICTION

ESSAYS

The Feel Good Life

FOR TEENS

A GIRLFRIEND'S GUIDE TO BOYS SERIES

Putting Boys on the Ledge
Studying Boys
Who Needs Boys?
Smart Boys & Fast Girls

STAND ALONE NOVELS

The Fake Boyfriend Experiment

FOR PRE-TEENS

THE FORGOTTEN SERIES

Penelope Moonswoggle, The Girl Who Could Not Ride a Dragon
Penelope Moonswoggle & the Accidental Doppelganger
Release Date TBD

COLLECTIONS

BOX SETS

Alpha Immortals
Last Hero Standing

STEPHANIE ROWE BIO

Four-time RITA® Award nominee and Golden Heart® Award winner Stephanie Rowe is a nationally bestselling author, and has more than twenty-five contracted titles with major New York publishers such as Grand Central, HarperCollins, Dorchester and Harlequin, and more than fifteen indie books. She believes in writing stories where characters survive against all odds, fighting their way through to personal triumph, while discovering true love and sensual, hot passion along the way.

Stephanie is an award-winning and bestselling author of adult paranormal romance, and has charmed reviewers, receiving coveted starred reviews from Booklist for several of her paranormal romances. Publishers Weekly has also praised her work, calling her work "[a] genre-twister that will make readers...rabid for more."

In addition to her vibrant paranormal romance career, Stephanie also writes a thrilling romantic suspense series set in Alaska. Publisher's Weekly praised the series debut, ICE, as a "thrilling entry into romantic suspense," and Fresh Fiction called ICE an "edgy, sexy and gripping thriller." Equally as intense and sexy are Stephanie's contemporary romance novels, set in the fictional town of Birch Crossing, Maine

Stephanie is a full-time author who has been an avid reader since she was a kid (she even won the blue ribbon at her town library for reading the most books over the summer). She wrote her first book when she was ten, but abandoned that fledgling career when people started asking to read it. Fortunately, she now delights in people reading her work, and loves to hear from readers. With more than fifty completed novels to her name, Stephanie is well on her way to fulfilling the dream that started so long ago. Some of her favorite authors are Lisa Kleypas, Dick Francis, and Julie Garwood, but the list goes on and on

In her spare time, Stephanie loves to play tennis, take her rescue dog for walks in the woods, and to make up stories about the people she sees on the street with her daughter. Yes, the author's imagination is always at work.

Want to learn more? Visit Stephanie online at one of the following hot spots

WWW.STEPHANIEROWE.COM
HTTP://TWITTER.COM/STEPHANIEROWE2
HTTP://WWW.PINTEREST.COM/STEPHANIEROWE2/
HTTPS://WWW.FACEBOOK.COM/STEPHANIEROWEAUTHOR

CPSIA information can be obtained at www.ICGtesting.com
Printed in the USA
LVOW04s1004170515

438805LV00018B/672/P